Praise for Keeping Janie

"Keeping Janie is what romantic suspense dreams are made of... keeps you on your toes with unpredictable plot twists that have you begging for the next book."

@toriannharris, Book Tok

"Keeping Janie was an incredible follow-up to Call her Janie. I finished the book in two days and was completely shocked at the ending. So far, the trilogy is definitely bone-chilling suspense!"

Matthew J. Anderson, Author

"Wow. What a story. The first book was full of new beginnings, new love, and new experiences. This second book? It was full of love, trust, and heartbreak. Keeping Janie was so raw and powerful. This book contains so much love and heartbreak I was on the edge of my seat close to tears the entire time."

Sam, Bookstagram @court_of_reading

"S.R. Fabrico really outdid herself with this one. Keeping Janie is an intense masterpiece that you will not be able to put down."

J. Lane, Avid Reader

Also By S.R. Fabrico

Fiction:

The Secrets We Conceal

Call Her Janie

Keeping Janie

Janie's Hope – Coming Summer 2024

Non-Fiction:

My Firefly Journal

My Dance Journal

My Cheer Journal

My Gymnastics Journal

My Soccer Journal

My Swim Journal

My Basketball Journal

My Volleyball Journal

Keeping Janie

Book 2 of the Southport Series

S.R. Fabrico

SRF Creations

Hardcover ISBN – 979-8-9867938-7-0

Paperback ISBN- 979-8-9867938-6-3

For my nieces and nephews, I love you dearly.
Know that you can do anything you put your mind to.
I believe in you always.

Keeping Janie

PROLOGUE
Gray

Life has a knack for altering course in ways we can't possibly fathom. I believe that's why I, like other human beings, hold onto Hope, unwavering Hope and faith that things will work out how they are intended to carry us forward into tomorrow.

ONE

Lizzie

Gray was using my daughter to manipulate me, and I felt like a prisoner—caged inside my own life. Today was May 18, Janie's second birthday. Sitting at a table on the Johnston Lawn, I watched my daughter's two-year-old birthday party like an on-looker.

I knew I shouldn't have trusted him. This party's out of control.

Fort Johnston Museum was a large, two-story brick mansion with four, tall, white pillars adorning the entryway. Built in 1749 on several acres of land, the fort was the first one constructed in the state of North Carolina. Gray rented the Johnston Lawn to throw Janie her birthday party. When he asked if he could have a birthday celebration with her, I assumed he meant a cupcake at his condo. Little did I know that the entire Princess brigade, complete with pumpkin-shaped carriage rides, would be in attendance. White tables with Cinderella castle centerpieces and chairs decorated the lawn. Front and center stood an archway decorated with twinkling lights and white flowers. Through the archway was Janie's very own pink throne. Face painting, clowns crafting balloon animals, and magicians were scattered around the area for kids and parents to enjoy.

I rolled my eyes. *Thank God she won't remember this. How long am I going to have to play this game with him?*

"This is quite the party," Josh said, his comment interrupted my thoughts.

I looked at him with sullen eyes. "Sure is."

He leaned over and kissed my forehead. "We'll get through this. Have faith." Wearing his perfectly fitted jeans with a short-sleeved blue button-down, Josh was as handsome and kind as ever. His shirt accentuated his exquisite blue eyes, and the five o'clock shadow he was sporting highlighted his square jaw.

"I know we will. I'm just frustrated." Frustrated was an understatement.

Josh reached out, took my hand, and pulled me to my feet. "You're raising Janie every day. That's a wonderful thing. Let's try to enjoy the party."

I shot him a sideways glance and followed him toward the birthday crowd. Yes, I was raising Janie, but every day I lived with the fear that it could be the last one I would have with her. The custody battle was taking forever, and I couldn't relax until it was over.

"*We've* been raising Janie," I said as I wrapped my arm around his side. I pushed my thoughts to the back of my mind, leaned into his chest, and said, "I love you. Thanks for always finding the silver lining."

He squeezed me and said, "I love you, too."

Janie sat on her throne and clapped her hands as she watched the princesses dance in unison before her, their dresses bellowing out as they twirled.

"Look, Mommy," Janie squealed as I approached. "JJ, watch," she exclaimed. Her eyes glimmered in the sunshine as happiness oozed from her every pore. I scooped her up, rested her on my hip, and we danced to the music before sitting back onto the throne with Janie on my lap. Josh stood beside us, and we did our best to enjoy the moment.

I scanned the crowd, but I recognized only a few faces. I spotted Randy, Renee, and Helen, and seeing them brought a smile to my face. Helen sported an outlandish sun hat almost as wide as she was tall.

Dressed in a crisp white dress shirt, Gucci shorts, and a Gucci belt, Gray sauntered throughout the grounds and shook hands with each of his guests. As he approached us, Janie giggled. Holding out her arms to him, she squealed, "Daddy!" My heart sank low into my gut. I could practically taste each heartbeat as my blood pumped through it. *Daddy.* The words might as well be nails on a chalkboard. I had the urge to vomit. I kissed Janie on the cheek and reluctantly handed her to Gray.

Gray proceeded to parade Janie around the party and show her off to his friends. The child he never wanted—the child he used to control my life. *I've got to get out of this tangled web of bullshit.* I watched as Gray waltzed toward the carriage rides, and my eyes darted toward Josh. "I'm not letting him take her without me."

Josh hesitated, but eventually urged me to go. I quickly headed toward the carriage.

"Do you have room for one more?" I asked Gray as he and Janie climbed into the carriage.

"I always have room for you," he said, his menacing green eyes piercing right through me. I climbed into the carriage, looked back at Josh, and smiled nervously. Josh supported me every step of the way, but I could see concern and maybe even hurt in his eyes. He had the patience of a saint, but even Josh Miller could only take so much Gray Stone.

I love him so much. My cheeks burned red hot as my heart swelled.

Veering forward, the carriage snapped me out of my daydream as we headed down Bay Street along the water. Janie was propped onto her knees and gripped the open window as she looked out at the seagulls diving into the water. She pointed her little finger. "Gulley's, Mommy, gulley's."

"That's right, Janie. Seagulls," I said and leaned forward to get a better view. Gray sat on the opposite bench and snapped pictures of Janie and me.

"She's beautiful, you know. Gets it from you," he said as he looked at the photo he had just taken.

I sighed. "She's beautiful and smart."

"I've fallen in love with her. I know you don't want to hear it and don't believe me, but I have. I'd love nothing more than for us to be a family."

"You don't know what love is," I snapped. "We've already discussed this. I'm engaged to Josh. You agreed to let us raise her."

"Well, I changed my mind. I'm crazy in love with you both, and the thought of not having you in my life makes me sick to my stomach. The thought of not spending time with Janie makes me feel like I'm suffocating."

"You can't do this. Gray, we've been over this a million times. I'm marrying Josh. Janie will live with us. There's no family here," I said, pointing my finger at him, then toward myself, and back to him again. "There's never going to be an *us*."

The carriage came to a stop by the picnic tables. The stagnant and hot air caused sweat to form perfect beads on my forehead. "Come on, Janie. Let's blow some bubbles," Gray said as he stepped out of Cinderella's pumpkin. Rolling my eyes, I trailed behind them.

Exhaling sharply, I asked, "Why are we stopping? We should get back to the party."

"I want to talk for a minute."

I crossed my arms and said flatly, "Talk."

"I understand I hurt you." Gray unscrewed a cap on a bottle of bubbles and handed the bottle to Janie. Then, placing his hand gently on my shoulder, he continued, "I know I don't deserve a second chance, but I'll do whatever it takes to win your trust." He looked at Janie, who was distracted, playing with her bubble wand. "Our daughter has changed me. I want to be a better man. I love you both and will fight for you, Lizzie."

"There's nothing to fight for. You *say* you love us. Love isn't pony shows and diamonds, Gray." Shifting my weight, I tried to escape his hold and forcefully shrugged his arm off. "It's unconditional. It's being there for the hard parts. It wasn't long ago you didn't want anything to do with us, especially Janie. I moved on, and *now* you want us in your life." Exasperation flooded my chest as I lifted my eyes to the heavens. I exhaled a weary sigh. "I gave you a chance, and you called security."

Gray's eyes, usually so guarded, shimmered with a nugget of raw desperation. "You need time. I get it, but I will prove that I've changed."

Janie giggled as she smashed bubbles with her hands.

"Sure, Gray. Time. Time's what I need." I crossed my arms and turned away from him. "We should get back."

He was really something. After everything he had said and done, how did he think he could just waltz back into our lives like nothing had ever happened? Gray believes that because he commands it, it will be so. Well, it will not be so this time. I'm with Josh, and he needs to get on board with that.

"I'll be part of my daughter's life, whether you like it or not. She's my daughter," he said firmly. "And need I remind you, I can take her from you at any time."

His words filled me with rage, and I balled my fists and gritted my teeth. *Calm down, Lizzie. Don't make a scene.*

"You're spending time with her now because, as her legal guardian, I've allowed it," he said.

Not for long, hopefully.

"And there it is. That's the Gray I know." I put the cap onto the bubble jar and lifted Janie into my arms. "Come on, sweetie. We need to return to the party."

"Par – teeeeeeeeeee," Janie said as she wrapped her arms around my neck.

"If you're genuine and want to be a better person, you can start by not threatening me whenever I don't do exactly what you want. Janie needs stability. She needs her mother. If you love us, you'd understand that and stop using her as a pawn." I placed Janie into the carriage and climbed in behind her.

Gray's face reddened, a vein throbbing at his temple. His eyes, previously an icy calm, now blazed with a fiery mix of anger and frustration. His hands, clenching and unclenching, betrayed his struggle to maintain composure.

Before he could utter a word, I swiftly and pointedly slammed the carriage door shut, effectively barring him from joining us. "You can walk. It'll give you time to think about what I said." Turning to Janie, I forced a cheerful tone. "Wave bye to Gray, Janie."

I'll be damned if I'll refer to him as her daddy.

Later that night, Janie was exhausted. She passed out in the stroller on the way home. I felt terrible admitting I hated the party, especially since Janie loved it and had a blast. Even more, I hated she had such a good time. Josh and I tucked her into her crib and sat on the balcony attached to our bedroom and overlooking the water.

"I'm exhausted," I said.

"I know, babe. Gray being in the middle of our lives is exhausting."

"Gray threatened to take away the power of attorney today."

"He did what?" Josh gasped.

"He wants to be a family. He threatened to take Janie away if I don't do what he wants." I rocked slowly in the chair and rubbed my temples. "Please don't say I told you so. I know. I know. Everyone thought a power of attorney was a bad idea. What was I supposed to do, let them put my child in foster care? Let Gray have her?" *I made the best choice out of the shitty choices I had.*

"Just focus on today. For today, Janie is with us."

Part of me feels a little sorry for Gray. He had been married, but was alone and trying to divorce Catalina for over a decade, but she won't sign the papers. I often wondered if Catalina became the psycho she is because she was married to Gray. Maybe she was always crazy. Who knows? Either way, she stole my child and created a fake birth certificate, naming Gray as the father and her as the mother. I have no parental rights to my daughter except the power of attorney Gray agreed to grant me. The legal system has been slow and daunting.

"The entire situation sucks," Josh said as he took my hand into his and squeezed. His touch sent warmth pulsating through my body, melting my worries away. He stood and pulled me toward him. He wrapped his arms around my waist and pressed his lips to mine. He cradled me and carried me into our bedroom. Laying me on the bed, his hands caressed my skin like a masterful surgeon as he slathered lavender lotion onto every inch of me. His lips tenderly traced from my neck, down my shoulder, and onto my back, lingering with every kiss.

Releasing the stress I had pent up, I groaned. "Ugg, you're so good to me," I whispered. "I'm tense all over."

"Tense all over, you say?" he teased. "I can certainly help with that."

He massaged my hips and buttocks, down my hamstrings, then my calves, and onto my feet. Barely able to speak, I muttered, "That feels amazing."

"I'm glad. You've had a tough day," Josh said in between kissing his way up my leg. He gently rolled me over and kissed my stomach. He placed his hands on my thighs and spread my legs. A rush from his touch stretched down to my toes. His lips were like perfect dew drops upon my skin as he worked his way downward.

Working his tongue back and forth, I gasped. Tingles shot through my body, and I cried out for more, but guilt crept in and took over. I ran my fingers through his hair and pulled him toward me.

Josh looked up, his eyes clouded with a mix of confusion and concern. "What, babe? Are you upset?"

"I'm not upset. I'm sorry. You're incredible, and I practically have zero self-control with you."

A hint of sarcasm tugged at the corners of Josh's mouth, his eyes taking on a teasing glint. "Your self-control seems pretty on point to me lately," Josh remarked. Despite the playful tone, there was an undercurrent of hurt that made his words sting.

I don't want to hurt him, but he's right. Lately, I had been unable to allow myself to be with him. I was sure my denials were hurting him, but that was not my intention.

His eyes softened and revealed a vulnerability he often tried to hide. "I'm starting to think you don't want to be with me any-more."

"That's not it at all," I said and kissed his lips. "I love you. I love you so much. It's just..."

"It's just what, Lizzie?" He stood from the bed and dressed. "You won't set a wedding date. You spend most of your time with Janie. We haven't had sex in months." He pulled up his pants and looked me dead in the eye. "I'm trying to do my best here. I'm trying to be patient and understanding. But I can't help but feel like you don't want me."

"You're right. I'm sorry." I rolled onto my side to face him. "I feel guilty."

His shoulders slumped, and he said, "I don't understand. What do you have to feel guilty about?"

"I feel like I don't deserve to be happy with you. I'm a mother doing my best to hold on to my child, and I feel every ounce of me should focus on that." I scooted toward the middle of the bed to make room and patted the sheets. "How can I be intimate or celebrate a wedding when Janie isn't legally ours?" A tear trickled down my cheek. "Come, lie with me. Hold me. I do want to be with you, always."

I've got to get through this before it takes over my life. But how can I let myself be with Josh when all I can think about is keeping Janie?

Josh climbed into bed, wrapped his arms around me, and pulled me against him, his desire still at attention and poking me. My tears continued to burn my eyes as I lay quietly in his arms.

I genuinely don't deserve this man.

TWO

Catalina

Bob, the corrections officer, walked me back to my cell. His receding hairline made his forehead look gigantic. He opened the cell door and signaled for me to enter. I turned around to face him as the cell door clinked shut. "Thanks, Bob," I flirted and batted my eyelashes.

His cheeks reddened slightly, and he puffed out his soft chest.

"After dinner in the laundry room?" I gently touched his hand with my fingertips.

He winked. "I wouldn't miss it for the world."

I had just finished with my visitor when I returned to the cell. Gertrude was lying on her bed reading *The Notebook*. Oddly, she was a sucker for sappy novels.

My cellmate Gertrude was a large woman with unruly sandy blond hair who believed she was in charge when I arrived. My slender frame gave her the wrong impression, but she learned quickly that I was the Alpha female. Gertie was in for killing her boyfriend. She popped him in the head when she caught him with a hooker. We became great friends after Gertie realized I wore the pants in our relationship. I told her not to get too attached because I would be getting out soon.

She looked up and said in her thick, redneck accent, "Was it da usual?"

"Yep." I raised an eyebrow.

Our cell was small, and the air was dank with the aroma of piss and shit, and the walls were dingy and a grayish-tan. The only saving grace was the sliver of sunlight that peeked through the tiny slit of a window under the ceiling. Sleeping on two inches of foam was not doing my back any favors. The sacrifice was worth it, though. Soon, I'd be free, out on good behavior, and I'd have my daughter back.

"What ya got dere?" she said, pointing to the photograph I held in my hand.

I ignored her and climbed onto the top bunk. Lying on my back and staring at the ceiling, I held the picture up so I could stare at it in the sunlight. *My beautiful little girl. Mommy's coming to save you.*

The photograph was a clear shot of my daughter Sophie sitting on her princess throne at her second birthday party. I could see her dimples as clear as day and her wide smile in the close-up of her face. My heart broke that I couldn't attend, but her father made sure it was the most extravagant birthday party ever. Suddenly, bile rose from my stomach into my throat as I caught sight of Sophie's wicked want-to-be mother lurking behind her. I couldn't see her face in the picture, but I could tell it was her. I wanted to spit on the bitch. *Her time will come.*

I used the small piece of tape Bob gave me and stuck the new picture to the wall next to the others. I now had a collection of photos of my sweet girl.

I could feel Gertie's breath on my neck as she stood beside my bed and pointed. "Got a new one?"

I rolled to face her. "Yes," I said flatly.

"Do ya miss her?"

"Yes."

"She's cute. And her daddy's hot." She slid her tongue across her teeth.

I rolled my eyes. "He's taking care of her for me until I get out. We'll be a family again soon." I hopped down from my bed, walked over to the toilet, and began to whiz. "Sophie must miss me terribly. It makes me sad."

Gertie fixed her gaze on me. "Yeah. You'll see her real soon."

I pulled up my pants and sat on Gertie's bed. "She's the best thing that ever happened to me. I'm lucky to be her mom."

"I've never had da kids. What's childbirth like?"

I clenched my teeth and pictured myself slamming Gertie's head into the wall for asking that question. But I had to control my temper.

"I don't know about childbirth. I can't have children," I said between deep calming breaths.

"But, you…"

I cut her off. "My mother was a drug addict, and my father left when I was a baby. I was raised on the streets and pulled myself out of the gutter and married into wealth. All I ever wanted was a child to love and who would unconditionally love me back." I pressed the palm of my hand into Gertie's throat and squeezed as I spoke through clenched teeth. "She's my daughter. The woman who gave birth to her doesn't deserve to be her mother, and that's all you need to know. We clear?"

Gertie's eyes were as wide as saucers, and her head bobbed up and down as she acknowledged just how clear she was.

THREE

Lizzie

Sprinting up the stairs, I tripped on the last step and almost fell. I quickly regained my footing as I burst into the bookstore and squealed. "I've missed you!"

"Lizzie! I feel like we haven't seen each other in a year. I've missed you too," Helen said as she rushed toward me and threw her arms around my neck. Her shiny, black leggings squished as she ran.

"It's only been a week, but I agree it feels like an eternity." The bookstore looked fantastic. Josh's construction company did an incredible job putting everything back together after Catalina destroyed it. He had to drive to an antique shop in Georgia, but he managed to find the exact chandeliers. Even the pirate armoire looked good as new. He installed new hardwood floors with the help of Randy and his latest hire, Drew. Drew recently retired from the Marine Corps and worked part-time to help Josh with smaller projects.

"How about that birthday party, huh?"

"Gray's really something." I let out an annoyed sigh. "It's a difficult situation. We got into an argument, and I let him have it. I don't want to admit it, but I can tell he's really trying." I walked toward the counter and set down my purse. "I'm excited to be here."

"I'm glad you're here too. I need help setting up for popsicles and poetry." Popsicles and Poetry was my latest event. It was an adult-only evening of poetry reading, BYOB, and Hawaiian Punch popsicles, each filled with vanilla vodka.

"How are things with you? What's new?" I said.

"Oh, you know, the usual. Bunko and the bookstore."

The door buzzed, and I turned to see who had entered.

Flushed, Helen smoothed her hair down with her hands and walked to greet Drew. *What's he doing here? And why's Helen so flustered?*

"Good morning, gorgeous," Drew said. His work boots clomped onto the hardwood floor as he walked. His white hair was neatly trimmed, and his eyes lit up the second he saw Helen.

"Hi, Drew." Helen gave him a flirtatious glance, and a smile as wide as the Grand Canyon spread across her face.

"I've fixed the sign out front for you and figured I'd stop in and look at the sink in the break room while I was here."

"You're so kind," Helen said, her smile lingering across her face. She fluttered her eyes as she nodded toward the back corner of the bookstore and said, "You know where it is. We'll be out here working if you need anything."

Helen turned around, and my jaw hit the floor. She looked at me and shrugged. "What?"

"What do you mean, what? Clearly, there are some things you haven't been telling me."

She walked past me toward the poetry section and waved her hand. "I don't know what you're talking about."

"Don't play coy with me, missy. I know flirting when I see it," I said as I darted after her. Stepping in front of her so she couldn't dodge my question again, I put my hands on her shoulders. "Do you have a man?" I could barely contain my excitement.

"Lizzie, don't be ridiculous. He's doing some handy work around the store."

"I see. Well, it's obvious he likes you. And I'm pretty sure you like him, too." I dusted off the podium we planned to use tonight, flicking the feather duster side to side with a little extra attitude as I waited for Helen to respond.

Suddenly, her shoulders slumped slightly as she dropped her head and stared at the floor.

Shit, did I offend her?

"Helen, what is it? I'm sorry. I didn't mean to upset you," I said gently as I stopped dusting and walked toward her.

She took a deep, calming breath and looked up with tears filling her eyes. "I do like him, Lizzie. He makes me laugh. Every time I see him, my stomach does cartwheels. I broke the sink on purpose so he would come inside the store today. But, I...” Her voice trailed off as a tear trickled down her cheek.

“But you feel like you’re not ready, or maybe like you’re cheating on Kenny?”

“I want to be ready. Drew seems like a decent, kind man. He lost his wife, too, so we have that in common. But I don’t know if I can be with another man.”

“You told me once to open my heart so I wouldn’t miss out on life’s moments, and now I’m giving you the same advice.”

“I’ll think about it.”

Helen and I cleaned and organized for the next hour, preparing everything for Popsicles and Poetry. We organized a variety of small, medium, and large vases with red and white roses and sprigs of baby’s breath. I tied a black tulle bow on each, and we scattered them throughout the store.

Helen put the last vase in its place and said, “How’s Janie? Are you managing okay?”

“Janie’s amazing. She says a new word almost every day. Her smile could light up the darkest room. Oh, and those dimples.” A mother's love flooded my heart. “She’s a pretty cool little girl.”

“That’s wonderful.” Helen began pulling her favorite poetry books off the shelf to add to the display table we created for tonight. “Any word on the custody yet?”

“We’re supposed to have a hearing in a few weeks. It keeps getting postponed, so I’m trying not to get my hopes up.”

"I know this must be difficult for you. It'll work out. How's Josh handling everything?"

I let out a sigh. "I don't know. He's supportive, but distant at the same time."

"It was only the two of you before. Now it's the two of you, Janie, and Gray. It's an adjustment."

"Yeah. I guess you're right."

Helen was my first friend when I moved to Southport, and she's been my best friend ever since. Supportive and loving, she's been there for me from the beginning. It dawned on me that I never asked why she didn't have children. Maybe she did, and I didn't know about them, but that didn't make sense. Surely, I'd have met her children if she had them.

"Did you and Kenny ever try to have children?"

"We tried for years, but I guess us being parents wasn't part of God's plan." Helen looked peaceful and sad at the same time. I was a bad friend for not asking her sooner.

"After a decade of disappointment, we stopped trying and accepted the inevitable. We prayed that someday God would grant us a child to love, even if it wasn't in the traditional way. I never told you this, but God heard my prayers when you showed up at the bookstore last September. I love you, Lizzie, like a daughter or little sister, and I'm proud of you for pulling your life back together."

I stepped forward and bear-hugged her, twisting her body from side to side as I growled, "I love you, too." Helen has most definitely been like a sister or mother figure. She helped me to open up about my past and move on. I was grateful that our paths had crossed.

"Oh my God," Helen gasped as she jumped back from our embrace and laughed. We both paused as the sound of footsteps approached.

Pointing at the wrench he was holding in his hands, Drew appeared, slightly sheepish. "I'm sorry. I didn't mean to startle you. I need to get a different tool to finish up the sink."

"Lizzie, you should see Drew's truck. He's equipped it with a motorized fold-out toolbox with more gadgets and gismos than I knew existed."

Drew laughed. "You can't get a job done right without the proper tools."

Later that night, Bayview Books was filled wall-to-wall with people eating, drinking, and buzzing about the delicious adult popsicles. Helen wore a green cotton dress that flowed down her ankles. She greeted everyone as they entered.

I stood in the center of the store, clutching the microphone with excitement. "Thank you for joining us tonight. Grab a plate of snacks, a drink, and a popsicle if you haven't already. We've had several people sign up in advance. When your name is called, step up to the mic, tell us a little about yourself, and read your poem. If you didn't sign up but would like to read, find Helen or me, and we'll do our best to add you to the list."

I paused for a moment to ensure I had everyone's attention, and then gestured gracefully toward the display table. "The poetry books we have in the store are available for you to purchase throughout the night, and you can order anything we don't have."

Catching movement from the corner of my eye, I turned to see a man hovering hesitantly near the front. With an encouraging smile and a sweeping gesture, I beckoned him closer. "First up, we have Tom. Come on up, Tom."

The crowd clapped as Tom stepped forward and took the microphone. He appeared to be in his mid-thirties, wearing khaki shorts and a navy-blue golf polo. His reddish hair poked out from underneath his trucker cap. He shifted uneasily from one foot to the other, swaying slightly as a visible sheen of perspiration formed on his forehead.

"Thank you, Lizzie. I've never done this before, but my beautiful wife Laura and I are visiting from out of town. We've heard so many good things about the bookstore and your event this evening, and we had to come." He pointed to a brunette woman sitting midway through the crowd. Her eyes overflowed with adoration as he spoke. "Laura, my love, this one's for you."

As Tom finished his poem, Laura stood with tears in her eyes. The crowd cheered as she embraced her husband.

"Kiss!" someone shouted from the crowd.

"Yes. Kiss. Kiss. Kiss." More cheers came.

Tom wrapped his arms around Laura, pressed his lips to hers, and dipped her as they kissed.

"What a way to start the night," I said. "Let's see who's next."

The evening continued with poems about Southport, sunsets, and ocean waves, funny joke poems, and poems of everything in between. The crowd seemed to be having a blast. Drew even came and helped the entire night. I could see the pride in his eyes for Helen and her bookstore.

I whispered in Drew's ear as I walked by. "I'll let you in on a little secret. The store's usually very slow on Monday mornings. Bring her breakfast or coffee." I winked and headed over to find Josh.

Squeezing me, he said, "Another successful event, babe. I'm proud of you."

"Thanks. I love helping Helen bring the store to life." I tapped Josh on the nose with my index finger. "I need to wrap things up."

I ran my fingers through his hair and headed toward the podium. "I hope everyone had a wonderful time. Helen has created something extraordinary here at Bayview Books. Let's all give Helen a huge round of applause." The audience burst into enthusiastic cheers. "I think we can squeeze in one more. We appreciate everyone coming out. You don't have to go home, but you can't stay here."

I gestured to the door and laughed. "Our last poetry reading of the night, drumroll, please..."

The guests simultaneously broke into drumrolls while I flipped through the list to find the name. I froze and glanced at Josh, who grabbed his keys and started for the door. He paused at the exit and turned, anger written all over his face. Dread pooled in my gut.

Reluctantly, I said, "Let's hear it for our final reading of the night, Gray Stone."

Gray sauntered to the microphone, and I could feel my heartbeat ramming against my ribcage. *What's he going to say? This could be a complete disaster.*

He stood behind the podium and rested his hands on the edges. His smooth, dirty blond hair was slicked back, and not a hair was out of place. His gray linen blazer hung perfectly over his black silk shirt and jeans. A few women in the crowd giggled and whispered to each other as he walked by. It was hard not to find him attractive.

Looking out into the audience, he paused, lowered his head, and took a deep breath.

"Hello, as Lizzie said, my name is Gray Stone. I've recently relocated to Southport to be closer to my daughter. I've spent most of my life treating people like shit and am what most people would consider an asshole." The crowd chuckled at his honesty. Helen looked at me, her eyes wide. I shrugged as Gray began to read...

"I am a flawed man.

But I see clearly now the man I want to be.

Your eyes shine bright like the sun.

Sometimes the feelings I feel make me want to run.

I don't understand these feelings that consume me.

I guess this is what you call unconditional love.

My life belongs to you now—the one who calls me daddy.

My little girl, you have changed me in ways you'll never understand.

You make me want to be a better man."

Gray's gaze met mine. His green eyes shimmered with a sheen of unshed tears. An unexpected softness transformed his features as he stood before me, cloaked in a tenderness I hadn't witnessed before. "Thanks for the opportunity to share my feelings. I'm not a poet like most of you, but I needed to share these words for my own personal growth. Helen, your event's been a wonderful way for people to come together and spend their evening. Thank you."

Is this genuine? That's the question. I just don't know yet.

FOUR

Gray

I used my palm to wipe the steam that clouded the bathroom mirror.

Damn, I look good.

Flexing my chest muscles had become an essential part of my morning routine. I enjoyed my simple life in Southport. Living here made spending time with Janie easier. I converted the second bedroom into an office, and I paid a decorator to create the perfect sleeping space for Janie in the third bedroom. The walls were painted a warm light green and purple with white beadboard around the bottom half. The theme was sea creatures with beautiful coral, fish, and a smiley face octopus.

Janie wouldn't be allowed to stay with me anytime soon, but I was convinced she'd eventually need a room at my house. I had fallen completely and totally in love with my sweet little girl. Her innocent eyes shined bright in my mind. I laughed out loud as I thought about her inquisitive discovery of the world. She captivated me, and I was determined to be a better man for her.

Shaking the sentimentality away, I took one more admiring glance in the mirror. Sure, on the outside, I was a force to be reckoned with. On the inside, I still had a lot of work to do. Acknowledging my flaws was the first step toward being a better man—right? I shaved, dressed, and sat at my home office desk.

"How much longer until the office building is ready?" I snapped at the man on the other end. "I can't hire staff without an office." Pacing the small room, I practically wore a hole through the hardwood. "It was supposed to be done weeks ago. I'm starting a business. I need a proper space. An executive's office."

The contractor hesitated for a moment before responding, "I understand your frustration, Mr. Stone. We've faced some unexpected delays, but we're doing our best to expedite things. I assure you we're pushing hard to get it finished for you. Give us another two weeks, and I promise we'll have it ready."

"Two weeks? That's not what I was promised! Every delay is costing me money and opportunity. Get it done, or I'll find someone who can." Slamming down the phone, I went into the kitchen and grabbed a glass from the cabinet. I filled it with water and gulped the liquid down.

Back in my office, I sifted through applications I received for the new southern annex of Gray Stone Marketing, South. I'd wanted to expand my business for a while, but never took the plunge. Now, everything seemed to be falling into place.

I sorted the applications into piles: hell no, maybe, and possibly interview. Tossing the hell no's into the trash bin under the desk, I leaned back in my chair and thoroughly reviewed the pile marked 'possibly interview.' Glancing up, I became overwhelmed with my dank surroundings. Frustrated, I groaned. "I need my office building finished." I stood to go outside for a walk. *Maybe some vitamin D will help my mood.*

As I walked toward the door, lights flashed on my cell phone, alerting me to a call from a prison facility. My heart sank; there was only one person it could be. "Gray Stone," I answered.

A robotic female voice chimed in, "You have a collect call from Catalina Stone. Will you accept the charges?"

Gritting my teeth, I replied, "I'll accept."

Silence ensued, punctuated only by my increasingly restless pacing. I knew she was listening. "Sign the divorce papers, and I'll do what I can to help you."

More pacing.

Her lack of response agitated me further. "Sign!" I shouted and pressed the end call button.

Bitch.

Stifling a string of curses under my breath, I snatched the boat keys from the hook on the wall. I decided to take the boat out for a spin and headed to the docks. As I walked, my unbuttoned linen shirt flapped in the breeze, showing off my washboard abs. Deep in thought, I almost didn't notice Josh standing on the dock.

"Hello, Gray," Josh said. Looking up as I neared, he paused from washing his boat, which was anchored next to mine.

Fuck you.

I wanted to respond with a quick-witted insult, but I thought better of it. The bitterness I harbored toward him filled the pit of my stomach. He's the one who gets to make Janie breakfast every day. If I'm completely honest, I'm not angry with him. I'm angry with myself. It's my fault he's Janie's everyday father. I created this mess. The pain squeezed my heart like a vise every time I was around him. Wincing slightly, I looked away and hoped he didn't notice the look of disdain that flashed across my face.

"It's a beautiful day," I said. *It's a beautiful day? Seriously?*

Josh set down the hose and walked toward me. He wore a hat and sunglasses, which made it difficult for me to read his expression. I could see why Lizzie loved him, and that pissed me off, too. I inhaled a large breath to make myself an inch taller, and stiffened as he approached.

"I know we aren't friends and probably never will be. But I'd walk through fire for Janie, and I hope you would, too. For her sake, we need to find some middle ground," he said, reaching out to shake my hand.

I looked down at his hand, not sure how to respond. I considered spitting on it, but that wouldn't go well. My shoulders slumped as I exhaled a deep sigh. I didn't want to find the middle. I preferred to punch him in the nose and watch the blood drip down his face. He's right, though, and I know it. Every fiber of my being knows it, and that makes me hate him even more. Deep down in my core, I know he's everything I want to be.

Reluctantly, I reached out and shook his hand. "I'll try," was all I could muster. Josh sensed the difficulty I had speaking those two words. He looked at me with understanding.

"Janie's a great kid. Her existence has changed everything for me."

I couldn't agree more. I'm not sure how it happened or when, but loving Janie changed everything for all of us.

I was a father.

He was a father. I winced again at that thought.

Lizzie was a wonderful mother, and we both loved her dearly.

Looking to escape the conversation, I said, "It has indeed," and stepped onto my yacht. I needed to be alone with my thoughts. The rage grew inside me with fierceness, but I didn't want to lose control. My skin was suffocating me like a blanket, snuffing out the flames, but the fire threatened to break free. "I'm headed out."

I could hear Josh walking behind me. "Do you need a hand shoving off?"

What's with this guy? He can't possibly be this stupid. Take a hint, bro. I'm trying to get away from you.

Without looking back, I raised my hand over my head and shouted, "I'm good. Thanks."

The sun was unrelenting, scorching my skin as sweat trickled down my body. I lay there, mind swirling with memories I'd buried deep. I never quite grasped how messed up my childhood was until Janie came along and showed me the real reflection in the mirror.

Memories flashed crisp, clear, unapologetic. A tidal wave of regret, shame, and sadness slammed into me. My business, money, and power materialistically filled the void in my heart for so many years that I didn't notice I had become a piece of shit, a person not capable of giving or receiving unconditional love. Deep down, I was a screwed-up guy, blind to the mess inside. The truth hit hard. I brought an amazing little girl into the world, with a woman worth her weight in gold, and I had botched it. Big time.

I spent every minute of my time building my empire and filling the void in my heart with "things." I married Catalina because she was exquisitely beautiful, the perfect trophy wife. She was easy to get along with, and in the beginning, I enjoyed spending time with her, but I never loved her. I didn't know how. I had no idea back then that she was batshit crazy.

All my life I'd been a hollow man, full of nothing and everything simultaneously. But now I had a daughter. I wanted to be a better man. A better *father*. A father that my daughter deserved, a father that she could look up to. I needed her in my life like a human being needed oxygen. My emptiness had been replaced with immense love. A love I don't quite understand. One that burns me from the inside out every day as I watch Josh live the life I was supposed to have: a life with Lizzie and my daughter.

I was sweating profusely, and I didn't notice the tear that slid down my cheek. Years of regret bubbled up and boiled over. I took a sip of wine and then another. "Fucking shit," I said out loud to no one. "You have work to do." I took another sip, more like a gulp this time. I will do the work and have the life I want. I am Grayson Ethan Stone, the man, not the little orphan boy.

Gray Stone only knows victory.

FIVE

Lizzie

As the water rolled gently onto the sand, a subtle slapping sound graced my ears. Josh and I sat on the balcony that connected to our bedroom. This was our morning ritual, and I loved the sound of the waves washing in and out, accented by the birds singing their morning greetings. The serenity brought me peace. Shirtless, Josh stared from across the little bistro table. I enjoyed that view, too.

"The office building's ready in Wilmington," I said. Josh glanced at me and took a sip of his coffee. I loved how his eyes peeked over the rim of his mug as he sipped. "We talked about this a few weeks ago, but I'm reminding you I start working there today."

His square jaw tightened slightly, and his back stiffened. I should have reminded him yesterday, but I knew this news would bother him. What was I supposed to do? I worked for Gray Stone Marketing, South, and we agreed this was necessary until custody of Janie was sorted out.

"On the bright side, no more trips to New York." I tried to sound reassuring, to lighten the mood.

"I know," he said. He turned to face me; his ice-blue eyes glistened in the morning sun. His intense gaze showered so many unspoken words down upon me. "Gray's part of our lives now. He's Janie's father, or, at least, he wants to be."

Josh dropped his head and stared at his feet. He looked back up at me. "I have to find a way to accept this."

Pain shot through my chest like an arrow hitting its bullseye. Gray was generally a piece of shit, but Janie loved him, and he was her father. I wanted nothing more than for Josh to have custody of her and legally be her father, but even then, it didn't mean that Gray wouldn't be a part of her life.

Gray has been trying to do better. He hasn't taken away the power of attorney and has allowed Janie to live with me and Josh, but he spends at least half a day with her each week. When he looks at her, I can see genuine love in his eyes. I see the same genuine love when he looks at me, but it's also mixed with regret and shame.

"I love you, Josh. Janie loves you. The truth is, she loves you both." I stood and stretched and then sat in Josh's lap. I placed a delicate kiss on his lips and ran my fingers through his hair.

He exhaled softly.

"I miss your touch."

"I'm sorry. I've been distant lately. You've been so supportive. You don't deserve any of this."

"You're my person, Lizzie. I'm part of you, and you're part of me. We're in this together." He slid his hand up my thigh, wrapped his arms around my waist, and pulled me closer into him. I rested my head on his shoulder and let his warmth spread onto my skin.

"I don't know how I'd do life without you," I said softly. I lifted my head to look into his eyes, and he kissed me. I could feel the longing in his lips as they touched mine. He cradled me in his arms and carried me into the bedroom. He laid me on the bed and removed his shorts. I savored the image of his naked body as it glowed in the sunlight that peeked through the windows of our room.

He kissed me slowly and sensually. Each press of his lips ignited a deeper fire within me, one that consumed every part of my being. I wanted him, but the guilt crept into my heart.

I battled with my emotions, silently screaming for the guilt to go away. Josh ran his fingers gracefully, like a feather, under my shirt as he removed it and exposed my bare chest. His touch on my skin was like magic, bringing my defenses down, and it wasn't long before my doubts faded. Succumbing to the moment, I drew him closer and wrapped him in a tight embrace.

His gaze held a silent plea, and I answered it with my own as I urged him to continue. He took his time and continued to caress me. Slowly, he shifted to rest on top of me, and with his arms extended, his eyes met mine. "You're beautiful, Lizzie," he whispered, pressing down onto me and thrusting his hips forward, forging our bodies into one. It had been so long since I had allowed myself to let go of the guilt. My mind, body, and soul cried out, for I felt so much pleasure wrapped in his love.

Later that day, at Gray Stone Marketing, South, I sat with Gray at the conference room table, interviewing several potential candidates. He budgeted to hire an executive assistant and a marketing director. The office building smelled of fresh paint and new furniture, and the faint but persistent sound of construction echoed from a distant corridor. Designed with a modern feel, everything in the space was sleek and edgy. The lobby was decorated with large silver vases topped with red wicker balls and modern leather lounge chairs. GSM, South titanium letters hung on the wall behind the white marble welcome counter. Gray called this annex facility GSM, South. The full name was a mouthful.

We spent four hours interviewing candidates, and Gray wasn't satisfied with any of them. "What about Marco for the assistant position? He seemed to have a decent amount of experience and some fresh ideas he could bring to the table," I said.

Gray flipped through the stack of resumes again. "I don't know. He was okay. But I want the best."

I nodded in acknowledgment. He wasn't the best, I agreed.

"Up next, we have Alexandra. She's fresh out of college but majored in marketing. She might make a great assistant. Someone we can mold and shape for the future."

I grabbed her resume from him and looked it over. She did seem promising. I looked up from the paper and glanced at Gray. As much as we'd been through, it was hard to believe that we could fall so easily into the groove of working together. I had to recognize that Gray had changed, at least a little. He stopped trying to pursue me. Maybe he had moved on or decided I was a lost cause and gave up. I wasn't sure which, but I appreciated him giving me space either way.

Gray had softened these last few months, and it was unexpected, but my guard was still up. I wondered how long this version of him would last. Part of me rooted for him to fail because it would make my life with Josh easier, but the other part of me rooted for him to succeed because Janie deserved to know her father.

The conference room where we conducted the interviews was floor-to-ceiling double-pained glass located in the center of the office building. Blinds hung from each panel for privacy, but Gray preferred them open.

Startled by a knock on the door, I jumped in my seat. "Hello?" A voice from the front lobby called.

Alexandra was tall and slender. Her navy-blue blazer fit like a glove and toned down her rainbow-checkered trousers. She looked confident, put together but a little on the quirky side, and eager to get the job. Her bleach blond hair was thick, wavey, and hung long to the middle of her back. Her face appeared to be painted on, and her lips matched the shade of pink in her rainbow pants, but she wore the look nicely.

"Have a seat." I motioned to her to sit down at the conference room table.

"Thank you for taking the time to interview me today," she said. She sat up straight like she had been properly trained at a finishing school and rested her hands on her lap. Her portfolio lay on the table in front of her.

"Why do you want to work for GSM, South?" Gray asked, kicking the interview off without hesitation.

"I want to be the best, so I want to work for the best." She smiled and looked at both of us as she said the words. "Gray Stone Marketing is the best. I was ecstatic when I learned about the opportunity to work at a new office in Wilmington. Eventually, I'd love to work in the New York office, but to have the opportunity to work here first would be amazing."

I instantly connected with her, and by the look on Gray's face, he did, too. I wasn't sure if the look on his face was because he was genuinely excited about her potential or something else. She reminded me of myself when I searched for my first job. I was determined to do whatever it took to succeed.

"I don't think we introduced ourselves. I'm Gray Stone."

Alexandra quivered when he said his name. She tried to hide her excitement, but her eyes gave her away.

"I know who you are, sir. Do you work from this office?"

"Yes, for now, at least. I'll be spending most of my time here, getting this annex up and running." Her eyes lit up with a childlike glee as if she were five and Gray was Santa Claus, delivering her the most anticipated gift.

"I'm Lizzie Levine." I stood to shake her hand.

"Yes, ma'am. I know who you are, too. I'm truly honored to have the possible opportunity to work for both of you."

"Your resume says your name is Alexandra Sunshine, and you attended the University of North Carolina at Wilmington. Why did you choose marketing for your major? What do you hope to accomplish in your career?" I asked.

"I prefer to be called Andra," she said. She shifted nervously in her seat. "I enjoyed UNCW. I chose marketing because I want to help businesses thrive. I'm creative, and I think my talents can help businesses grow and expand, which is what I'm most passionate about. Someday, I'd like to run my own marketing firm or a branch of your firm, Mr. Stone." Her body language suggested she was nervous, but her tone was nothing short of confident. I liked this girl.

Holding her resume, I said, "I see here you have photography experience."

Andra beamed. "Yes, ma'am. It's mostly a hobby, but I think a bonus attribute for a marketing position."

Setting her resume back down, I said, "I'd love to see some of your work."

"I didn't bring any photos with me, but I can certainly show you next time. Assuming there's a next time." She smiled.

We continued asking her questions, and she perfectly articulated her answer for each one. Her portfolio was incredible. I couldn't imagine finding a better candidate than Andra. I was getting excited and ready to hire her on the spot. When Gray asked her if she had anything else she wanted to share with us, she pulled a thumb drive from her purse. She had brought a presentation to show us, and I think my jaw hit the conference room table and bounced closed. I was floored. She was perfect.

After the presentation, Gray made sure Andra understood the position was for an executive assistant and that she would be at his beck and call. She acknowledged her understanding of the long hours and high demand. He said, "If you do an exceptional job, the possibilities are endless. And if you're serious about the New York office, that could be a possibility in the future, too."

Andra nodded excitedly. She seemed ready for the commitment. "I couldn't imagine two people I'd rather learn from. I'll do whatever you need."

Gray asked if she had any questions for us, and we thanked her for coming. "We have a few more candidates to interview. We'll contact everyone next week, so expect to hear from us by then."

I walked Andra to the door and closed it behind her. Turning around, I pumped my fist in the air and shouted, "Woohoo! I think we found our girl." Gray walked toward me and we high-fived. The exchange felt normal. Gray moved closer and paused.

"What?" I said.

He shook his head. "Nothing."

"What?" I said, more forcefully this time.

He stared at me the way only he can. He had put me through hell, said despicable things to me, used our daughter against me, but I couldn't deny that he was incredibly handsome and had a magnetic pull I worked hard to fight against. In the end, he was the reason I had Janie now, even if he had made it difficult.

Dropping his head, he said, "I'm trying to be better."

That's odd. "Gray, what's the matter? Are you okay?"

"We had a great day. We high-fived, and my instinct was to pull you into my arms and hug you, but I stopped myself. That's all. I'm doing my best to fight those urges and respect you."

"I appreciate that, Gray. In time, this will get easier for all of us."

"There's so much I want to say. Things I need to say to you. I want to correct my wrongs. I truly do, Lizzie. I love Janie, and I want to be in her life."

I could hear the despair in his voice. He could have taken her from me, but he didn't. He seemed so exposed and genuine. But a voice inside my head urged me to stay guarded and not allow myself to fully trust him. He's done so much to hurt me I didn't know if we could ever come back from the past.

"We need to do what's best for Janie. This isn't about you and me anymore; it's about her. Everything's about her," I said.

"I agree, but for me, it's about you, too. I treated you horribly, and I'm truly sorry for that. I'm a flawed man. I own that, now. I'm going to be a better man for Janie. And for you."

The one thing I knew for sure was that when Gray Stone set his mind to something, he followed through no matter how much work and effort it took. I wanted to believe he meant it for Janie's sake.

"It's in the past, Gray. You hurt me, and your actions changed things between us, but all of that is in the past. We have a daughter now. We need to work together to figure this out for Janie. I don't want to lie to you. I don't completely trust this new you. I'm not sure this version of you is here to stay. But I'm trying. I need time. And you need to keep trying. We'll see where it all goes."

I packed up my things to head home for the evening. Gray moved closer and stopped beside my desk. He pressed his palms on the top as he leaned forward. "Today was a good day," he said with a huge smile.

"It was. We need to find your marketing director, and we'll have a good team to get started."

"I'll set up some more interviews. In the meantime, I'll handle the job," Gray said.

My phone dinged. It was a text from Josh.

Josh: What time will you be home?

Gray looked at the phone, his lips subtly curving into a frown. He turned to leave the room, seemingly masking his true feelings.

I picked up my phone and replied.

SIX

Lizzie

Josh left for work early this morning. He had a new project starting and wanted to be the first on the job site. I had the day off and looked forward to spending time with my girl. Janie and I lay in bed and enjoyed a lazy morning watching cartoons.

Bubble Guppies blared on the television, and Janie was entranced. I stared at the ceiling fan spinning round and round like the thoughts in my head. Was Gray genuine? Or was this another ploy to use Janie against me somehow? I didn't trust myself to know the difference. I wasn't sure I would ever know. The last few years had been a crazy rollercoaster, and I was ready to get off the ride. I looked over at Janie, my beautiful baby girl. I know she's mine in every way that matters, but not having legal custody was wearing on me. According to Mr. Stallard, Catalina didn't stand a chance of getting custody, and as long as I played nice with Gray, everything should be okay.

Should be wasn't good enough.

The custody hearing was postponed again until July, and now I waited. I snuggled Janie closer and kissed the top of her head.

"I think we should go for a walk. What do you think?"

Janie clapped her hands and smiled widely, causing her dimples to crease on both cheeks.

I got dressed in a pair of black running shorts, a purple tank top, and running shoes. The humidity in the summer was brutal. I tied Janie's hair in a ponytail that sprouted off the top of her head like a sparkler on the Fourth of July and dressed her in a pink flowered t-shirt with matching pink shorts. Scooping Janie up to rest on my hip, we walked down the stairs into the kitchen. Josh had brewed a fresh pot of coffee. Next to the coffee pot was a small blue vase with a single purple rose and a note.

Lizzie,

> *I can't wait to spend forever with you and Janie. I hope you girls have a fantastic day.*

All My Love, Josh

My heart instantly swelled as I leaned toward the flower and took a long, slow breath. Inhaling, the fresh scent of the single rose was intoxicating. If Josh's compassion and love could have a scent, this would surely be it. *I love him so much.*

I put Janie in her high chair and handed her a blue sippy cup of milk while I cut up a banana for her to eat. I could see Len sitting in the sunroom reading. I pushed Janie toward him, making rumble noises with my lips like the Daytona Five Hundred of high chair races.

"Good morning, Len. How are you feeling today?"

I didn't know Josh's dad was sick when I met Josh. Since we had been dating, Len's coronary heart disease seemed to worsen daily. He was a sweet old man with a heart of gold, and he loved to spend time with Janie. He would often rock her on the front porch or in the sunroom as he told her make-believe stories.

"How's pop pop's special girl?" He walked over and kissed Janie on the top of the head.

While Janie ate, Len told her a story about his Great Aunt Tilley. He was full of stories, and I didn't know which were real or fiction, but Janie loved them all the same. He was talking in a pirate accent as he explained that Aunt Tilley was a vibrant soul who corralled the pirate's booty to load onto their ships.

Janie giggled and threw banana pieces on the floor. "Booooty," she said and patted Len on top of his head. This had somehow become their thing. He would bow down to her, and she would pat or rub his head.

"We're going to head out for a walk in a minute. Do you need anything?" I said as I cleaned the bananas off the floor.

"I'm good," Len said. "Thanks for asking."

After Janie finished eating her breakfast, I wiped her hands and face and buckled her in the stroller.

Len waved goodbye to Janie. "Oh, wait. An envelope came for you this morning. I put it on the counter."

"Great. I'll grab it on the way out."

I pushed Janie through the kitchen and tossed the envelope into the stroller on our way. Grabbing my phone, I texted Josh.

Me: Dad seems good this morning. Heart emoji. Thank you for the coffee and the flower. Janie and I are headed for a walk.

Me: Love you.

I slid the phone into the pocket of my shorts and off we went.

As we walked along the water's edge, the sun danced in the sky, soaking Vitamin D into my pores. The day was glorious. I stopped for a moment to watch the barge pass through the waterway. Crouching to be at eye level with Janie, I said, "Look, honey."

Her eyes wide with wonder, she pointed her little finger at the ship and said, "Wassat?"

"It's a ship."

"Shit," she repeated.

I chuckled and said, "No Janie. Ship p p p," emphasizing the p sound.

Filled with excitement, she clapped her hands and kicked her feet up and down. "Shit. Mommy, Shit." Shaking my head, I laughed.

We continued walking along the water until we came to Caswell Avenue. Turning right, I said, "Let's go visit Uncle Randy and Aunt Renee."

Janie clapped her hands with excitement.

Caswell Avenue was lined with beautiful oak trees that must have been hundreds of years old.

If these trees could talk, the stories they would tell.

Spanish moss draped from massive limbs like tinsel on a Christmas tree. The beauty was exquisite, and I'm not sure how I hadn't acknowledged that before. As I walked down the street, passing cyclists, golf carts, and other walkers, each waved and said hello. You couldn't walk down any street in Southport without greeting everyone you see.

Sweat was pouring down my back, and I stopped to take a sip of water and check on Janie. Tilting my head back, I poured the cold liquid into my mouth and spotted a bird's nest tucked into the corner of a tree branch hanging over my head. I carefully moved closer to get a better look. The mama bird was feeding the little hatchlings whose heads were barely poking out of the nest. I leaned down and whispered quietly to Janie, "Look, Janie. Can you see the baby birdies?"

She raised her hand, pointed toward the nest, and whispered back, "Wassat?"

"That's a mama bird feeding her baby birdies."

Janie smiled and flashed her dimples. Her light brown sprout atop her head bobbled around as she wiggled with excitement. *How did I get so lucky to be your mom?* I leaned in, rubbed my nose to hers, and kissed her forehead. "Eskimo kisses. Love you, Janie Bug."

She wrinkled her nose and then smiled.

When we approached the house, Randy was sitting in the rocking chair on the front porch. His bright-colored Hawaiian shirt stood out like a beacon in the middle of the ocean. Removing his tan fisherman's hat that hid his auburn wavey locks, he said, "Well, hello, Janie girl. How are you today?" Janie flapped her hand to wave at Uncle Randy.

"Janie and I decided to go for a walk this morning. We figured we'd come by and say hi."

"Hey, sis, I'm glad you stopped by. Ren and I wanted to ask you guys to come to dinner tonight."

"I need to make sure Josh will be home from work in time, but sure. Sounds great. We'd love to."

"Awesome. Call Helen and invite her, too."

"Sounds great. Will do. What's on your schedule for today? Do you want to join us on our walk?"

"Nah. Can't. Waiting for Ren to get ready, and then we're headed down the road to help Mrs. Jackovski with her windows. She needs them resealed and cleaned. Told her we'd come by today."

"Okay. See you later tonight."

Janie and I strolled around the block and headed towards home. Not long after we stopped to visit Randy, a red-faced Janie was passed out in the stroller. I paused on a bench by the water to enjoy a moment of peace while she slept. I pulled the cover down on the stroller to provide her some shade and turned her fan on high. I rested my head on the back of the bench and let the sun's rays tickle my face. With my eyes closed, I listened to the sounds of ships as they passed by, people playing and talking at the waterfront, and birds calling their mates. I leaned forward and peeked inside the stroller. Innocent, sweet Janie was sound asleep. I could watch her sleep all day. She looked so peaceful and content.

The edge of the manilla envelope caught my eye. I had already forgotten about it. Bending over, I grabbed it from underneath the stroller and ripped open the flap. Inside was a note that said, *I'm watching you.* My hands flew up to cover my open mouth as I gasped. My eyes darted side to side, and I spun on my heel. I could not shake the feeling of being watched.

I peered inside the envelope and pulled out two photographs. Both pictures were of me, Josh, and Janie sitting on the balcony at our house. I remember the night because Janie was fussing about not wanting to go to bed. She was sitting in my lap crying as she reached for Josh. I shoved everything back in the envelope and took off like a bat out of hell toward the house.

SEVEN

Lizzie

Running late, we rushed to get ready to hang out with Randy and Renee tonight. I showed Josh the photos. "This came today," I said and held the picture up to his face. He was pulling up his jeans and almost fell over as he tried to get a good look.

"What the hell?"

I threw on a cute plum sundress with white flowers splashed across the top. "It came with a note that said, 'I'm watching you.'"

Buttoning his shirt, Josh said, "You seem pretty casual about it."

"I don't like being threatened, but at this point, I think I'm numb to it. I've learned to ignore it and move on." I ran my fingers through my hair, swiped on some lip gloss, and said, "I can't let the fear paralyze me. *I won't.*"

"Well, I don't like it. Catalina's already tried to kill you once."

Josh took Janie by the hand, and we headed to the golf cart. "That's the scariest part. She's in jail. So where did the envelope come from?"

"It has to be her," he said.

"I don't know. I already called Deputy Wilson and Mr. Stallard. I'm taking the note and photos to the police station tomorrow."

Josh buckled Janie into the car seat attached to the golf cart, and I climbed into the back seat next to her. I didn't like the idea of her riding in the back by herself.

"In other news, Helen's coming tonight." Janie waved to everyone on Bay Street as we passed by. "She's bringing Drew."

"Drew?" Josh turned to look at me in the back seat.

"You know, Drew. Your new retired guy."

"You don't say." Josh raised an eyebrow as we made eye contact in the rear-view mirror.

"He totally has the hots for her, but she's taking it slow."

Josh laughed. "Well, good for Helen. What a sly little devil Drew is. Who knew?"

The golf cart lurched to a stop as Josh pressed the pedal into park. The front porch was adorned with newly hung bows covered in birds and birdhouses. Climbing out of the golf cart, I smiled at Renee's attention to detail when it came to her home.

Helen and Drew slid into the driveway behind us.

"Perfect timing. I'm so glad you guys came," I said as I waved to them.

"Miss a chance to see my girl Janie? Never," Helen teased.

"I love your dress, Helen." Helen liked to wear sporty clothes most of—if not all—the time. She once told me she was tired of wearing stuffy paralegal clothes, and now that she didn't have to anymore, she liked to be comfortable. Tonight, she chose a fabulous, mid-length, powder blue cotton dress.

"Thanks, girl." She winked.

I opened the door and announced, "The gang's all here. Let's get the party started."

Renee hollered from the kitchen. "Woohoo." Janie pulled her hand free and took off running toward Renee.

"Re Re," Janie exclaimed as she jumped into her arms.

"Hello, Janie girl," Renee said as she twirled her around in a hug. "Where's Josh?"

Confused, I turned around to look for him. I didn't notice he hadn't come in yet. "He's here. Probably getting something from the golf cart."

As usual, the kitchen island was covered with food, and various delicious scents wafted through the house, causing my mouth to instantly water. Cheese and crackers were nestled perfectly on a sunflower-shaped dish. Sitting in the mini-Crockpot next to a large bowl of chips was the most delicious buffalo chicken dip ever to grace my lips. Helen brought a tray of beautifully cut veggies picked fresh from her garden. Josh and I brought several bottles of wine, hotdog and hamburger buns, and Burney's.

"Yes! You brought Burney's," Renee said.

"Heck yeah, I did. We can't have a party without it."

"This is my friend, Drew," Helen announced as she placed her hand gently on Drew's shoulder.

Renee tilted her head slightly and smiled. "Nice to meet you."

Doing his best to help Helen avoid any unwanted questions from Renee about Drew, Josh asked, "Where's Randy?"

"At the grill, cooking up the burgers," Renee said.

A few minutes later, Randy came into the house wearing a black apron with white block letters that said SMOKING HOT across the chest. "Hey guys, glad you made it. Who wants cheese?"

"Smoking hot, eh?" I said and slapped Randy in the gut.

He folded at the waist and grunted. "You know it, sis."

Renee playfully rolled her eyes and said, "Yeah. Yeah. Smoking hot." She shook her head and whacked Randy on the back. "Everyone, grab a plate. Let's eat."

I loaded food onto my plate and sat at the table.

Randy leaned back and balanced his chair on its two back legs. Rubbing his belly, he said, "I love when people come over because I get to eat all this great food." His eyes widened as he took in the food on his plate.

Renee squinted at him from across the table. "Just ignore him. Clearly, he eats fine." I cut food into tiny bits for Janie to eat when Renee asked, "Any news on the custody hearing?"

I sighed. "It was pushed back to the end of the month, so in a few weeks. Mr. Stallard says we have everything we need, and with Gray's support, he doesn't see any reason I shouldn't get custody." Josh's jaw tightened at the mention of Gray's name or, more specifically, the mention of *Gray's support*. "He said that we may not have an answer that day. Sometimes the judge likes to review the case and will call us back for a final verdict." I wiped Janie's hands clean and handed her a stuffed unicorn to play with so I could eat. "I'm anxious about it. I don't want to get my hopes up. I pray the judge will do the right thing and grant me custody."

"It's going to work out. I know it will," Randy said. His words were garbled between chewing.

I could sense how complex this topic of figuring out how to navigate our lives while raising a child with Gray was tough for Josh. "Let's talk about something else, if that's okay."

Renee took this opportunity to get the scoop on Helen and Drew. "Yes, let's." She tented her hands on top of the table and turned toward Drew. "Tell us how you met Helen." Helen's face immediately turned bright red, and she glared at Renee.

Drew gently placed his hand on Helen's and said, "I helped renovate the bookstore."

"I haven't been able to get rid of him since." Helen laughed and looked up at Drew. "He might start working a few days a week at the bookstore when he isn't working for Josh."

Shaking his finger at Helen, Josh said, "Don't be taking my man now. He has more tools than Southport has sunsets. This man can fix anything."

Helen beamed with pride and said, "Randy, you should check out his truck. I'm sure he has some gadgets that you don't have. He carries them around so he's ready for anything at a moment's notice." She stood from the table and mimicked Drew. Her arm in the air and finger pointed, she mocked. "You need to have the proper tool to do the proper job."

Everyone laughed, including Drew.

"Make fun all you want. It's true." Drew glanced at Josh. "When I'm not building shit for you, I'll be at the bookstore slinging books. Bayview Books is pretty cool, and I get to help this fine lady." He gently pinched Helen's arm and took a sip of wine.

"I think that's great since I can't be there as often now," I said as I lifted Janie from the table. "I need to get this one ready for bed."

"You boys can go compare tools. I'll help Renee clean up the kitchen," Helen said, a sly grin on her face.

"Who's ready for game night?" Renee shouted from the living room. "Get your drinks and let's get ready to play. I have a fun-filled night of games planned. We need to make teams, ladies. What do you think? Boys against girls?"

"Hell yeah. Look out, boys. We're gonna open up a can a whoop ass on ya," Helen shouted as she clapped her hands like a physical education teacher trying to get the class motivated.

Randy circled up with the boys, turned to us, and said, "You're going down."

"Oh shit, this is serious business," I said. I was laughing but was also slightly scared.

"First game, Face The Cookie," Renee said, her voice booming. She explained the directions loud and clear, and we each selected our team members to sit at the table and play the game. Renee and I played for our team, and Josh and Drew for the boys. We each placed an Oreo cookie in the center of our forehead and waited. The goal was to wiggle the Oreo down my face and into my mouth using only my facial muscles. The team to have both players successfully complete the challenge first won the round.

"On your mark, get set, go," Helen shouted. Cheers erupted from Helen and Randy. Each encouraged their teammates to finish. Drew was the first to finish and then jumped out of his chair to high-five Randy. He immediately joined in on the cheering, and the volume cranked even louder.

Renee was close to being finished until her Oreo plunged to the ground. Helen groaned. "Come on, girls, you can do this!"

Two seconds later, I successfully wriggled my Oreo to the corner of my mouth. Like a giraffe, I slid the tip of my tongue to collect the cookie and pull it into my mouth. I stood and cheered. Shimmying side to side, I pointed at the boys. "Come on, Renee. Get that cookie in your mouth."

Renee was working her facial muscles hard. She smiled and frowned to lift and drop her cheeks and slid the cookie toward her lips.

Josh was so close he had chocolate cookie crumbs dancing into his mouth when bam—the cookie hit the floor. Jumping up and down, the rest of us screamed at our teammates, hoping our cheers could will them to finish. Finally, Renee popped her cheek with a puff of air and caught the Oreo in her mouth. We fell back into our seats and burst out laughing.

"Whew, that was exhausting," I hissed out in between gulps of air.

The games went on for the next hour. We played Jenga un-stack to see which team could remove the most pieces before the stack fell down. Next was Marshmallow stuff. Each team nominated one player to see how many marshmallows they could put in a bowl by sucking them up with a straw. Renee had planned ten games, and we had two left to play. Josh seemed to be going through the motions. He played and laughed, but I could tell his mind was somewhere else.

The score was five to three, with the girls in the lead. The boys had to win the last two games to tie and, of course, in the event of a tie, Renee planned a tiebreaker.

"Okay, gang. The next game is called Junk in the Trunk," Renee announced as she placed a bag of ping-pong balls into two empty tissue boxes. "We need one member from each team to play. Decide your victim." She laughed. I was nominated for my team, and Josh was nominated for the boys.

"You're going down," I said and then kissed him.

Renee tied the tissue box around my waist as she reviewed the instructions. "Basically, the name of the game is to shake what your mama gave ya. When I say go, you twerk until all the balls have fallen out of your tissue box. The first one with an empty box, wins."

Engaged and ready to go, I settled into a double squat with my hands on my hips. Josh's face was as red as a tomato, and he couldn't stop laughing. *Maybe I was overthinking it. He seems to be having a good time now.* I whispered to Renee and Helen, "This should be easy, like taking candy from a baby."

Renee held her arms out in a T. "Are you ready?" Josh and I nodded. "Go."

I thrust my hips back and forth aggressively, popping my butt in the air, and ping-pong balls flew one after the other from my tissue box. After fifteen seconds, I had one ball left and the stubborn little shit did not want to come out.

"Done!" Josh yelled as he embraced Randy and Drew in a bro hug. "One more to go, and we tie, ladies. The game isn't over yet."

I groaned. "I totally had you beat. That one ball didn't want to come out."

"A win is a win. Sorry, babe," Josh said as he tried to come in for a hug.

"You're the enemy. No hugs for you." I crossed my arms in front of my body.

Renee emerged with two sets of baby bottles taped together at the neck to form a sort of hourglass-type mechanism. Inside, one bottle on each set were pink and blue M&M's.

"This one's called Baby Rattle. A team member from each team will use one hand to rattle the bottle until all the M&M's shift from one bottle to the other. The first team to do this wins the game. Select your victims."

Randy and Renee were selected for this game. The rest of us stood beside our respective teammates to cheer them on to victory, and the game began. Renee and Randy violently shook their arms up and down over and over while we cheered boisterously. "You can do it. Shake. Shake. Shake. Let's go."

Randy was close, but Renee pushed ahead to clinch the win for the girls.

"Yes. Victory tastes so good," Helen said as she sipped her wine. The girls did a little victory dance and high-fived. The boys pouted.

Taped inside the now empty baby bottles was a piece of paper. Randy held the bottle up to get a closer look. "Look. There's a message inside."

"Oh Lord, Renee. What are you going to have us do now?" I laughed.

Randy pretended to squint so he could see the message more clearly. "Mine says, 'We're having'." He shrugged as if he didn't know what it meant.

Renee beamed and said, "A baby. We're having a baby."

Clasping my hands over my face, I said, "Wait. What? Did I hear you say you're having a baby? As in, you're pregnant."

Renee and Randy, both smiling from ear to ear, simultaneously said, "Yes. We're having a baby."

"Oh, my God. That's wonderful news. I'm so happy for you guys." I squealed and jumped up and down. I hugged them both and tears filled my eyes. "I thought it wasn't possible."

Renee squeezed my arm. "We thought so too, but I guess God had other plans."

"Our babies are going to be best friends."

Josh shook Randy's hand and congratulated him. "Wonderful news, man. Be ready to become second fiddle."

Renee was glowing. Helen asked, "How far along are you?"

"I'm four months. We've been dying to tell you, but there never seemed to be a good time with everything going on. And we really wanted to get through the first trimester before we told anyone. We didn't want to jinx anything."

"This is amazing news. Just amazing. I'm so excited." *Aunt Lizzie has a nice ring to it.*

EIGHT
Josh

The last few months had been challenging, but exciting at the same time. Janie had entered our lives like the most blessed tornado and turned things upside down, but in the best possible way.

It had been too long since Lizzie and I had time to ourselves to talk about our future and our future with Janie. I fell more in love with that little girl and her mother every day. At the same time, I felt less and less connected to Lizzie. Motherhood was her priority now and it should be, but where did that leave me? As I sipped my coffee, I inhaled my gratitude for what life had brought me and exhaled my fears. I stood to stretch and twisted my back from side to side in the morning light.

Quietly, I tip-toed into the bedroom where the woman of my dreams was fast asleep. I watched her lying there in the bed we now shared. Her mouth was slightly agape, making the faintest and cutest snoring sound. I whispered, "I love you, Lizzie, more than you'll ever know." Janie would be awake soon, and I wanted to savor this moment.

I carefully slid into bed beside Lizzie, and with gentle strokes, I caressed the top of her head. Her eyes opened slowly, and she looked at me. A smile spread across her face. She had been through hell and back, and I was proud of how she had handled everything. I was angry with myself for being frustrated that we hadn't got married yet or talked about my custody of Janie. But I knew she was doing the best she could. I smiled back at her and fought the urge to force the conversation.

"Good morning, beautiful."

"Good morning, handsome."

"How about we go on a date tonight? Renee offered to babysit." I bopped the tip of her nose with my finger.

She scooted closer to me and tucked her head under my arm. I often pretended I didn't like to cuddle, but secretly I loved it when she was snuggled in my arms. My heart felt full. Her love was like oxygen, and I didn't think I could breathe without her and Janie.

"I'd like that. What'd you have in mind?"

I trailed my fingers along the small of her back, and she leaned in closer. Placing my thumb and forefinger on her chin, I tilted her head and touched my lips to hers. Kissing her slowly, my desire burned from the inside out as she kissed me back. Her lips sent tingles down my spine like tiny synapsis firing shockwaves to every part of my body. Her kiss drove me wild, and it was difficult to control my impulses. I could lie in this bed with her every second of every day.

"I was thinking we could go out on the boat at dusk. I've hired a captain and a chef. All we have to do is show up. They'll take care of the rest."

"Sounds wonderful," she murmured and pressed a gentle kiss to my chest. Her eyes glimmered invitingly.

Unable to control myself any longer, I shifted atop her, drew her close, and savored the warmth of her skin. I sucked her nipple into my mouth and was rewarded with her moans. I could feel the pent-up rush of endorphins pulsating through my veins. Her breathing hastened, and I trailed kisses along her neck, the delicate scent of lavender enveloping my nostrils.

She entwined her legs around my waist, drawing us impossibly close, our bodies fitting together seamlessly as she kissed me. Inside, I was wild—raging to be inside her. Yet, on the outside, I remained patient, wanting to cherish every second. Taking a deep breath, I gently pushed inside her. A sigh of relief escaped her and filled me with a profound sense of fulfillment.

Suddenly, cries exploded through the baby monitor, and our bodies went flaccid. I continued, but I could feel Lizzie disconnect from the moment, so I stopped.

"I'm sorry. I need to get her." Her body dropped, and her eyes showed disappointment. Our lives belonged to Janie now. We had a daughter, and she came first in everything because that's what parents do.

"It's okay. Janie comes first." I kissed her forehead. "I'll go. You stay in bed for a few more minutes."

Lizzie

Later that evening, I dropped Janie off with Randy and Renee. "We'll be back in the morning to pick her up. Thank you for keeping her tonight. Josh and I really need this time alone."

Renee set the diaper bag down and grabbed Janie's hand. "Are you kidding me? We love having her. Glad to help. Let's do breakfast when you come back to get her."

"Sounds great. Are you sure you guys will be okay?"

"We'll be fine. Everything's going to be fine."

"You feel up to it? Maybe we should take her on the boat with us."

"Lizzie, don't be ridiculous. We love having Janie. It's all good." She flicked my arm with a pointed finger and commanded, "Go. Take care of your man."

I nervously picked at a small scab on my arm and bit my bottom lip. "You're sure?"

Renee pressed her hands to my shoulders. "For the love of God, woman, go. We're going to be fine." She pushed me toward the door.

I hugged Renee and gave Janie a giant bear hug and a twirl. "Okay. We'll see you in the morning for breakfast."

I kissed Janie on the head. "I love you, baby girl. Be good for Re Re, and Unkie." I waved and hurried to the golf cart, afraid that if I didn't move swiftly, I'd burst back through the front door and cancel the entire evening.

At my house, I scoured my closet for the perfect outfit to wear. Butterflies fluttered furiously in my stomach like it was my first date with Josh. After trying on half my closet, I settled on a jean mini-skirt, a white, low cut, V-neck tank top, and a sheer black chiffon blouse and topped off the outfit with my favorite red wedges.

I was in the bathroom putting the final touches on my make-up when Josh entered the bedroom.

"You ready, babe?"

"Almost."

"Okay, we should leave in a few minutes."

He was changing into a pair of clean jeans and a button-down crème shirt when I walked into the bedroom. "I'm ready."

A short golf cart ride later, we stepped onto the *Hammer of the Sea*. The sky was perfect for an evening on the boat. There wasn't a cloud to be found. We were just in time to watch the sunset and the dazzling stars of the universe fill the night sky.

The back deck twinkled with lights. The lounge chairs had been replaced with a small table for two. "I'll let the captain know we're ready to shove off. Be right back."

My lips parted slightly, and I arched my back as memories of my favorite date with Josh on this very boat flooded my mind. He took me fishing, and I ended up in his bed. We made love for the first time on this vessel. Feeling my temperature rise, I fanned myself and caught sight of the vase of freshly cut roses in the center of the table. Sitting to the side of the table was a bucket of ice, and a bottle of champagne was nestled inside. I considered tossing the ice over my head.

I slid into a seat at the table and looked toward the water. I was lucky to have Josh in my life. Butterflies and knots battled in my stomach. I wanted to be in the moment and appreciate the evening with my fiancé. He deserved a night with my undivided attention, but I was also worried about Janie. When she wasn't with me, I worried. I couldn't help but feel I would wake up one morning, and she'd be gone. Taken. I tried to shake the feeling.

Don't be ridiculous. Everything's going to be fine.

I pulled my phone from my purse and texted Renee.

Me: How's Janie? Everything going ok?

Renee: Everything's fine. Enjoy yourself.

I breathed a sigh of relief and dropped my phone back into my purse. *Relax. Janie will be fine.*

Josh returned and ran his finger along my shoulder as he walked past and sat across from me. His soulful green eyes reflected the twinkle lights strung around the deck. "Let's toast." He popped the cork and poured champagne into our glasses. "To us."

Hoping the alcohol would kick in and force me to relax, I said, "To us," and then downed my glass.

Josh hadn't set down the bottle yet, he tipped it over and poured me a refill. "The salad will be out soon."

"Thank you for putting this evening together. I want to spend time with you, but I'm struggling to be without Janie by my side twenty-four-seven. If I take my eyes off her, I'm afraid she'll disappear, and this will all be a dream."

Josh moved to stand behind me and massaged my shoulders. "I understand, Lizzie. This has been a lot for all of us." He tilted my head to the side and pressed his thumb into my neck. "Randy and Renee love Janie. They'll take great care of her."

I knew the words were true. His magical hands were releasing all the tension in my shoulders. Maybe it was the champagne, I'm not sure but, I started to relax. I grabbed his hand and kissed his palm. He pulled me to my feet, wrapped me in his arms, and said, "I love you, Lizzie."

"I love you, too." He took my hand in his and twirled me out, our arms extended. He twirled me back in, met my lips with his, and then dipped me. We danced to the music only we could hear as the sunset, and night draped over the sky.

The chef appeared behind the cabin door and set our salads on the table.

"Let's eat," Josh said, twirling me to my seat. "More champagne?"

"Yes, please."

Pouring more champagne into my glass, Josh said, "We haven't talked in a while about us. About our marriage plans. Lizzie, I love you. I want to spend the rest of my life with you. I want to set a date. I'd marry you tonight, right here on this boat, if you'd let me."

A lump formed in my throat. My shoulders slumped, and I looked away from him. The last thing I intended to do was hurt Josh. But I didn't feel right getting married and moving on with my life until things were settled with Janie.

"Lizzie?"

The silence was deafening. I practically chewed a hole through my cheek.

"Lizzie?"

I turned to face him. The inner corners of his eyebrows were raised, and his eyes were soft. "I love you, Josh. I do. I love you with all my heart. I want to marry you." He pressed his lips together, and the corners of his mouth pulled downward slightly.

"I have to consider Janie now with every decision that I make. How can I celebrate our marriage and have a wedding when she could be taken from me any day? I don't know how to move forward until I have legal custody of her." I chugged my champagne to dull the ache creeping into my chest. "I do want to marry you.

I know you want an official wedding date. Hell, I'll marry you the instant I have custody of Janie."

I knew this must be hard for Josh. I love him so much. I wanted our wedding day to be special. I wanted to be completely focused on him and our future together. Until Janie was legally mine, I felt like I couldn't give my full heart and attention to anything else.

He looked away. I could see his eyes welling with tears in the moonlight. He took a quick breath and rubbed his lips together. "You know, I'm concerned about custody of Janie, too. You aren't the only one afraid. But I still want to marry you."

His words sliced through my heart like a paper cut. Small and recoverable, but painful until it heals.

"I need you to try to understand. My heart's a mess with fear every day. I'm doing my best to hold it together. When I say I do, I want the only feeling in my heart to be my infinite love for you." *How do I make him understand that my reservations have nothing to do with him?*

"I want to believe you, Lizzie. I do. I don't want to let this doubt creep into my heart. But I can't help it. I can't help but feel like you want to postpone things because you aren't sure anymore. Gray's a part of our lives now and Janie's biological father. Do you want to be with him so you can be a family?"

My heart sank. Our lives were complicated, and I couldn't deny that Gray was Janie's biological father. I also couldn't deny that he has been doing everything he could to prove that he loves her and wants to participate actively in her life. My throat felt dry as I fought hard to suppress my tears.

"It's complicated." Two words were all I could muster. Gray will undoubtably be part of Janie's life, and Josh will be part of her life, too. As a mother I can't split my heart in two. I can't say I do, while I worry about custody of my daughter.

"So, you do want to be with him?" There was a tremor in his voice.

"No. I want to be with you." My voice elevated in pitch as I spoke. "I don't know how to make you believe that, but it's the truth." I pushed my salad plate aside and buttered a piece of bread. More out of nerves than hunger because my stomach did not want food. "Gray is Janie's father. That's a fact. He's the only reason that we both get to raise her every day. We owe him a debt of gratitude for that."

Josh scoffed. "We owe him nothing."

Taking a deep breath, I organized my thoughts, my priority always being Janie. "Look. He might have started off with the wrong intentions, but now he seems genuine. I don't know what to believe, and I'm not letting my guard down, but what I do know is that we need to play nice until I have custody of Janie."

Searching for an answer, his gaze grew more intense as he asked, "What about me?"

"What about you?"

"Where will I fit into Janie's life? Into your new life?"

An exasperated sigh escaped my lips. "You're being ridiculous." Reaching across the table, I tried to bridge the gap by placing my hand over his. "Josh, you're my forever person. My best friend. I want to marry you as soon as we get through this. The day I have custody, we can go straight to the justice of the peace and say our vows. I don't care when or where. And you are Janie's father in every way that matters. She loves you."

The chef discreetly interrupted and placed the next course in front of us. Josh glanced at the dishes and then back to me. His eyes had softened but still carried traces of uncertainty. "I'm sorry, Lizzie. You have enough going on, and I shouldn't add my insecurities to your struggles." His gaze dropped, perhaps in shame or maybe introspection. We continued our meal in contemplative silence.

After dinner, we lay on the lounge chairs and watched for shooting stars in the sky. Wrapped in his arms, I felt safe. I wanted to reassure him, but I didn't know how. "I don't want to love anyone else but you. I want the rest of our days to be filled with morning coffee on the porch overlooking the water and quiet evenings at home. I want you to make love to me in every room in the house. I want to share the good and bad times with you, Josh. I want to marry you and only you." I nestled my head into his chest and wrapped my arm around his waist.

"I know, Lizzie. I feel the same." He pointed toward the sky. "Look, I saw one. Did you see it?"

"I missed it. I was looking at you."

NINE
Gray

The long, brick building looked more like a school than a prison except for the barbed wire fence surrounding the perimeter. Bouncing balls smacked against the pavement as women in gray shorts and shirts played basketball. The grass was immaculate, like it was the ninth hole at Pebble Beach.

I was stunned by the events that had unfolded over the last year. My batshit crazy wife tried to kill my girlfriend. If that wasn't insane enough, she stole our baby. I had my head up my ass and was oblivious to all of it.

It didn't take long for Janie's beautiful blue eyes and radiant smile to win me over. I was a father. I had probably ruined any chance of ever being with Lizzie again. I had treated her like dogshit, and I'll regret it for the rest of my life. I'd ruin any man who treated my daughter the way I treated Lizzie.

"Sir. Please empty your pockets into the tray and step toward the metal detector." I threw my wallet and keys into the tray and handed it to the guard. "Step forward, sir."

Geez, give me a second. I nodded and stepped in between the edges of the metal detector. Green light.

"Step through, sir." I collected my belongings and proceeded to the counter.

"I'm here to see Catalina Stone."

I was ushered into a waiting area. Taking in my surroundings was an old habit from my days at the orphanage. Suddenly, my mind was catapulted back to a memory of me sitting on a bench in front of Nathan Rose Mortuary and staring up at the man speaking to the crowd. Loneliness engulfed me, and icy cold ran through my veins even though the sun still kissed my skin. I was seven years old in this memory, and that was the day I became an orphan. I think that was the day my heart turned to stone and brought new meaning to my name: Grayson Ethan Stone.

My life was spent in and out of orphanages, never being the "chosen one," but I was determined to have the life my mother wished for me. Her smile willed me forward each day. I was an outsider of sorts most of my life. Looking back, the isolation was my fault.

My thoughts were abruptly pulled back to the present when I spotted a man seated across from me on a bench in the prison waiting room. Absorbed in his phone, he didn't notice my gaze. His white, long-sleeved, button-down strained at the buttons, hinting at recent weight gain and perhaps a reluctance or inability to invest in a better-fitting shirt. His black tie was loose around the neck and hung slightly to the left. The tie and the distraught look all over his face lead me to believe he probably spent a lot of money defending someone inside this prison. I didn't want to strike up a conversation with him, but I was a little curious to know more.

On the right side of the room was a middle-aged woman. Flanking her on either side were two young boys. *Poor kids, I wonder if their mother's in here.* I took my seat in the corner and responded to emails on my phone while I waited.

About fifteen minutes later, my name was called, and I walked the long hallway with glass compartments filled with loved one's talking to other inmates. The guard pointed me to a station, and I sat in front of the thick glass. Catalina entered the hallway from her side. Her long brown hair was cut short and rested barely above her shoulders. Her milky white skin was paler than normal. She looked almost translucent. Her cheeks had sunken in and gave her a bit of a skeletal appearance, and her frame was as lanky as ever.

I picked up the phone on the wall. "The gray matching shirt and pant set suits you."

She gave me the finger. "What do you want, Gray?"

I took a moment to weigh my words. I had to get this right. "Kitty Cat," I said, as I tilted my chin and flashed her a flirtatious smile. "You look like hell. But I hear you have a parole hearing coming up soon."

Not taking the bait, she snarled, "Yeah, and?"

"I assume you're going to want your daughter back." She leaned forward as I mentioned her daughter. *That got her attention.*

"Back? She's my daughter. I have the birth certificate to prove it. Your bitch, Lizzie, can say whatever she wants, but Sophie is my daughter." She lifted her head and puffed out her chest. Her smugness made me want to punch through the glass and choke her.

I exhaled and spoke calmly, "She's my daughter, actually. But I'd like to offer you an olive branch."

"I'm listening." She raised one eyebrow and steepled her fingers.

"Sophie's custody hearing is coming up in a few weeks. I'll do everything in my power to swing the judge to side with you. I'll suggest you're the most suited to continue raising Sophie." It sickened me to call her Sophie, but I had to play along. Janie was a much better name.

Her pupils dilated, and she leaned forward, then looked me in the eye, and pressed her palm to the glass. "Are you suggesting that we be a family?"

"I'm suggesting that we share custody, but I have a few conditions." Her blue-ish gray eyes glistened as she envisioned her freedom and raising Janie with me. I severely miscalculated her obsession. After everything, I assumed she'd moved on. *Shit. Shit. Shit. Think, Gray.*

I exhaled, slowly lifted my palm, and pressed it to the glass to meet hers. "Oh, Kitty Cat. I think our ship has sailed. You don't love me. I know you don't, and I've made peace with that. But I believe you love our daughter." I looked into her eyes and watched as the twinkle faded. "I'd like you to sign the divorce papers. If you agree to sign the divorce papers, which state you get zero of my estate, properties, and businesses, I'll pay you alimony of two hundred thousand dollars annually." She glared at me and smacked the glass. "Now hold on, Kitty Cat, I'm not done." I tilted my head and gently curled the corner of my mouth. I spoke in a soft, understanding tone. A tone that would send butterflies whirling in her insides—at least I hoped it would. "I wish things could be different for you and me, but you know there's nothing left between us. I'll make sure that we get shared custody of Sophie. I know how much you love her. We can raise her together. I have the power to do this if you'll sign the divorce papers."

Catalina hunched in her chair, taking in everything I had suggested. "You'll have money and your daughter. And technically, you'll still have me. We'll raise her together, but I want the divorce."

She dropped her head and said, "I'll sign."

"You won't regret this. I'll have my attorney come by with the papers this afternoon."

She snapped her head up, her eyes black as night now. With pursed lips, she said, "If you fuck me over, I'll kill her. If I can't have her, no one can have her. Do you hear me, Gray? I'll fucking kill her and your bitch, Lizzie, too."

"Guard," I shouted. Pressing my hand against hers again, I slowly slid it down the window, and her hand followed.

"Goodbye, Kitty Cat. You can trust me. You'll be with your daughter soon."

Fuck. She's insane. My heart raced as I made a swift exit.

TEN

Lizzie

Mrs. Donahue was sitting on the couch reading the newest Nora Roberts novel, and Helen was working behind the counter. Her brown hair hung down in a perfect set of beach curls. She was once again wearing a dress. I did a double-take. *Yup. She's wearing a dress.* Mr. Paul and a man I'd never seen before were in a very intense chess game.

"Hi. What's the occasion?" I said as I stepped behind the counter beside Helen.

"I felt like wearing a dress. Is that a crime?"

"Not at all. You look great. You've been wearing dresses a lot lately. That's all." I smiled. I reached for the stack of mail under the counter and started sifting through the pile. I submitted an article to Vogue Magazine about the bookstore and was eager for a reply. "I came to see if you want some lunch."

A moment later, Drew emerged from the staff room with a drill in his hand.

"Just felt like wearing a dress, huh? I see."

"Oh, stop it, Lizzie." She nudged me with her elbow. "He's building some new bookcases for the store."

Drew greeted us at the counter. "Hello, ladies. I need to grab my camera from the truck. I want to take pictures of my work. I'll be right back."

"Lizzie's grabbing us lunch. Do you want something?"

Drew stepped behind the counter, twirled Helen around, and kissed her right on the lips. My jaw hit the floor. "I'd love a hot date with you, but I'll settle for a sandwich. Something with turkey works." He kissed her again and walked out the door.

"Umm, what just happened?" My smile widened with excitement.

"A lady doesn't kiss and tell," Helen snickered.

I slapped her shoulder. "You sly little devil."

"I took your advice. We went for coffee and then dinner and then, well..."

"Helen!"

"Oh, Lizzie. He's wonderful. I didn't think I could bring myself to think about another man, let alone be with one. But he's wonderful."

I hugged her tightly and we rocked back and forth. "I'm so happy for you."

She stepped back and grabbed my hands. "At first, we took it slow, but I realized I'm not getting any younger. So, I jumped right in, and here we are."

"If you're happy. I'm happy, and he seems very nice. Not too shabby looking for almost sixty, either." I laughed. "Write down what you want from Sand Witches, and I'll go get it."

Helen scribbled her and Drew's orders on a small piece of paper and handed it to me. "Leave Janie here. I'll read to her while you're gone."

"Okay. Be right back."

Sand Witches opened a few weeks ago, and I was excited to try the food. Word on the street was that they had an enchanting secret sauce that made their sandwiches taste magical. The door jingled as it opened, and in walked Andra. Tied up in a messy bun, her hair was as bleach blonde as I remembered from her interview. Her shorts were so short her vagina was practically chewing on her shorts. Although she looked like she'd been at the beach most of the day, her face was perfectly made up.

"Hey, Andra. You're a long way from home. What brings you here?" I said as I waved hello. She seemed oddly nervous. Her first day at GSM South was tomorrow. I guess I'd be nervous, too.

She laughed. "My roommate raves about Southport. I had to visit before work took over my life."

"You have to get some Burney's before you head back to Wilmington. Their croissants are divine. Are you excited for your first day?"

She shifted her weight. "Yes, ma'am. I'm excited. A little nervous, too. I really want to do a great job."

"You'll do wonderfully," I reassured her. "And please, no need for the 'ma'am.' Call me Lizzie."

She hesitated and then smiled, "I'm sorry ma'am — I mean, Lizzie."

I chuckled, "It's all right. We'll get there."

I placed my order at the counter with a young girl named Nikki. She suggested the Abracadabra special, a turkey concoction on a toasted panini. I ordered for Helen and Drew and stepped to the pickup window at the end of the counter.

Andra hesitated for a moment and then bravely ventured, "Can I ask you something personal?"

I was taken aback by her directness, but I admired it. "Of course," I replied with a welcoming smile.

"Are you and Mr. Stone...you know...together?"

I nearly choked in surprise. What a forward question for a young girl. But I must admit she had guts.

"Not that it's any of your business, but no. I'm engaged to someone else." I raised my eyebrow and looked her up and down. "Let me give you a piece of advice, woman to woman. If you're thinking of barking up that tree, don't. As a matter of fact, if you even have the slightest notion you want to bark up that tree, find a new job. He isn't worth it. You're young. Don't screw up your life for Gray Stone."

She looked visibly taken aback. "Oh, no, ma'am. I don't want to be with Gray Stone. I just assumed…"

I raised my hand in objection and stopped her mid-sentence. "You assumed incorrectly. Didn't your mother ever teach you not to assume?" Confused, she blinked, so I explained. "Never assume. It makes an ass out of you and me. Get it?"

"You're right. I shouldn't have assumed. My apologies. It's just that Gray seems to want your opinion, your expertise. He respects you. I assumed…"

"There's that word again."

"I'm sorry. I figured you were together, is all, since he listens to you."

There were so many things to unpack from her words, but I didn't have time, so I gave her the cliff notes version. "Work hard, use your brain, set your standards, and men will respect you. Two, you don't need to be with a man to earn his respect. In fact, that's the opposite of respect. He should respect you first before anything else. And three, you don't know what you don't know, but please know that you have a lot to learn. Good chat. Gotta run. See you tomorrow."

I grabbed the bag of food, a few bags of chips, and drinks. I paid the sweet old man behind the cash register and left.

I didn't want Andra to make the same mistakes I did. She was ambitious, had a good work ethic, and seemed to have a good head on her shoulders. She needed to stay focused on work. She could succeed on her own two feet. And she certainly doesn't need to add a tussle in the hay with Gray. Although I didn't think she was his type, stranger things had happened.

Back at the bookstore, Helen and I sat at a table in the children's corner so Janie could play while we ate. "So, tell me about Drew."

"There's nothing to tell. I already told you everything. Well, there might be a little more." She wiped her mouth and took a sip of her drink.

"More?"

"He wants to take me to the mountains. Not any time soon, but he said he goes every fall when the leaves change, and he wants me to go with him."

"I think that's perfect. You don't have to commit right now."

"I agree. If things are going well, I'll go. If not, I won't."

Janie toddled over to us and raised her arms while opening and closing her hands.

I picked her up and sat her onto my thigh as I kissed her cheek. I reached down, rummaged through the diaper bag, and pulled out a container of Cheerios for her to snack on. "I can't stay too much longer. Her lunch is at home."

"I'm glad you stopped by. It's always nice to see you," Helen said as she patted the bottom of Janie's foot. "How are things?"

"What things? There's so many." I laughed, but secretly I wanted to cry.

"Is Josh coming around? It has to be hard for him to have Gray around all the time. You're working with him. He's spending time with Janie. Custody isn't final yet. I'm sure Josh's nervous, too."

I sighed. "He's doing okay. We had an argument about setting a wedding date." I bounced Janie up and down on my knee and handed her a book to play with. "Len's not been doing well, either. He refuses to go to the doctor. It's hard. Worst of all, Catalina has a parole hearing soon. Stallard thinks there's a good chance she'll get out with time served and community service."

Helen's eyes narrowed, and her jaw clenched. "I can't believe that's true."

"Well, believe it. It's still a few months away. I'm praying the custody is settled before she gets out." Janie threw the book onto the floor and started to squirm.

ELEVEN

Lizzie

Andra, the new hire, settled into her role nicely after the first week. Gray hired an interior designer who classed up the place with paintings, large floral vases, warm and inviting lobby chairs and couches, and even some finishing touches in the bathroom. GSM South was coming along. Initially, I didn't expect many clients to want to meet with us at this location, but we'd already had several reach out to schedule their appointments. They wanted to couple their visit with a mini-vacation. Gray probably had already figured this would be the case, but I was just catching on. I walked into the lobby where Andra sat at the front desk. Her brightly colored, short skirt shined through the glass top. Her skirt accented her lime green low-cut blouse. Her face was, as always, adorned with flawless makeup. Today, however, she had accentuated her eyes with a shade of green eyeshadow that matched her top perfectly.

I handed Andra a list of all the clients we needed to schedule appointments with. "The list is in order of priority. Please work your way down from the top to fill these appointments." Emails and phone numbers were on the page, making it a simple job. "Please make sure to schedule my appointments on the days that I am here."

"Yes, ma'am. I'll get right to it."

I raised my eyebrow.

"I'm sorry. No problem, Lizzie. I'm on it."

"Perfect," I said and walked around the corner to Gray's office.

"Hello, gorgeous," he said as I entered the room. "I'm sorry. Old habits die hard. Let me start over." He grinned sheepishly. "You look nice today."

My new black slacks were perfectly pressed and paired well with my white sleeveless blouse covered in tiny black polka dots. They were the perfect combo for my power red heels and ruby earrings Josh gave me last Christmas. Josh especially liked the heels, and I promised him I'd wear them later.

"Thanks, Gray. It's nice to dress up a few days a week." I sat in one of the large plush armchairs in front of his desk.

"Have you decided on a daycare for Janie, yet?" he said as he sat down in the chair beside me.

"No. I'm not sure what I want, but Renee can't watch her forever."

He crossed his leg over his knee. "I can pay for her daycare. I want to help."

"I appreciate that. I don't need you to pay for it. I just need to decide where to send her. Honestly, I need to get comfortable with the idea."

"You'll figure it out."

I nodded in agreement and shifted my weight in my chair. "What do you think of Andra so far?"

Gray strolled over to the door and closed it. My insides squirmed as the door clicked into place. Being behind clothes doors alone with Gray was something I tried to avoid.

"I think she's working out great so far. She's been on the ball, completed her tasks, and is pleasant most of the time. I have this nagging feeling about her, though."

"What do you mean?"

"I don't know. Maybe it's too early to tell. Ask me again in a few weeks." He sat back in the chair. "How are you enjoying being back in the swing?"

I rested my arms on the chair and crossed my legs. "Honestly?"

He laughed. "Yes. Honestly."

"So far, so good."

"You sound surprised," he said.

"Well, I'm a little surprised. Yes, there was a time when we worked well together and set the world on fire, but there was also a time when you were pretty much an asshole and made me feel like a pile of shit. How's that for honesty?" I laughed. He shrugged apologetically.

"I'm not convinced you've changed, but I'll admit you've been good to Janie, and you haven't crossed the line at work. I appreciate that, Gray. I really do."

"I've told you a million times. I love Janie. I know I was an ass. I wish I could take it back. But it wasn't long before our baby girl wrapped me around her little finger." He opened his mini-fridge and grabbed a bottle of water. Holding it up, he said, "You want one?"

"Sure," I said. "I know you love her. I try not to let the custody hearing consume me, but I don't think I've gotten a full night's sleep since all this has happened."

Gray settled back into his seat and placed his hand atop mine. I quickly withdrew my hand from beneath his. "Look, I know I tried to manipulate you by using our daughter. I want to punch myself in the face for that. Janie needs you. I promise I won't take her away from you. Have faith. The custody hearing is going to work out."

I wanted to believe him. Every fiber of my being wanted to believe he was genuine, but I couldn't. There had been so much hurt, so much pain. I wanted custody of Janie, and I hoped Josh could adopt her. *Maybe I should discuss this with Gray now?*

"Lizzie, our daughter, is the greatest thing that ever happened to me. You gave me that. You gave me Janie. I'll always be grateful to you."

Probably now's not a good time to bring up parental rights for Josh. I sighed. *How could I even ask Gray to give up his parental rights? He is her father.*

Knowing my sighs, Gray said, "What's on your mind?"

I looked up, and his heartfelt, genuine, green eyes locked onto mine. I couldn't conceal the pain radiating all over my face. He must have recognized the pain, too, because understanding swept through him, and he said, "I truly am sorry, Lizzie. For all of it."

I don't know why, but I wanted to hug him. I didn't, but I wanted to.

"I'm happy with Josh. He's so good to Janie. I want you to know that."

Gray dropped his head and shuffled his feet. "I don't want to admit it, but I know he loves Janie. He's one lucky guy."

I smiled, but I didn't miss the slight resentment in his tone.

I stood and clapped my hands. "All right, we have lots of work to do. Beach Front Properties is coming in a few days, and we need to seal the deal. Let's see what Andra's made of. Conference room brainstorming session."

"Ah, shit. It's going to be a long few days. We should've scheduled that meeting a week later."

"Yes, we should have, but your mister 'we've got this' bit off a little more than we could chew."

He laughed. "Yeah, I guess I did. We don't have a business without business, so we need this client. They are a big fish if we can land them."

As I walked out of his office, his words trailed off in the distance. Andra was working at her computer when I approached the lobby. Passing her desk, I said, "Come to the conference room when you're done."

Curious, she looked up at me. "Will do."

Gray followed me into the room and sat at the head of the table. I plugged the jump drive into the laptop connected to the seventy-inch television that hung on the wall. After I cued up the presentation, I took a seat next to Gray at the table. Andra hurried in shortly after and chose the chair across from me.

"Great. The gang's all here," Gray said. "This is our first shot to land a very big client. We need to be prepared. Beach Front Properties is a local realty company. They handle most of the rentals for the Carolina coast and also deal in real estate. They feel like Airbnb is kicking their ass and hired us to help beef up their marketing strategy."

Beach Front Properties logo was front and center on the screen. A large dune covered in sea oats with a basic Times New Roman font in blue that said Beach Front Properties.

"I think the first thing we need to do is encourage them to rebrand with a new logo," Andra suggested. "Something more modern and sleek."

"I agree," I said. "We need to capture the essence of their business, their culture, and what they want to convey to the world in this new logo."

Gray took a sip of water and said, "Agreed. Lizzie, we'll work that into the presentation."

I clicked on the next slide, which showed the percentage of business they did on each beach along the coast. "It appears they have a good foothold locally in Southport, Oak Island, and Wilmington, but I think we should encourage them to expand out from those locations to capture more market share elsewhere." I made a note to look at the map, do some research on the coastline, and determine which target areas would be best to go after. "I'll work on some suggestions."

Andra was staring at the television. I could see her wheels turning. "What if we partner with local businesses and do weekend giveaways for the properties they already own? We could also put together for the guests a welcome basket that showcases all the available rental and sale properties Beach Front has available."

"Love it. Keep the ideas coming," Gray said. After two hours of brainstorming, we had a full deck to present to our first clients. "Andra, clear your schedule. You'll assist Lizzie with whatever she needs the rest of the day and tomorrow." He turned to look at me. "Lizzie, I'm sorry to ask, but we might need to pull a late night tomorrow if we don't finish."

"Understood. I aim to have everything ready by close of business tomorrow, but if not, I know the drill. We work until it's done. I'll make arrangements."

TWELVE

Lizzie

Like a perfect watercolor painting coming to life before my eyes, the sunrise was breathtaking, painting the sky brilliant shades of orange, yellow, and pink. Josh was asleep in the bed. He looked so peaceful. I slipped into the shower and got myself ready to attack the grueling day that lay before me. Sitting on the edge of the bed, I stared at Josh for a moment before leaning into him. My lips gently touched his forehead. His eyes opened slowly, and he wrapped his arms around me, pulling me on top of him. He brushed the hair out of my face and kissed my lips. I longed for his sensual touch. His kiss. His love. All of him. I was completely and madly in love with him.

"I have to go. It's going to be a long day. I've arranged for Janie to stay with Renee. I'll pick her up on my way home from work. Don't plan on us for dinner."

He whined and kissed me again. "Do you have to stay late? I miss you. We've been so busy lately." I pushed myself off the bed. Josh growled, flew out of bed, scooped me up, and wrapped my legs around his waist. "I can get Janie when I leave," he said in between kisses.

"I've already made arrangements with Renee. It's okay. Spend some time with your dad. You two can have a guy's night." He twirled me around and pressed my back against the wall. He kissed my chest, working his way down the V in my shirt. "I love you. Have a good day," he whispered into my ear.

"You're making it hard for me to leave," I whimpered as his kiss lingered at the top of my breast. Forcing myself to stay focused, I said, "Renee will swing by to pick up Janie soon. The diaper bag's already packed and sitting by the door."

Smirking, he put me down and patted my butt. "You're lucky you're wearing pants."

He, however, wasn't wearing any.

The entire day was a blur. Andra, Gray, and I worked tirelessly preparing storyboards, logo concepts, marketing and growth strategies. Gray practiced the pitch at least a dozen times, but we still weren't done. Everything had to be perfect. At one-thirty, Gray ordered pizza, and we worked through lunch. At four-thirty, we took a quick break. At six-thirty, we still weren't finished.

I started packing my bag.

"Andra, you can go. Plan to be here at seven tomorrow morning in case we have anything else to finish. Beach Front arrives at 10:30 AM."

"Thank you. I'm exhausted. I'll be back bright and early in the morning." She didn't waste any time and was out the door a few seconds later.

"I know we still have a lot of work to do." I put the last binder in my bag and threw it over my shoulder.

"Are you willing to bring Janie to the condo? She can sleep in her room at my place, and we can keep working. We have quite a bit to finish."

A knot tightened in my stomach. Taking Janie to his condo would undoubtedly upset Josh. But on the other hand, the looming deadline was undeniable, and our work was far from over.

Deep in thought, I recalled the many nights Gray and I had spent working late, burning the midnight oil. This wasn't too different, was it? It was about the task at hand, not the setting. And yet, I couldn't shake off the unease, the feeling of trespassing some invisible boundary.

I wasn't comfortable with the plan, but we needed to finish. Reluctantly, I said, "Yes. I'll pick up Janie and meet you at your place, but Gray," I paused and looked him directly in the eye, "this is strictly business."

He held his hands up and nodded. "Strictly business."

On my way to the car, I texted Josh.

Me: We aren't done with the pitch. Picking up Janie and going to Gray's. We have to finish tonight. I love you. Kiss Emoji.

I waited for three dots to appear. Nothing.

Thirty minutes later, when I arrived in Southport, I rechecked my phone. Still no response from Josh. I closed my eyes and exhaled. *He's pissed.*

I started a new text message.

Me: I'm sorry. I know this sucks. I LOVE YOU!

I stared at the text and considered whether to send it. *Screw it.* Send.

Me: I'll be home as soon as I can.

Gray

I could see Lizzie and Janie approaching the door and opened it before she could knock. "Come on in." I extended my arm and welcomed them into the house.

"Dad-deeeeeee," Janie squealed. She ran to me with her arms wide, and I picked her up into a warm embrace. My heart exploded at her genuine excitement to see me. She put her hand on my mouth and squeezed my lips. I made a motorboat sound, and Janie giggled. Her giggle was like a symphony filling the room with joy.

I don't know how anyone could not smile at the sound of her boisterous laugh.

"I should give her a bath before bed," Lizzie said as she set the diaper bag onto the kitchen table. She checked her phone and set it back down. "I like to stick to her routine."

"No problem. I'll get you a towel."

"Thanks."

"Are you hungry? I can whip something up while you're doing bath time." With Janie still in my arms, I rummaged through the pantry to see what I could find. "I have some pasta. Does that sound good?"

"Quick and easy. Perfect." Lizzie took Janie from me and headed toward the bathroom.

Don't mess this up. If you ever want Lizzie to trust you again, you can't screw this up. I set the pot on the stove and waited for the water to boil. I poured two glasses of wine and spread our work across the kitchen table.

I could hear Lizzie in the bathroom singing to Janie. I couldn't help myself; I had to peek. Standing quietly in the doorway, I watched as the mother of my child sang softly to our daughter. My heart instantly swelled.

"Dad-deeeeee," Janie said as she kicked her legs wildly in the water.

"I'm sorry. I didn't mean to disrupt you. I could hear you singing, and I—,"

Lizzie turned to face me, and her white shirt was drenched, cupping her breasts and accentuating her nipples that now stood erect and poked through her black lace bra. Water dripped from her hair.

"I'm soaked. Do you have something I can change into?" I could hear the tension in her voice.

I could feel my loins tingle as my eyes devoured the beautiful woman standing in front of me.

Easy Gray. Easy. Just get her something to change into. Don't be an asshole.

"Yes. I'll grab you something."

"Thanks. I'll be right out," she said.

I dug through my closet and found a pair of workout shorts and an old Beatles T-shirt. I grabbed a navy-blue Southport hoody in case she might get cold. Lizzie and Janie were coming out of the bathroom on my way back. Janie was nestled in a towel with her head resting on Lizzie's shoulder. I pulled my phone from my pocket and took a picture. This was a moment I would remember forever.

"Gray. What are you doing?" Lizzie said, eyeing me with the slightest bit of contempt.

"I was lost in the moment. She looks so sweet and content resting on your shoulder." I leaned over to show her the picture. It was a darling photo. Janie, our sweet baby girl, was happy as a clam in her mother's arms.

My mom's face flashed into my mind like a faded old picture. I squinted as if it would bring the image into better focus. My memory of her was so long ago that I struggled to see her face clearly. We were at the playground near my house; I think I was around six. She wore a pink floral dress and white cloth sneakers. Her blond hair was tied into a ponytail at the nape of her neck. The sun made her eyes sparkle, and her smile always made me feel safe and secure. The warmth of my daughter resting her head on her mother's shoulder made my heart full.

Reluctantly, Lizzie said, "It's a great picture. Send it to me."

A hissing sound erupted from the kitchen. "Shit. The pots boiling over. Be right back."

In a flash, I ran to the kitchen and dumped the pasta into the strainer I had placed in the kitchen sink. I poured some pink salt, oregano, and garlic into the sauce and stirred. *So far, so good, Gray. Keep it up.*

Lizzie had already changed when I walked into Janie's room. *Damn, she looks good in my clothes. It's so hard not to touch her. God help me, I want to kiss her lips. I can taste them.*

She was putting on Janie's pajamas when I entered the room.

"Thanks for the clothes. Want to say good night?" She picked Janie up and carried her to the crib. I walked to the bookcase and pulled The Very Hungry Caterpillar off the shelf. I stood beside the crib and began to read. "In the light of the moon..."

Lizzie stood by my side and rubbed Janie's arm as I finished the last page. As I closed the book, Janie touched her palm to her lips, threw her arm up with her fingers spread wide, and smacked her lips.

Lizzie laughed. "That's her blowing us kisses."

I reached down and rubbed Janie's head. The moment overtook me. This was the first time I had put my daughter to bed. Overwhelmed with pride and joy, my eyes filled with tears. I looked down, hoping Lizzie wouldn't notice. I wasn't generally a sap, but since becoming a father, I couldn't help myself.

"Good night, Janie bug. Mommy loves you so big." Lizzie squeezed Janie's toes, and we walked out of the room. Lizzie looked at me and squinted her eyes. "Are you crying?"

"I'm not crying. You're crying." I laughed it off.

"You're definitely crying. I don't think I've ever seen you cry." Lizzie punched my arm.

"I've never put Janie to bed before. It meant a lot that I could do that. That's all." Flooded with emotions, I wanted to change the subject. I still hadn't quite mastered the art of processing and sharing my feelings adequately, but I was working on it. "Dinner's ready. We should eat. We have a lot of work to do."

Lizzie rechecked her phone before sitting at the counter, and I handed her a glass of wine. Glaring at me, she said, "One glass only."

"Are you waiting for a call or something?"

"Josh hasn't texted me back. It's odd. That's all."

"I'm sure he will. Don't worry about it." I put a bowl of pasta in front of her and walked around the counter to sit in the chair beside her. "I want you to know that Catalina and I are officially divorced. She signed the papers a few weeks ago."

"That must be a relief. How the hell did you do that? Did you see her?" Lizzie took a bite of her pasta. Her eyes lit up like a Christmas tree. "I forgot how good your sauce was. This is delicious." She raised her glass and took a sip of her wine.

"I did see her." Lizzie's body tensed. I didn't want the truth to ruin the evening, but it was important to tell her. My inner voice wouldn't shut up and urged me to spill my guts. "You won't like it, but I need to tell you something."

Lizzie turned to look at me, and I saw the slightest bit of contempt in her eyes. "What did you do, Gray?"

"I need you to know that I'm being honest with you. There's no manipulation here. I'm doing my best to earn your respect and trust." I rubbed my hands on my thighs. "Please hear me out before you lose it. Okay?" Concern immediately flashed through her eyes, and she inhaled slowly.

"I can't promise you anything. I'm sorry. We've been through too much. Tell me or don't tell me." She held up her hands as she spoke.

"That's fair." I reached out and cupped her cheek. My words caught in my throat. "I love you, Lizzie."

She immediately put her hand to mine, and for an instant, I thought she might say it back. I could see that deep down, she still had a flicker of feelings for me. Maybe it was only as the father of her child, but I could see it in there. That small little spark was something I could work with.

As she pulled my hand from her face, she said, "Gray. No. I'll leave right now." She stood. "We've been over this. I'm completely and entirely in love with Josh." Like a punch to the gut, the wind blew out of my sails. I didn't just know she was in love with him, I saw it with my own eyes. I saw it in how she looked at him, and how he looked at her.

I was too late.

Swallowing the lump in my throat, I continued. "I understand. Please don't go. I won't be able to finish the work without you. I didn't mean that I love you." I fidgeted with my pasta. "I mean, I do love you, but as the mother of my daughter. I'll always love you. I'm telling you this because I need you to know." I gulped down my wine in hopes the liquid courage would propel my words forward. *Gray Stone, nervous to speak to a woman. What on earth's happening to me?*

"I told Catalina I'd help her get custody of Janie if she signed the divorce papers." Lizzie's face turned three shades of red as she clenched her chest and moved toward her bag. Anger radiated from her eyes like daggers. *If looks could kill, I'd be six feet under.*

She gasped. "You did what?"

"I needed the divorce. I have no intention of helping her. I said it so she'd sign the papers." I pleaded with her to understand. "Please, Lizzie. You have to know how much I love you and Janie. I would never take Janie from you. Never."

Lizzie collected the papers I had laid out on the table and put them in her bag. "I thought you'd changed. I'm the fool." Tears rolled down her cheeks. She looked at me and said, "How could you? You used our daughter again. You used her to get what you wanted."

I moved quickly to block the door; my arms stretched out wide to barricade her path. Tears filled my eyes as panic rushed through my body like a tidal wave.

"Lizzie," I pleaded, my voice trembling. "I was wrong. I didn't think it through. Janie means everything to me. I'm begging you to understand. I'm trying to be better. I'm trying every day to be someone Janie can be proud of. Someone you both can be proud of."

Desperate for her to hear me, I dropped to my knees and wrapped my arms around her waist. Trembling, I looked up at her and said, "I'm on my knees asking you for forgiveness. For all of it. I'm a flawed man kneeling before you and acknowledging the hurt I've caused."

I buried my head into her stomach and squeezed her tighter. "I never knew my father. My mother was all I had. Life was tough, but she gave her all. I want so much for Janie. I want her to know her dad.

"I can't undo the past. But I promise I want to be a better man for our daughter. I don't know how to fix what I've done. I can only move forward. There's a good chance I'll mess up again, but I swear to you, I'm trying." I could feel her body soften. She reached down and wiped my tears away with her thumb. Her exquisite blue eyes met mine, with deep pools of understanding and empathy. She pulled me to my feet.

"This is a process for me too, Gray. I want to believe you. I want to trust you, but I'm afraid. I don't want you to hurt me again. And I swear if you hurt our daughter, you'll never see either of us again." Her jaw tightened. "You've made it difficult for me to trust you, but I do see you're trying."

I wrapped my arms around her, and we embraced. "I could never hurt you or Janie. If you can believe anything, believe that." Her warmth was like a cocoon of protection, and I didn't want to let go.

"You need to try harder. You cannot use our daughter as a pawn to get what you want." She stood tall with her hands on her hips. "If I'm staying, we need to work."

Side by side at the kitchen table, we worked tirelessly for hours, perfecting every single detail of the pitch for tomorrow. She was brilliant. Together we created profound plans that I was confident would land the client. I was bummed that Lizzie couldn't be part of the pitch, but she didn't work on Thursdays, and after the long day today, I couldn't expect her to be there. "I think we're almost done," I said, content with our work.

"I think so, too." She high-fived me and let out a sigh of relief.

"How about a little wine to celebrate?" I was already pouring two glasses before she could answer.

"You know what, yes. That sounds great. I'm exhausted." She took her glass and kicked her feet up on the lounge chair in the living room. "What time is it?"

I wasn't sure myself. I looked at the clock on the wall. "Holy cow, it's almost midnight."

"Josh's going to be angry with me for being here so late. I'm not looking forward to the fight brewing at home." Exhausted, she sipped her wine and leaned back in the chair.

"Lizzie, I need you to know that I do love you. I've spent the better part of my life being a complete asshole, and it cost me the best woman I've ever known—you. I can't imagine loving another woman as much as I love you. I didn't know what I had until you were gone, and I'm truly sorry. I want you to know that your happiness means more to me than anything else in this world. Josh is a good man, and I know he loves you. I see how happy he makes you and how much he loves Janie. It's hard for me to control my desires with you, but I won't do anything to hurt you. I love you too much." I looked over toward the chair. "Lizzie?"

I could hear the faintest little snore. "Lizzie?" I walked over to the chair. She was sound asleep, still holding her wine glass. *Great, I finally get the nerve to pour my heart out to her, and she's sleeping.* I stared at her for a moment. Her perfect radiant beauty. I gently pulled the wine glass from her hand. Leaning over, I kissed her forehead and covered her with a blanket. "I love you."

Lizzie

"Oh, my God. Oh, my God. What the hell? Oh, my God." *How could I have fallen asleep?* Freaking out, I shouted, "Gray, how could you let me fall asleep?" Frantic, I started throwing everything in my bag. I went into Janie's room and put my clothes back on. I reached down into the crib and pulled her up. Carrying her to the dresser, I shouted again. "Gray. Get up. How could you let me sleep here?"

I changed her out of her nighttime diaper and headed into the kitchen to gather our things. Gray walked out. He yawned. "Good morning."

"What do you mean, good morning? This is a mess. Josh's going to kill me. Where's my phone? I can't find my phone."

Blinking, Gray reached over the counter and grabbed my phone. "Here. It's right here."

I snatched the phone out of his hand and tapped the screen. "Great. It's dead." I let out a scream of frustration. "You did this on purpose, didn't you? Of course, you did. You'll never change." I flung my bags over my shoulder and reached for the door.

"Lizzie, settle down. I didn't do this on purpose. We worked late. You were exhausted." He put his hand on the door. "I didn't want to wake you or Janie. It's going to be okay. Nothing happened."

I threw my hands in the air. "Nothing happened." I groaned. "Nothing happened. Everything happened. Of all places, to fall asleep. I can't believe this. Josh will never forgive me." I pushed Gray to the side. "Get out of the way. I need to go. Now."

Janie waved her little hand. "Bye, Daddy."

THIRTEEN

Josh

I glanced at my phone screen in the hallway by the front door. I'd sent twenty text messages to Lizzie with no response. My pacing was about to wear a hole in the hardwood floor when the front door flew open. "Lizzie!" Tears immediately slid down my cheeks. "You're okay. You're both okay." I wrapped my arms around them and didn't let go.

"I'm so sorry. I fell asleep and I..."

Sadness, anger, and disdain welled in my gut. "Wait. What?" I pulled away and looked at her. Janie was still in her arms. "You fell asleep? You fell asleep, where?" I started pacing again. *I can't handle this shit right now.* Lizzie walked past me to the kitchen and put Janie in the pack-and-play.

Janie peered over the top and smiled. "JJ"

I sighed. Her sweet face relaxed me a bit, and I took a breath. She was still in her pajamas, and her hair was a mess, sticking up every which way.

"Please don't be mad. We had to finish the pitch for today. It took all night, and I fell asleep. Nothing happened, I swear." She tried to wrap her arms around me. I pulled away.

"I texted you twenty times. I needed you last night. And you were asleep at Gray's." I threw my hands in the air. Frustration took over, and I wanted to scream. I had only gotten maybe two hours of sleep and was hanging on by a thread. "My dad's in the hospital. He had a heart attack last night." I fell into the closest chair. Putting my head into my hands, I started to cry. "They had to resuscitate him, and it doesn't look good."

Lizzie's face was etched with fear and sadness as she approached. With tears brimming in her eyes, she tenderly ran her fingers through my hair. "I'm sorry, babe," she whispered. "I truly didn't know."

I looked at her. Blinking away my tears, I said, "No, you didn't know. You were busy doing God knows what with Gray. I can't believe you took Janie to his house. I can't believe you didn't answer me." She tried to embrace me. Normally, I'd welcome her touch to take my pain away. Normally I'd want her to console me and reassure me that everything was going to be okay. Instead, when I looked at her, I felt only anger and confusion and pushed her away. Should I believe that nothing happened because she said so? I could see that she was hurting as much as I was.

"I was worried sick that my dad was going to die. I was worried sick that something happened to both of you. I was sure that something happened when you didn't respond. I was about to call the police when you walked in."

She tried again to sit on my lap and wrap her arms around me. I refused. "I texted you I was at Gray's. You didn't answer me, either." A smorgasbord of emotions whirled through me.

I clenched my teeth together to keep myself from yelling. "I didn't answer you because I was rushing my father to the hospital. I did text you back eventually, but apparently, you were too busy to notice. You've been too busy a lot lately." That was harsh, but I didn't give a shit. My world was collapsing around me, and the one person I should be able to count on was with another man.

Janie started to cry. Her arms reached up toward Lizzie, and her cries filled the room as they grew louder and louder. Lizzie picked Janie up onto her hip and bounced her up and down. "Shh. Shh. It's okay, Mommy's here." She wiped the tears from her eyes and hoisted her up so Janie's head could rest on her shoulder. Rocking back and forth, she said, "Josh. I'm sorry. You're right. I got caught up in work and didn't check my phone. It was late, and I fell asleep. My phone died. I still haven't seen any of your missed calls or messages. I truly am sorry." Her eyes filled with a combination of guilt and compassion. "How's Len? What can I do?"

I leaned back in the chair and crossed my arms. "I'm sorry, too. I'm upset and scared, and I took it out on you. I'm glad you're home safe." I sighed. "I really did think something happened." She reached out for my hand, and I took hold of it. She squeezed my fingers. "It's not good, Lizzie. It's not good at all." She weaved her fingers between mine and kissed the top of my head. A tear slid down her cheek.

I raised my eyes to meet hers. I loved her more than my own life, but how can I just take her word for fact? *Is that what love is?* She said she didn't sleep with Gray, and I believe her. I didn't want to be angry or jealous, but I couldn't help it. She was the love of my life, my soulmate, my ride or die. Lately, she hadn't been anything but Janie's mom. I shuddered at that last thought because it was hateful. Of course, I loved that she was Janie's mom. And I loved Janie. This was all too much right now with my father in the hospital. I winced again, and Lizzie noticed.

"This is awful, babe. I'm so sorry," she said with a tenderness that made my heart hurt a little bit less. Janie was still fussy and squirming in Lizzie's arms. "Janie hasn't eaten breakfast. Have you eaten anything? Let me make you something. You need to eat." She went into the kitchen and put Janie in her booster seat.

"I haven't eaten. I've hardly slept. I'm not ready to say goodbye." Fighting back the tears, I poured myself a glass of water. My stomach was nauseous. How did a man live without his father? *Who'll guide me through life?*

"Don't give up hope. Len's a fighter. Plus, he won't miss any chances to give you a hard time. He'll get through this. I know it." She cracked the eggs and put a few pieces of toast in the toaster oven. Maybe Lizzie was right. My dad was a fighter. Perhaps, it didn't have to be the end. I scooted closer to Janie. Covering my face with my hands, I peeked out and shouted, "Boo!" She giggled, and my heart was less heavy for a moment. We continued playing peek-a-boo while Lizzie cooked breakfast. Janie's giggle was a great distraction from the vile feeling that took up residence in my stomach. *I love this little girl so much.*

"Where's JJ?" I said, and Janie laughed a full belly laugh.

"I'd like to go back to the hospital later today. Do you want to come?"

"Of course. I'm not sure Janie should go, though. I'll need to see if Renee can keep her for a few hours. Or maybe she can hang with Helen at the bookstore." Lizzie set a small plate of eggs on the tray for Janie and handed me a plate. She glanced at me reassuringly and smiled.

"Lizzie?" I said, taking her in for the first time since she walked in the door. Her clothes were slightly damp, and her hair was unbrushed and knotted. "Did you sleep with Gray last night? I need to know the truth."

She froze, and her body tensed. *What does that mean? Why is she tense?*

"Are you seriously asking me that?"

"Yes."

"Absolutely not. I did not sleep with him."

"Would you tell me if you did?"

"I didn't sleep with him," she said more sternly. "What can I do to convince you I'm telling you the truth?"

I don't know if she can convince me. "I believe you." But my tone was not genuine.

Lizzie used her foot to push my chair out from under the table. She straddled me, wrapped her arms around my neck, and kissed me.

"I love you and only you. Gray's my past. You're my present and my future, and every lifetime we may live. I did not sleep with him. Nothing happened." She kissed me again. My insides melted, but a tiny prick of doubt lingered. Sometimes a tiny prick of doubt is all it takes for a man to come unglued. "Let's focus on Len for today."

Clapping her hands, Janie interrupted our kiss and said, "Mommy and JJ." Her feet kicked the air excitedly. She placed her ketchup and egg-covered hand on her mouth and threw her arm out to blow us a kiss. I reached out, pretended to catch her kiss, and placed it on my cheek.

FOURTEEN

Lizzie

The next day, I dropped Janie off with Randy and Renee. Randy had no jobs today and was excited to spend the day with Janie. When I arrived, he was outside filling the bird feeders. "Hey bro," I hollered out the window as I pulled into the driveway. Dressed in his usual mix-matched attire and a baseball cap, he waved.

"Renee's waiting for you inside."

I unbuckled Janie from her car seat and went to the front porch. Randy set down the bag of bird feed and said, "You ready for the Fourth of July festivities in a few days? You guys should come here in the morning. We can do breakfast."

"Sounds great. I'll run it by Josh, but I'm sure we're in." I walked into the house and found Renee in the kitchen cutting up strawberries. Her baby bump was barely showing.

"There's my girl," Renee said.

Janie bobbled her way over to her, yelling, "Renny."

"I can't believe she starts daycare next week. We're going to miss hanging out with her." Renee put Janie into her booster seat and set several little strawberry pieces on a unicorn plate.

"I know. I'm not sure I'm ready, but it's time. You've been so gracious. I appreciate it." I poured some milk into Janie's sippy cup.

"Are you kidding? We love having her."

Randy burst through the front door, kissed Renee on the cheek, and popped a strawberry into his mouth. "How's Len doing?"

"He's okay. He's awake, so that's good. He isn't eating much, and they don't know when he'll be able to go home. He's still in intensive care."

"I'm sorry, sis. That's a bummer. We'll say some prayers for him to recover quickly."

"I should get going. We've had a busy week, and I need to catch up on a few things. Thanks again. See you later."

As I pulled into my parking spot at GSM South, the exterior had been decorated with red, white, and blue streamers, and a welcome sign was added to the front door. I entered the building and greeted Andra. She looked like Barbie with her bleach blond hair tied up in a high ponytail and she wore a hot pink cotton sundress with matching hot pink lipstick. I put my things onto my desk and hurried to Gray's office.

"Knock knock," I said as I entered. "I'm dying to know how it went."

"Hey, Lizzie. There's fresh coffee if you want some. I even got you some caramel drizzle." He walked to the coffee bar across from his desk and handed me a mug. "I tried to call and fill you in, but your phone kept going to voicemail."

"Sorry. It was a rough day. Len, Josh's dad's in the hospital."

"Oh no. Is he okay?"

"Not sure." I squirted some stevia into my mug, poured in the creamer, and drizzled the caramel on top. "Josh's pretty upset. He's there now. He's also pissed about our sleepover."

"That's ridiculous. Nothing happened," Gray snapped.

"Put yourself in his shoes if the situation was reversed. I don't think you'd be too pleased either."

Gray nodded in agreement. "Fair point."

"I'm doing my best to keep it together. Let's stick to work. How'd it go with Beach Front?"

"We landed the job. All of it. They will pay a monthly stipend for us to implement every idea we pitched." His gigantic smile stretched from ear to ear, and I suddenly had the urge to jump into his arms. I was proud of him. Whether I wanted to feel it or not, I did—full-blown pride for Gray Stone rebuilding his life here in Southport as the father of my child.

"Oh my God, that's amazing news." I embraced him triumphantly. Realizing that I was getting a little too close for comfort, I backed away and ran my hands down my dress to collect myself.

"It's exciting. Now, we need to deliver." Gray sat back down at his desk. "Lots to do."

"I'll leave you to it." I headed for the door.

"Wait," he called after me. "Did you decide on a daycare?"

"I did. She starts next week." I forced a smile. My stomach had been in knots since dropping her off at Renee's.

"Which one did you go with?"

"A spot opened at Apple A Day. I have to pay for the entire week, even though she'll only be there for two or three days, but it's better than nothing. It was my second choice. But it'll do for now."

"It'll be good for Janie to play with other kids." I could tell by the look in his eyes that he could see through my fake smile. Sometimes, I wish he didn't know me as well as he did. He got up and stood in front of me. He placed his hands on my shoulders and said, "I know you're nervous. She's going to have a great time. You're doing the right thing, Lizzie. Don't doubt yourself. You're a great mom."

You're a great mom. Those were precisely the words I needed to hear, and I appreciated hearing them from him. I pulled him into me and hugged him tight. "Thank you. You don't know how much that means to me. Sometimes I question every decision I make. I don't always feel like I'm a good mom."

"Don't say that. You're an excellent mom. Janie's happy and healthy. I hate to say it, but even Josh is wonderful with her." He wiped a small tear from my cheek.

"I never thought I'd say these words, but you are a good father, Gray. Janie adores you."

"I'd love to continue being her father, if you'll consider it. I understand what I'm asking, but I'm her biological father. I'll do whatever it takes to prove to you I'm worthy. She can live with you, but I want to be a part of her life."

I inhaled deeply and sighed. "I understand. I'll consider it." The truth was, at this point, there was no good reason to keep him from her. Wanting Josh to be her father wasn't a good enough reason. Gray was her biological father. He loved her, and she genuinely loved him. I didn't know how to have this conversation with Josh. He loved Janie like she was his. He treated her like his daughter, but I wasn't sure our relationship could handle this blow, and I didn't want to lose Josh. *Aren't I doing the same thing as Gray by not saying anything?* I'm using Janie to get what I want or to delay the inevitable fight this conversation will cause.

"Lizzie. Earth to Lizzie."

"Sorry. I went inside my head for a minute. I'd better get to work. As you said, we have a lot to do." I turned to leave Gray's office. As I exited, I bumped into Andra, who seemed startled. "I'm sorry. Did I scare you?"

"Um... Well... No. I—" Her jaw dropped, her pupils flared, and her weight shifted backward.

"You are clearly flustered. Is everything ok?"

"You startled me. That's all."

"Sorry about that." Confused by Andra's reaction, my brows drew together, causing my forehead to crease. "I'll be more careful next time," I said.

That was odd.

FIFTEEN

Lizzie

The courtroom walls were stark white with oak wood trim around the ceiling. Matching oak wood wainscoting dressed the lower half of the walls. Two heavy wooden oak desks sat on either side of the room, each accompanied by two chairs. The air smelled of linseed oil and Pine Sol, an odd combination. Behind the judge's bench was an extensive oak wall treatment that met at a peak in the center.

As I walked down the aisle of pew-like rows of benches with my attorney, Mr. Stallard, to take my seat at the desk, I squirmed as if I might blow chunks all over the floor. My stomach was knotted and gnarly in ways I hadn't experienced before. My heart was pumping blood filled with anxiety through every vein in my body. Finally, the day of the custody hearing had arrived.

I caught sight of Helen and Drew first. They were sitting in the front row. Helen was dressed in a tan business suit, and Drew was holding her hand. Next to Drew were Randy and Renee, who were also holding hands. We all anticipated today's outcome. Josh kissed my cheek. "It's going to be okay."

His eyes were tired. Dark circles and bags hung underneath them. Between work and spending time with Len, Josh hadn't been able to get much sleep. He'd spent most nights at the hospital since Len was admitted. He took Janie from my arms, and they sat in the second row behind Helen.

Representing himself, Gray was seated at the other table across from mine. He said he didn't need an attorney, and Mr. Stallard was fine with that. Next to Gray sat Catalina's attorney, Mr. Jacobs.

"All rise. With the honorable Judge Marshall presiding, this court is now in session." The bailiff made his announcement, and we all stood. My heart was pounding against my ribcage. I had to remind myself to breathe so I didn't pass out.

The judge, cloaked in a neatly pressed black robe, entered the room and took her seat.

"Please be seated and come to order," the judge instructed.

My legs were numb, and I was afraid they might slide out from under me like Bambi on ice. Mr. Stallard took my hand and squeezed. He whispered, "It's going to be okay. Breathe, Lizzie."

Judge Marshall put on her glasses, shuffled some papers, and looked up. Her eyes peered over the top of her spectacles. "Okay. We're here to discuss the custody of Sophie Stone. Counsel, you may present your case."

Mr. Stallard stood and smoothed his tie. "This is a complicated situation, your honor. Sophie's name is Janie. I'd like to refer to her as Janie."

"I didn't ask you for her name. Her birth certificate says Sophie Stone. I asked you to present your case."

Mr. Stallard stopped in his tracks, cleared his throat, and continued. "Yes, your honor." He picked up a document from the table. "I have in my hand a petition to establish maternity that I previously filed. Attached to the petition is a genetic marker test that indicates with 99.97% legal certainty that Elizabeth Levine is the biological mother of Sophie Stone, or as she's called now, Janie Levine."

Mr. Jacobs, Catalina's attorney, stood and waved a document in his hand. "Your honor. I have the birth certificate for Sophie Stone, which clearly lists my client Catalina Stone and her ex-husband Grayson Stone as the parents."

Mr. Stallard took a few steps forward. "Your honor, my client never gave up custody of her daughter. I'd like to stay these proceedings until such time as we can be heard on the petition to establish maternity. Once maternity is established, my plan is to file a motion to remove Catalina Stone as a party to this custody hearing because she is not the mother. She's only listed as the mother on the birth certificate because she stole Elizabeth Levine's child. Catalina Stone is currently in jail serving time for this crime. My client has been caring for Janie with her fiancé, Josh Miller, for over a year. She's a happy, well-balanced child living with her rightful mother."

"Your honor, Sophie Stone is only living with Elizabeth Levine because Grayson Stone signed a power of attorney giving her the ability to raise Sophie. Catalina Stone, the mother of record, is concerned about her daughter's safety. She has been wrongly accused of her crimes, and her ex-husband willfully gave her daughter away in an attempt to get back at her for the divorce. My client intends to file a motion for Sophie to be in the care of her sister while the situation is sorted out. Poor Sophie has been through enough." Mr. Jacobs looked at me and sat back down at the desk. *Does this guy believe his own shit?*

"Your honor, Mr. Stone gave my client, Elizabeth Levine, the only legal opportunity he could for her to raise her own daughter. He wasn't giving his daughter away to harm his ex-wife. He was trying to do the right thing within the law. I'd like to call him to the stand for questioning."

Mr. Stallard nodded to Gray to take his seat.

Janie screamed excitedly, "Daddy." Like a deflating balloon, the room murmured with laughter that broke the silence that previously filled the air.

"Your honor. I know it's unorthodox to have a child present, but it's important for the court to witness firsthand the minor child's interactions with her biological mother and father."

"Understood," the judge said and continued. "Mr. Stone, Catalina Stone is your ex-wife, correct?"

"Yes."

"And you are the biological father of Sophie Stone."

"Yes. Janie Levine is my daughter."

"Who's Janie Levine?"

"Janie Levine is Sophie Stone. My ex-wife named her Sophie, but her biological mother named her Janie."

"Did you and Catalina Stone have a daughter?"

"No. Catalina cannot have children."

"Are you sure?"

"After several rounds of invitro and tens of thousands of dollars, yes, I'm sure." He chuckled.

"Did you know that Elizabeth Levine was pregnant with your child?"

"Yes."

Judge Marshall's dark hair was pulled back into a tight bun that lifted the skin around her face. She appeared to be in her mid-fifties and a no-nonsense kind of judge. She turned to face Gray, curiosity spread across her face like a rash.

"Why did you grant Elizabeth Levine power-of-attorney to raise Janie? Didn't you want to raise your daughter yourself?"

"I'm ashamed to admit this, but in the beginning, I didn't want to raise my daughter. I loved her mother, Lizzie. I mean, Elizabeth. She deserved to have her daughter back, and I wanted to spend more time with Elizabeth." Gray looked at the judge. "Lizzie was told she'd lost her child. She'd fallen down a flight of stairs and was told she had lost the baby. She had suffered enough. Signing the power-of-attorney gave her the opportunity to get her daughter back. She'd lost enough time with her daughter already. However, since then, I've realized that being a father is the greatest gift in the world, and I've fallen in love with my little girl."

I could feel Josh's eyes boring a hole in the back of my head. He's an incredible man to be here and support me today. I know Gray speaking on my behalf isn't easy for him.

"Mr. Stone, are you here today to fight for sole custody of Janie Levine?"

"No. I'm here because I believe that Elizabeth Levine deserves legal and rightful custody of our daughter. She and I would like to share custody." My heart constricted at his words. I had not talked to Josh about this yet. "Your honor. Catalina was my wife. We were separated when I was dating Lizzie. I didn't want the baby." Judge Marshall kept her eyes fixated on Gray. Her brows turned downward. Her face was sullen. "Lizzie moved away, and I didn't hear from her. I'm ashamed to say I assumed she'd had an abortion."

Gray looked at me. Tears shimmered in his eyes. "I received word about what Catalina had done and was told that I was the only person who could accept custody of Janie, or she'd be put into foster care. I met with the social worker and took custody of my daughter and then signed the power of attorney for Lizzie to raise her." Gray cleared his throat. "Your honor, I made the biggest mistake letting Lizzie Levine walk out of my life. I used our child to get her back. It was wrong. But I won't apologize because, in the process, I realized what it meant to be a father. I love my little girl more than anything else in this world, and I'll do anything for her. I want Lizzie to raise her. She's Janie's biological mother, and every child needs their mother."

"As Janie's father, do you believe in any way that she should remain in the custody of Catalina Stone?"

"No."

"Thank you. Nothing further."

I looked over at Gray with a sincere smile on my face. *He was telling the truth.* My reservations about him were fading, and I was proud that he was Janie's father. Randy reached out from the bench and squeezed my shoulder. Josh was clinging to Janie.

The judge peered over the bench at Mr. Jacobs. "My client has a right to make her case and fight for her daughter. She raised her from birth and feels that Sophie should remain in her care. I'll file an objection to the petition to establish maternity on behalf of my client to remain Sophie Stone's custodial parent."

Judge Marshall said, "Noted. We'll consolidate the petition to establish maternity with this custody action so they can be heard concurrently."

Mr. Stallard took a sip of water. He reached over and patted my hand assuringly. "Your honor, we're here today for justice and to grant Elizabeth Levine rightful custody of her daughter. Gray Stone agrees to this and would like his daughter to be raised by her biological mother. They are both employed and financially stable parents. Janie is thriving and surrounded by good family and friends. Gray Stone and Elizabeth Levine have a working relationship and communicate regularly. They are committed to working together to provide a safe and healthy environment for their daughter."

Judge Marshall stared at Janie for a few minutes. She was snuggled in Josh's arms with her head resting on his shoulder. She turned to look at me and smiled, flashing her dimples. Judge Marshall softened, and for the first time today, she smiled.

"We'll take a ten-minute recess." Judge Marshall rose from the bench and disappeared from the courtroom.

Gray rushed over and hugged me. "That was terrifying. It's going to be okay. I just know it." Josh stepped out from his seat with Janie in his arms and put himself between Gray and me.

"Lizzie, I have to go." Janie reached for me and wrapped her arms around my neck. Josh hugged us both. "Dad had another heart attack. He isn't responsive. I need to go right now."

Josh's gaze locked onto Gray's. Afraid of what might happen next, I held my breath. Gray extended his hand, an offer of peace, or perhaps understanding. Josh hesitated, his eyes never leaving Gray's. Reluctantly, he took Gray's hand and shook it, but I could feel the tension radiating from Josh's skin.

"I'm sorry to hear about your dad," Gray said.

"Lizzie, I really need to go." His eyes were full of sadness.

"Oh, Josh. Of course. I understand. Go. I'll be there as soon as I can." My emotions were all over the place as I watched him rush out of the courtroom.

Mr. Stallard turned to face my family and said, "I'm hopeful. Gray, you were perfect. I was nervous, but you really came through."

Gray smiled. "I was being honest."

"All Rise," the bailiff commanded as the judge entered the room.

"As a judge, my job in every custody situation is to determine what's best for the child. Sophie Stone appears to be a happy, healthy little girl surrounded by much love from family and friends. I'm inclined to agree that Elizabeth Levine should be granted shared custody with Grayson Stone.

"However, I'd be remiss if I didn't do my due diligence to ensure I understood the facts to make the best decision. Given the strange nature of the case, I'm taking the matter under advisement to review the information presented. I'll contact you when I'm ready to make a final ruling."

Judge Marshal banged her gavel, and the sound resonated through the courtroom like a clap of thunder on a hot summer's day.

A flicker of hope lingered that we may be one step closer to Janie legally being my daughter. But mostly, I felt unrelenting frustration and anger mixed with sadness for Len.

"This is ridiculous. You grew the child in your body and gave birth to her, for Christ's sake," Randy said in a stern whisper. "I want to punch my fist through the wall."

"Let's get outside," Mr. Stallard said as he ushered us out of the building onto the sidewalk. "I don't have any reason to believe that Lizzie won't get custody."

I was silent. Putting Janie into her stroller, I did everything I could to fight back my tears. Her beautiful face looked up at me and smiled, showing both her dimples.

Gray reached down and grabbed my hand. "It's going to be ok."

I hugged him. "Thank you for being a good father. Thank you for defending me in there. I know it'll come at a cost to you. Catalina's crazy. No doubt you just pissed her off."

Surrounded by family and friends, I was reminded of how lucky I was to have an incredible support system. "Mr. Stallard, I need to go to the hospital. Is there anything else?"

"I know waiting for the judge's ruling is nerve-wracking for all of you. I think it went well, and Janie will be legally Lizzie's before we know it." He looked at me and said, "I'll call you the minute I know anything at all."

Josh was slumped in a chair, sitting in the waiting room with his head propped in his hands. His dark hair was disheveled, and his typical five o'clock shadow had almost grown into a full-blown beard. His eyes were sullen. My heart ached at the sight of him.

I pushed Janie in the stroller, sat beside him, and reached for his hand. He put his hand inside mine, and I squeezed it. "Have you eaten?"

"No." He still hadn't looked up.

"What did the doctor say?"

"They're giving him some medicine right now and asked me to leave the room. They want to discuss end-of-life care." A small tear barely trickled from the corner of his eye. "They aren't sure how much time he has left. They want me to put him in an assisted living facility."

I didn't know what to say. Len was a good man, and he loved his son. I could see how much his illness hurt Josh, and it was too much to bear. "What can I do to help?" *I wish I could take the pain away.*

"There's nothing you can do. My father's going to die. I need to come to terms with that. Unless you can save his life, you can't help."

"Oh babe, I'm so sorry." I wasn't as good at controlling my emotions, especially right this second given the day I had in court. Tears spilled uncontrollably from the corners of my eyes. I was a mess. I loved Len. He was good to me, but seeing Josh in pain was like a searing hot iron resting on my heart.

"How'd it go today? I'm sorry I didn't even ask." Josh looked at me for the first time since I'd arrived. The dark circles under his eyes had deepened to a shade of brownish-grey.

"The judge said she was taking time to review the information before making a decision." I wiped my hair back. "I'm tired of waiting. I just want my daughter."

Josh put his arm around me and pulled me close. "It's going to work out. It has to." He kissed the top of my head. More tears spilled down my cheek. "I know you need to get Janie home, and I'd rather be alone right now, if that's okay. I have so much on my mind. I need to sort through it all."

He wants me to leave? "I can stay a little longer."

He reached into the stroller and rubbed Janie's head. "It's okay. I want to be alone for a while. I'll text you. I'll be home later." His tone was weak and somber.

"Can I at least bring you a book or something to keep you busy while you wait?"

"Lizzie, I'm good."

"Okay. I love you." I wrapped my arms around his waist and hugged him like tomorrow wasn't promised. He sighed and then rested his head on mine. "We'll get through all of this."

"I know we will." He grabbed Janie's foot and said, "Goodbye, sweet girl. JJ, loves you."

He looked back at me and kissed my forehead. "Love you too. Be home soon."

SIXTEEN

Lizzie

Today was the first day of the Fourth of July festivities, and the town was completely covered in red, white, and blue. Stars and stripes lined the street, hung from the streetlamps, and spread across front porches everywhere.

"Josh, we need to get going. We'll meet you at the Nine Eleven memorial around noon."

He barely lifted his head from his cereal. "Sounds good."

Janie stood in front of him with her hands raised.

Josh looked at her, and a smile shone through his eyes, but not on his face. Josh had always been the happy-go-lucky one. These past few weeks since Len's heart attack were hard for him, and seeing him in so much pain hurt my heart. "Bye Janie girl. Be good for Mommy." He kissed her cheek and then set her down.

"All right, Janie bug. We need to go see Aunt Helen."

"Helly." Janie giggled.

I buckled Janie into the car seat Josh had secured in the golf cart and off we went to Helen's. She waved at everyone we passed along the way. She said hello to a couple passing by on a bicycle, three golf carts, several families on a walk, and her favorite neighbor, Mr. Paul, the resident chess master. Janie brought joy to everyone. Each passerby smiled and giggled at her and commented on her cuteness or her dimples or how friendly she was. She'd never met a stranger, which terrified me.

The golf cart lurched forward as I stepped on the brake in Helen's driveway. Janie was singing, "La la la. La la la," when we arrived.

"We're here, Janie bug."

"Helly." She clapped her hands.

I walked with Janie to the front door and let her press the bell. No answer.

I rang the doorbell again. No answer.

I dug into my pocket and pulled out my phone to text Helen.

Me: We're here. Are you ready?

I pressed send on the text. I sat Janie in the rocking chair on the front porch. Using my foot, I rocked her back and forth. *This is so unlike Helen.* I decided to try again, and I banged heavily on the door and then waited.

Finally, Helen cracked the door, wearing a silk lavender robe. Sleep still covered her eyes, and her hair was matted on top of her head. She opened the door to let me in, and I caught a glimpse of

Drew walking to the kitchen. "I'm sorry, Lizzie. I overslept. I'll be ready in a jiffy."

My eyes widened, and a smirk appeared on Helen's face.

Jubilant, I said, "You little minx."

"Oh, for Pete's sake. Get in here."

Janie and I went inside and sat on the couch. Helen's house was small but exquisite. She recently renovated, or should I say Drew renovated, most of the living room and kitchen. The open floor plan made the space feel larger. Helen opened the blinds and then disappeared into her bedroom, leaving me hanging on the details. Sunlight poured into the room and showed off the freshly painted walls and kitchen cabinets.

Drew said, "Morning. Can I get you some coffee?"

"I'd love some," I said, staring at him like he was a monument in a museum. "You and Helen must be getting pretty serious."

"I think so."

"She's my dearest friend. You're the first man I've known her to have a sleepover with."

"Wow, you get right to it, don't you?" He laughed.

Blank-faced, I looked at him and said, "Yes. I suppose I do."

"Helen's an incredible woman." He lowered his voice to a whisper. "Can you keep a secret?"

"Depends on the secret." I didn't want to be rude, but I was still sizing up Drew's intentions.

"I'm falling madly in love with your friend, Helen." His eyes flickered nervously.

I relaxed into my chair. "That's wonderful. Why's that a secret?"

"Because I haven't told her yet. I'm also not sure if she feels the same way." He handed me a blue-green mug filled with piping hot coffee.

"Trust me, if she let you stay here, she feels the same way." I stirred creamer into my coffee. "Helen doesn't do casual relationships, so don't screw this up. As her friend, I have to say, if you break her heart, I'll break your face."

Drew laughed. "I don't intend to break her heart. Quite the opposite."

I peered over my mug as I sipped my coffee. "Good. I like you, Drew. Let's keep it that way."

A few minutes later, Helen emerged dressed in black leggings and an American Flag tank top with matching American flag sneakers. "You ready?"

She kissed Drew goodbye. Their lips lingered longer than I was comfortable with. It was like watching your mom and dad kiss. I squirmed a little. "All right. All right. That's enough."

Drew patted Helen on the ass and sauntered into the bedroom.

"Dish," I said outside as I strapped Janie into the stroller.

"Good grief, Lizzie. We're barely out of the house." Helen playfully slapped my arm.

"I mean, you had a man, an actual man, in your house. I need all the details immediately."

Helen grabbed the stroller and began walking. "Drew's sweet."

"Sweet, huh?" My lips curled into a half smile.

"He makes me laugh. He can fix anything, which is a bonus. I enjoy spending time with him, and yes, I enjoyed last night." She gave me a side-eye.

"You enjoyed last night, did ya?"

"I did. My evening is none of your business." She stuck her tongue out at me. "Let's get some croissants."

"You know I'm always down for Burney's."

We overindulged. I ate a Boston crème, two plain croissants, and half of Janie's that she didn't finish. Helen ate a chocolate crème and one plain. "God, these things are so delicious," I mumbled between bites.

"Yes, they're heavenly," Helen said as she shoveled in her last bite.

The town was mobbed with crowds of people meandering down the streets. American Flags and American flag prints were everywhere. American flag dresses, tops, pants, hats, shoes, glasses, you name it, everyone was wearing red, white, and blue.

We took our time wandering down Moore Street. The air was thick, and sweat rolled down my face and back. Helen and I took turns shoving our faces in the fan I hooked to Janie's stroller. It was as though we had entered the Devil's lair, and no amount of water would keep us hydrated. Finally, we approached the Naturalization Ceremony on the Fort Johnston Lawn just in time to see the five applicants take The Oath of Allegiance.

In unison, we could hear them recite, "I hereby declare, on oath, that I absolutely and entirely renounce and abjure all allegiance and fidelity to any foreign prince, potentate, state, or sovereignty, of whom or which I have heretofore been a subject or citizen…" They continued to proudly say the words as we watched with admiration.

Each new citizen was then presented with a Certificate of Naturalization and was now considered a Citizen of the United States. Pride oozed from their pores as they beamed with joy for their country and their citizenship.

"I've never seen a Naturalization Ceremony before. It's very moving. They're all so proud to be Americans." I sipped my water and fanned myself with a book from Janie's stroller.

"It's really something. The extensive process the applicants must go through. They probably know more about America than most Americans these days," Helen said.

We continued to stroll along the streets, checking out the shops as we walked, mainly to get into air conditioning and take breaks from the heat. My skin was on fire. I think I could have used it to fry bacon.

My phone buzzed in my pocket. It was a text from Josh. I clicked open the message.

Josh: Do you want to meet for lunch?

I contemplated his question. I had swamp ass, and my hair was sticking to my neck. I didn't want to blow Helen off for the memorial, but lunch indoors sounded glorious.

Helen was nose deep in sniffing a vanilla peppermint candle. I moved beside her and said, "Josh wants to meet for lunch. Any interest?"

"I'm good, but thanks for asking. Drew will meet me at the memorial, and then we'll go to the bookstore. You go."

"You sure?"

"I'm sure. Have you guys talked much since the custody hearing?" Helen put the candle down and picked up a large tan sunhat with an American Flag band around the brim.

"We haven't, really. Len's been so sick. Josh's been at the hospital most of his spare time. Between work, Janie, and Len, we haven't seen each other much."

"Well then, lunch is the perfect date." She hugged me good-bye and waved to Janie.

I texted Josh back.

Me: Lunch sounds great. Where?

Immediately, three dots appeared.

Josh: How about pizza? Dry Street?

Me: Great. See you there!

Janie and I walked back to Helen's to get the golf cart. We took back roads most of the way and then crossed over to Howe Street. According to the teenage host who greeted me, I arrived first. He had a mop full of brown curls on top of his head, and his skin appeared dry from the sun. With a massive smile on his face, he said, "Would you like a table?"

"Yes, please. Table for two and a half," I said and pointed to Janie in the stroller.

The restaurant was a small house converted into a pizza joint, and the food was delicious. The host sat us at a four-top in the corner by a window and placed a booster seat on one of the chairs.

"Can I get you something to drink?" he asked.

"Two waters would be great and a glass of cold milk for the little one. And could I see your adult beverage menu?" I winked at him.

Janie banged her hands on the table, entertaining herself with the noise it made. I reached into my purse for a baby wipe and cleaned off both of our hands. The host returned with our drinks. I ordered a cheese fry appetizer and some sort of fancy Independence Day cocktail.

Looking at my phone, I noticed I had a missed text message from Randy.

Randy: You still good for breakfast, parade, and fireworks tomorrow?

Me: Thumbs up emoji. Can't wait.

I looked at the time on my phone. 12:30 PM. *What's taking Josh so long?*

Janie was starting to squeal and squirm in her seat. She needed a nap, and honestly, I could use one, too. The heat drained the life out of me. A few minutes later, our server arrived with the cheese fries. "Bless you." I laughed. "I'm still waiting for someone, but can I order for my little one?"

"Sure. What'll you have?" She addressed the question to Janie who smiled, wrapped her hands together, and giggled at the waitress.

"Can we do the kid's cheese pizza?"

"One kid's pie coming up."

I grabbed an appetizer plate and started cutting some fries into small pieces for Janie. Doing my best not to get irritated, I took a deep breath and cleared my throat. Janie stuffed a piece of fry into her mouth. Then she tapped her fingertips together, letting me know she wanted more. Ten minutes later, the waitress returned with Janie's pizza, and I ordered a large pepperoni pizza to go.

Still no Josh.

Janie finished eating, and I took the to-go pizza and drove home. When I arrived, Josh was walking out the front door.

"You didn't wait for me?" he said in a huff.

"Seriously? I waited over forty minutes. I brought home a pizza."

He stormed back into the house, grabbed paper plates from the pantry, and sat at the kitchen table.

I set the pizza on the table. "Janie needs her nap. I'll be right back."

"Yep. Go take care of Janie." I didn't like the tone in his voice, but chose to ignore it.

By the time I returned, Josh had already eaten two slices.

"I'm sorry. I got tied up with work, and then the hospital called."

I sat down across from him and put a slice of pizza on my plate. "I understand. You could've texted me."

"You know, Lizzie. I don't need this shit right now," he snapped.

"Woah..."

He cut me off. "I'm sorry. I've got so much on my mind. I didn't mean to snap."

I didn't know how to respond, so I stuffed my mouth with pizza.

"Have you heard any news from Stallard?"

"Nothing," I mumbled with my mouth full.

"I guess your boy Gray saved the day in court, huh?"

My jawline tightened. *Is he trying to pick a fight?* "What's that supposed to mean?"

"It means good 'ole daddy Gray, saved the day." With arrogance dripping from his face, he leaned back in his chair.

Anger boiled in my veins as I stared at him, speechless. "I don't care who saves the day as long as I have Janie. You remember that all of this is for her, right?"

"Don't throw Janie in my face. I love that little girl. I'd do anything for her."

"I know you love her. Are you mad that you didn't save the day?" No longer hungry, I pushed my plate away. "I still don't have custody, remember?"

"I hate that Gray's in our lives. He treated you like garbage, and you allowed him back into your life. Back into Janie's life." Josh slammed his hand on the table, causing Cooper, Len's goldendoodle, to bark.

"I don't know what you want me to do. He's Janie's father. Yes, he was an ass, but he's still her dad." In an instant, I could see the hurt my words caused. I might as well have stuck a dagger directly through his heart.

Enraged, he yelled, "That's it. That's it, right there. He's Janie's father. He'll always be Janie's father. And because of that, I have to put up with him. I have to be okay with you sleeping at his house, and I'm expected to trust that nothing's going on behind my back. I have to let him be a part of our sweet little girl's life."

I stared at the man before me. He was barely himself. His beard grew thicker by the day, the bags under his eyes had grown to the size of suitcases, and his hair was sticking up in all the wrong places. I took a deep breath and chose my words carefully.

"We're both going through a lot right now. Before either of us says something we might regret, perhaps we should take a deep breath and calm down."

He stood up from the table and slammed his hands down. "Of course, you conveniently want to change the subject now. You didn't do anything wrong. Perfect little Lizzie."

I did my best to remain calm and not let his anger surge me into full-blown attack mode. "Josh, what do you want to talk about? If you want to talk, then let's talk. I'm right here."

He groaned. "Dammit, Lizzie. Dammit, dammit, dammit."

I remained still and looked at him as a tear trickled out of the corner of my eye. "I didn't sleep with him. I'm not in love with him. I'm in love with you." I reached across the table and placed my hand on top of his. "I made a child with him. My only concern is getting custody of Janie. After that, we can figure out what comes next."

He pulled his hand away. "There's no next. There's just Gray. I need to figure out how to accept our new family reality."

I knew my words would hurt him, but there was never a good time to tell the man you love that he wouldn't legally be able to adopt your daughter. "I love you with all my heart. I want you and me and Janie to be a family. She'll live with us, and you'll be her father in every way that matters." I reached for his hand again. He let me touch him. "That doesn't change the fact that Gray is her biological father. He loves her, too. Yes, he was an asshole to me, but he has done nothing but love Janie. The only reason we even have her now is because of him." I weaved my fingers inside of his and squeezed. "You were the one that was telling me we all needed to get along and that I needed to give him a second chance for Janie's sake. I did that. I did what you suggested. We should've had this conversation before we went to court. I'm sorry that we didn't." I looked into his eyes. Nothing but pain and hurt looked back at me. Then I delivered the final blow. "Gray's her father, no matter how much I love you. He has a right to be her father."

A tear fell down Josh's cheek. He said nothing. He simply got up and left.

My heart broke into a million tiny pieces. I know how badly he hoped to adopt Janie, but I can't ask that of Gray. He wanted to be part of his daughter's life, and he had a right to be.

My phone buzzed.

Josh: You're right. We should calm down before we continue the conversation. I need to get back to the hospital. I'll be home later.

Me: I love you. Heart emoji.

I waited a few minutes for a response. Nothing.

Me: I can go to the hospital. Do you need me to bring you anything?

Josh: Please don't.

Josh: I'll be home later.

I flopped into the kitchen chair, laid my head on the table, and sobbed.

SEVENTEEN

Lizzie

Renee made an egg, bacon, and sausage casserole, hash browns, pancakes, and fresh fruit. When I arrived, the food was beautifully laid out on the kitchen island, each in its own American Flag or red, white, and blue dish. The house smelled of bacon and deliciousness.

"Oh my. Janie, you look adorable," Renee said. Janie was decked out head to toe, ready to celebrate the Fourth of July. Her white sundress was covered in little American Flags with matching red, white, and blue sandals. Her hair was tied in pigtail sprigs on top of her head, each adorned with gigantic red bows.

"You outdid yourself," I said as I rubbed my stomach. "Janie cleaned her plate and had seconds."

"She sure did," Randy said as he shoveled more egg casserole into his mouth.

I looked at Renee and said, "How are you feeling?"

"Pretty good. The morning sickness has finally stopped. I feel like I'm getting my energy back. Doc says everything looks good." She took a sip of her orange juice.

"That's great to hear. I felt better during the second trimester. But you'll still be more tired than normal. You're growing a baby with bones, organs, fingers, and toes. It tires a person out, you know." I laughed.

"I never really thought about it like that, but I guess you're right."

"When you hit the third trimester, you'll feel like a stuffed pig, counting down the days until the baby arrives."

"Sounds amazing," Randy scoffed.

Renee laughed and said, "It'll be worth it. I can't wait for our babies to grow up together. They'll be besties for sure."

I squealed. "Oh, that'll be so great."

Randy cleaned his plate and disappeared upstairs to get changed for the parade.

Renee scraped her plate into the trash and said, "We set chairs out last night to save our spot."

I cleaned up the mess from breakfast and sang to Janie bug while I worked. "You are my sunshine, my only sunshine..."

She giggled and swayed her body back and forth. She loved music, and I loved singing to her, especially because she was my sunshine.

Randy and Renee reemerged a few minutes later. Randy's thick auburn hair was smashed under an American flag fishing hat, securely fastened by a string under his chin. He wore a tan polo with the United States Constitution sprawled across his chest and American flag print pants with matching American flag tall socks and red boat shoes. Topping off the outfit was a goofy smile full of excitement.

Renee wore an American flag print tank top, red shorts, and American flag running shoes.

"You two are a sight for sore eyes." I laughed.

Renee pointed to Randy and said, "At least he matches today."

"True."

Randy popped open Janie's stroller and said, "Ready to go? It's only two blocks, so we can walk."

"I'm ready." I cleaned Janie's hands and buckled her into the stroller.

Renee quickly tied her long black hair into a messy bun. "Is Josh meeting us there?"

I pressed my lips together and dropped my eyes to the floor. "I don't know. We had a fight yesterday, and he didn't come home. He was supposed to, but I haven't talked to him."

Renee's eyes softened with sympathy. "He's going through a lot right now. How's Len?"

"He isn't good. Josh's struggling. He doesn't want to discuss how he feels, and I think it's putting distance between us."

We strolled down Caswell toward the parade. As we passed Mr. Guffy's house, Gray spotted us during his run. Jogging in place, he said, "What are you guys doing? Just out for a stroll?"

Janie flashed her dimples and said, "Hi. Daddy."

"Hi, baby girl. Are you having a good day?" He rubbed her cheek.

"We're taking Janie to the parade," I said.

"That's fun. Maybe I'll join you." He glanced at me. "Would that be okay?"

No. It will not be okay. Not today. I inhaled a breath and thought about it. "I'm sorry. I don't think it's a good idea."

Randy and Renee stood frozen, watching our encounter and waiting for Gray's reaction.

"I understand. Maybe another time. Have fun." He kissed Janie on top of the head and continued his run, turning left at the corner.

"Wow. What was that?" Renee said, her eyes wide with shock.

"What do you mean?" I said.

Randy jumped into the conversation. "That's not the Gray we know. That's what she means."

"He's trying. He wants to be a true part of Janie's life."

"Between his proclamation on poetry night, the custody hearing, and his reaction today, I might actually find a place in my heart for him," Renee said.

Randy shook his head. "Do you believe he's genuine?"

"I didn't at first, but he's definitely wearing on me, which is increasing the tension between Josh and me."

Randy put his arm around my shoulders. "You're smart to keep your guard up."

We arrived on Howe Street and found our chairs. Sitting in the blazing sun, waiting for the parade to start, I wondered if Josh would eventually show up. I decided to text him.

Me: I missed you last night. Sad face emoji. Is everything okay? We're at the parade if you still want to come.

Three dots appeared and disappeared. No response. I waited a few minutes and then sent another message.

Me: Please, let me know you're okay.

Josh: Thumbs up emoji. I'm still at the hospital.

Me: Okay. Love you. Kiss emoji. Maybe fireworks tonight?

No response.

I slumped in my chair. *He's shutting me out.*

The parade kicked off with a local marching band blaring to the tune of "America The Beautiful." Cars passed one by one with local government officials, pageant queens, and town's folk waving wildly at the crowd. Cheers and claps erupted from the onlookers enjoying the celebration. Thousands of adults and children full of excitement lined the streets as each float rolled by. A small, antique fire truck drove past with wheels that looked more appropriate for a bicycle. Inside sat the retired fire chief, who was shooting candy from an air gun at the children sitting in the crowd.

I leaned over to Renee and said, "I can't believe that truck ever put out a fire. I guess a hundred years ago the buildings just burned." She laughed so hard she snorted. The truck was cool, but I couldn't imagine it being of any actual use, even back in its time.

Next in line was a high school drill team. Dressed in red, white, and blue, they maneuvered their flags and batons in perfect unison. Behind them was the cheer team, chanting for the U.S.A. and performing backflips down the street. A kilted man playing bagpipes dazzled the crowd with his musical talents. Beaming with excitement, Janie screamed and cheered.

As the Scotsman passed, I saw Gray, who stood along the sidewalk on the other side of the road. He waved and nodded and then pointed to his phone, signaling me to check mine.

I forgot I had set my phone inside Janie's stroller, so I didn't feel it buzz. I had a few missed text messages.

Josh: I'll try to catch up with you for the fireworks.

Me: Great. See you then.

Helen: Still on for a BBQ at Randy and Renee's tonight?

I checked with Renee to make sure we were still on, then responded.

Me: Yes. Still on. Bring a salad.

The last was a text from Gray.

Gray: I wanted to see our little girl experience the parade. I'll keep my distance. Wink face emoji. My heart broke. Gray was trying so hard to make things right. He was standing on the other side of the road just to glimpse his daughter's reaction to her first parade.

I elbowed Renee and showed her the text. She looked up at me with empathy oozing from her eyes. I shrugged. "What am

I supposed to do? The more I let Gray in, the further Josh slips away."

Renee put her hand up to her ear. "What? It's so loud. I can't hear you."

This was a bad time to have this conversation. I loved Josh. He was my soulmate, my everything. Gray, however, was my daughter's father. I also needed to remember that right now, I was legally nothing to Janie. Until I had full custody, I had to tolerate Gray. I may have tolerated him initially, but lately, he's been good to me and Janie. I wanted him to suck. I wanted him to be the bad guy, but he had only supported me and helped me be with my daughter. I sighed.

Music blasted from a large, brightly colored truck, and clowns on stilts danced around the street. The sound snapped me out of my head and brought me back to the parade. Two clowns wandered into the crowd and began high-fiving the children. Janie freaked out and started screaming. Her face turned red as tears flowed down her cheeks, and terror shown through her eyes.

"It's okay, Janie bug. It's okay. It's a silly little clown."

"No. Mommy. No," she shrieked and buried her face in her hands.

I lifted her out of the stroller and held her in my arms. I sang softly into her ear. "You are my sunshine, my only sunshine." My eyes locked with Gray's. I could see the concern on his face from across the street. I gave him a thumbs-up to reassure him that everything was okay. Janie soon passed out in my arms, her body like a furnace in the heat.

The parade lasted over an hour, with dazzling dancers and grown men driving miniature cars in figure eights and doing donuts down the street. Randy and Renee loved the Fourth of July parade so much it was the only parade in Southport they didn't participate in.

Still fast asleep, I laid Janie down in her stroller. We folded up the chairs while Randy walked home to get the golf cart, so we didn't have to carry them home. Renee said, "Look. I know this is difficult. Families come in all shapes and sizes. You and Josh will work it out. I think you should invite Gray to the BBQ tonight. He can spend time with Janie, and you and Josh can get used to him being an extended part of your family. It is what it is. The sooner everyone understands that, the better it'll be for Janie."

"I don't know. That might be a disaster." I folded the last chair and leaned it against the stroller.

"Maybe. But maybe not." Renee shrugged.

Gray made his way through the crowd of people and stepped onto the sidewalk next to us. He peeked in the stroller at Janie and smiled.

"She's so beautiful. Like her mother." He turned toward me. "I didn't mean—"

"It's okay."

"I said what popped into my head. I didn't think it through. I don't want you to feel uncomfortable. But she's beautiful, and she most definitely gets that from you."

Renee raised an eyebrow and nodded toward Gray.

"We're having a BBQ tonight at Randy and Renee's. Would you like to come?" I can't believe the words came out of my mouth. *What am I doing? That is an awful idea.*

"I have a steak and lobster at home with my name on it. I appreciate the offer, but I think it's best I decline. However, I'd love to join for a BBQ another day."

He grabbed my hand. "It's okay, Lizzie. We're all trying to navigate our lives with Janie. I've done so much wrong. I want to get the rest right." He peered into the stroller and stared at his daughter. "I love you, baby girl. Sweet dreams."

He waved goodbye and walked down the street toward his condo.

Renee stood with her jaw on the floor. "I wanted to hate him forever for all the awful things he did and said to you, but honestly, Lizzie, I'm proud of him."

I didn't want to admit it, but I was, too.

"Truth be told, I think he loves you. Maybe he isn't in love with you anymore. But he loves you enough that he wants to get this right. And there's no question how much he loves Janie." She pointed to Randy, who was turning the corner on the golf cart. "I can't freaking believe I'm saying nice things about Gray Stone. What in the actual hell is going on?"

I laughed, and then my laughter then turned into a groan. "I feel the same way, but he hurt me so badly. I think I'm afraid to let him in again. Hurt me once, shame on him. Hurt me twice, shame on me. You know what I mean?"

"Yeah. I get it."

Randy stopped in front of the curb. "Your carriage has arrived, ladies."

I helped load the chairs in the back. "I'm going to walk home and lay Janie down. I'll be over later for the party."

"Okay, sis. See you later."

EIGHTEEN

Lizzie

I returned home to an empty house and a heavy heart. *Maybe I should show up at the hospital?* I missed Josh. I missed his touch, our morning chats with coffee, and weekend cartoons with him and Janie. I missed my happy-go-lucky man, who made my heart sing.

I laid Janie down in her crib and crawled into my bed. An afternoon nap was exactly what I needed. I grabbed my phone from the nightstand and opened a text message to Josh. Staring at the screen, I contemplated what to write.

I typed, *I miss you*, then backspaced, and started over. *How's your dad?* I watched the cursor flash on the screen. My chest was tight with sadness. I deleted the message again.

Janie misses you. Delete.

Rolling onto my side, I groaned and tossed the phone onto the bed.

I woke up an hour later to Janie blabbering in her crib. I enjoyed listening to her sweet voice. I lay there for a few minutes while she talked to herself. *Screw it. We're going to the hospital.*

I changed, dressed Janie, and fed her some lunch. I got myself ready, and we drove to the hospital. My heart was pounding as I approached the information desk. I told the lady behind the counter I was there to see Len Miller. Her blue scrubs crinkled as she pointed me toward the elevator. "Take the elevator to the third floor, then turn right. Room 418 will be on your left."

"Thank you."

I followed her directions and stood outside the door. I don't know why, but I was terrified to enter the room. The last time I was in a hospital, my daughter was stolen. The time before that, a drunk driver had hit my parents. Maybe I was afraid of what Josh might say. Maybe I was afraid to see Len, or more accurately, see how Len was now. I convinced myself that he would enjoy seeing Janie. I lifted my chin and charged into the room. Only to find a sleeping Len and no Josh.

Where was he?

I quietly walked to the chair in the corner of the room and sat for a moment. I watched Len sleep. He seemed peaceful, his chest rising and falling in cadence. I walked to his bedside and grabbed his hand. "Len, we really miss you. You need to fight. Your son needs you. Your kind, strong, hard-working boy is a mess right now. He needs you. I need you. Janie needs you. You need to pull through this. The world is not done with Len Miller."

I wiped a tear from my cheek and squeezed his hand. I stood back up and walked toward the door when a quiet, gentle voice said, "Lizzie?"

I turned to see Len's blue-gray eyes. "Lizzie," he said again, more excited this time.

"Hi, Len. You're awake." I pushed the stroller to his bedside.

His eyes filled with joy at the sight of his granddaughter. "There's my girl."

"We've missed you. Honestly, we've missed Josh too."

"Josh?" His voice was almost a whisper.

"Yes. He's been here so often. We haven't seen much of him lately."

"Oh, dear." Len patted the bed to beckon me closer.

I scooted the stroller over to stand directly next to the bed. I grabbed Len's hand again. My stomach clenched with fear. *What's he about to tell me?*

"Josh hasn't been here in a few days."

I gasped. "What do you mean he hasn't been here? He hasn't been home, either."

"Lizzie, I'm dying. They'll be moving me soon to a twenty-four-hour care facility. Josh insisted he could take care of me. We fought about it."

"Oh, Len. I'm sorry." My heart stung with hurt hearing this news.

"I won't be a burden to Josh or you. I want to go into the facility, and Josh's angry about it. He loves you, Lizzie. He loves you so much. But ever since his mother died, he doesn't handle grief well." Len cleared his throat. I sniffed. "I don't know where he is, but he isn't doing this to hurt you. I know this about my son. He doesn't want to accept the inevitable, and he's drawing inward. Give him space, but not for too long. Don't let him push you away. He'll regret that decision later. He loves you more than anything in the world. Right now, you'll have to be strong enough to fight for both of you." He coughed again and inhaled a shallow breath.

I sat on the edge of his bed and laid my head on his chest. He wrapped his arms around me, and I cried. "We love you, Len. Thank you for welcoming me into your family. Thank you for raising a wonderful son."

"Oh, Lizzie. You're the gift. You make Josh so happy. You'll get through this."

"How long do they think you have?"

"Not sure. A few months, maybe a year."

I sat up and swiped my hands across my face. I looked at Janie, who was oblivious to what was happening. She looked up and said, "Papa." Her wide grin put a smile on Len's face, and we both laughed. She bobbled her head back and forth and made a muttering sound.

"What can I do to help you?" I said to Len as I stood.

"Love my son. And bring that beautiful baby girl to visit me." He pointed at Janie and smiled.

I kissed his head, squeezed his hand, and exited the room. I raced toward the elevator as fast as I could. Rushing to breathe fresh air into my lungs, I pushed the stroller through the exit doors and leaned against the building. I gasped for air as my heart filled with grief. The weight of everything was like an elephant bearing down on my chest. Len's impending death, Josh's grief, my own sadness, my fear and stress that I might lose my daughter. The reality Catalina could be released soon. Working with Gray. Building a new relationship with Gray, a relationship I wasn't sure that I could trust. All of it pressed down on my chest at once, and I clutched my shirt and tried to rip it off. *One foot in front of the other, Lizzie. Get your shit together.*

Janie started to cry. I think I scared her. I looked into my baby girl's eyes, and I knew I had no choice. Forward. That was the only option. I straightened up, took a deep breath, and puffed out my chest. "Janie. Mommy's okay. We've got this." I wrinkled my nose, puckered my lips, and made a funny face at her. Her cries turned into giggles, and just like that, I pulled myself together, suppressed those feelings of discord, and moved on with my day.

When we arrived at Randy and Renee's for the BBQ, I jumped right in and helped Renee prepare the food and set up for the party. Randy played with Janie while Renee and I worked hard in the kitchen. I cut vegetables for a veggie tray while she put together a cheese spread.

Every time someone came to the door, my heart fluttered. I texted Josh on my way over, practically begging him to come to the house for the party. He still hadn't responded. I was doing my best to have patience, but I must admit I was getting annoyed.

Over the next hour, the house filled with friends and neighbors. The kitchen table was full of people stuffing their faces with hot dogs and hamburgers that Randy cooked up on the grill. Helen, Drew, and I were still picking at the appetizers in the living room. Randy's Ax-throwing friends were sitting on the back deck. Music blasted from the Bluetooth speaker. Groups of people sat talking and laughing. It was a great night. Janie bounced from person to person, playing peek-a-boo, reading books, and singing songs.

As night fell, the party dwindled. One by one, the guests thanked Randy and Renee and said their goodbyes until Helen and Drew were the only people left. Dishes piled up on the countertop, and the trash overflowed. Randy and Drew carried out the bags while the girls cleaned up inside.

"No Josh, huh?" Renee said.

"I'm hoping he'll come by for the fireworks."

She pursed her lips and bit her tongue.

Helen said, "What'd I miss?"

"It's a long story. Basically, I've barely seen or spoken to my fiancé in a few days."

"What?" Helen gasped. "That's unusual."

"He hasn't been himself since his dad got sick." I set a freshly dried pot onto the counter.

"I'm sure he'll come by later," Helen said.

"Are you guys going to the water to watch the fireworks?" I wanted to change the subject.

Renee picked up the pot and said, "Yeah. You?"

"I think I'm going to stay here. Janie needs to go to bed. I can lay her down here if I watch from the front porch. Do you care if I stay the night, so I don't have to drive her home after?"

Renee said, "Of course, you can stay anytime."

"Thanks."

Helen washed the last dish, dried her hands, and said, "Thank you for a lovely evening, but Drew and I should get going. Speaking of, where is Drew?"

"Now that you mention it, Randy never came back inside either." Renee walked around the corner to check the bathroom. "No one's in the bathroom."

I walked to the front door and looked outside. Randy and Drew were inside the bed of Drew's truck, ogling the tools. "Found them."

The girls came to the door and laughed. "Boys and their toys," Helen said.

Helen said goodbye to Janie and gave me a hug. I waved to Drew and went inside to get Janie ready for bed. After her bath, we sat in the rocking chair in her room, and I rocked her to sleep. I was not ready to lay her down yet, so I sang three rounds of the sunshine song. As I held my daughter, I appreciated how precious this moment was. I didn't take any second with her for granted.

Randy and Renee were getting ready to ride their bikes to the waterfront for the fireworks when I walked into the kitchen. I checked my phone. I had a message from Josh. *Finally.*

Josh: I'll see you in a few for the fireworks.

Me: Come to Randy's house. I'm watching from here. I already laid Janie down.

Josh: K. Be there soon.

Me: Love you.

Josh: Love you, too.

My heart practically flipped out of my body. Hopeful that maybe everything would be okay, I smiled. I said goodbye to Renee and Randy, poured myself a glass of wine, and sat on the front porch eagerly waiting for Josh to arrive.

His truck turned the corner, and butterflies swirled in my stomach. His face was so handsome in the moonlight's glow. His dark hair was freshly washed, and his shaved face showed off his square jawline. Tingles shot through me at the sight of him. He parked the truck and hopped out. In his hands was a box of Burney's, a baked goods apology was coming, and everything would be okay.

He stopped on the steps and leaned against the porch railing. "Hi," was all he said.

"Hi," I said, wanting to hug him so bad it hurt. I didn't know what to do.

"I brought you some croissants."

"I see that." I caught his gaze and held it for a moment, a playful smile dancing on my lips—a silent flirtation, charged with the hope that he had felt my absence as acutely as I had felt his. I walked toward him and took the box. I tore off a piece of croissant and popped it in my mouth. My eyes rolled, and I moaned as the delicious pastry dazzled my taste buds. "You know the way to a girl's heart."

Josh stepped forward and wrapped his arms around my waist. His touch sent electrical pulses up and down my spine, but pain pumped through my heart. I yearned for his touch so much that it hurt. I leaned in and hugged him tightly. Squeezing with all my might, I didn't let go. I laid my head on his chest and breathed in his fresh scent. I closed my eyes and instantly wanted to forget the past few days.

"I love you," I said.

He hesitated. "I love you, too."

I brought my lips to his and for an instant, all my frustration, fear, and anger melted away until Josh pulled back. *What did I do? I don't understand.*

"Lizzie, I need you to know that I love you." He slid my arms back to my sides. "What I'm about to say is because I love you." Fear took over, and I immediately took a step back. Whatever he was about to say, I wanted him to look me straight in the face. *Oh my God, I think I'm going to vomit.*

He stepped toward me, closing the gap between us. "I have so many things going on in my head right now. I need time to process. I want to be the man you need me to be, but I'm not. I'm sick with jealousy over Gray, and you know that's not who I am, but I can't help it. I want to strangle him every time I see him. When he's near you, I want to kill him. Every day I feel like I will lose you to him, and it's turning me into someone I don't want to be."

He put his hand on my shoulder. I brushed him off and said, "I don't want to be with him. We've got to get to a place where we can co-exist with him, but he's not who I want to be with. You are."

"Please let me finish." He stepped onto the porch and leaned back against the railing.

I crossed my arms. "Go ahead. Finish."

"I hear what you say about Gray and how you don't love him. Somewhere inside, I believe you, but I'm not right in my head about it. I need time to process. On top of that, my father's going to die, Lizzie. I can't think straight. He's my best friend. It's all too much right now."

"What are you saying?" I pursed my lips and put my hands on my hips.

"I don't want to hate Gray. I don't want to hate that Janie loves Gray. I feel like I'm drowning in hate and need time."

I could feel my skin getting hot with anger. "*Say it*!"

Bang. Bang. Bang.

The fireworks exploded in the sky, drawing our attention upward. I stared at Josh's back and bit my lip. I refused to cry. I bit down harder and tasted blood in my mouth. He turned back around and wrapped me in his arms. I wanted to give into his hug, and for this to be a bad dream, but the pain made it all too real. I pushed him away.

"Just say it."

"I'm going to stay on the boat for a while. I may even take her out on the water for a few days." The fireworks continued to erupt in the sky, interrupting our conversation.

"Are you breaking up with me?"

He put his hands on my face and kissed my forehead. "I love you. I want to be with you. I need you to give me time. I need to find the man that you deserve to be with."

My jaw clenched, and I balled my hands into fists.

Boom. Boom. Boom.

Sparkles of fire and gunpowder lit up the sky. "I don't understand. You are that man. You're the man I want to be with. We're supposed to spend the rest of our lives together for the good parts and the bad parts. Your burdens are my burdens. We're supposed to do this together."

Glistening bright lights blazed the sky in a variety of colors. Then silence.

"I'm sorry, Lizzie. I need to be alone right now."

I exploded. "Go ahead and run. I may not be waiting for you when you get back." I didn't mean that. I'd wait forever for him, but right now, I was pissed.

"I hope you'll wait, but I'm willing to take that risk."

He's willing to take that risk. He's willing to walk away and lose me. Fuck him.

"Get out."

Bang. Bang. Bang.

More fireworks exploded in the sky. My legs felt numb, and my stomach bubbled with so many emotions. I screamed through tears, "Get out! Go. *Leave.*"

I started punching him in the chest. *Why won't he go? I need him to leave so I can fall apart.*

He wrapped his arms around me and I melted into his embrace. He was crying. "I love you so much. Telling you this has been the hardest thing I've ever done. I am physically in pain."

I looked up at him. "Then why are you doing it? Why? You're breaking my heart." I pushed away from him again and stepped toward the door. "Please, just go." I opened the door, walked inside, and closed it behind me. Unsure if my legs would support me, I leaned against the door for support. My hand rubbed my stomach in an effort to calm my nerves and avoid vomiting all over the floor.

Instead, I flung open the door, and frantically ran onto the front yard. Josh was halfway to his truck. He turned toward me, and I jumped into his arms and wrapped my legs around his waist. The fireworks were relentless, erupting in the air one after the other.

"Please don't do this. Please don't leave me. I need you. I love you. It's always been you. You've got to hear me." My lips burned as they touched his, and I could taste the salt of our tears as they trickled down our cheeks onto our lips. I kissed him again and again, moving him backward to keep his balance until we fell against his truck. His back collided with the door as the finale began with an endless blaze of lights bursting in the sky. I sucked in a long, intense breath, hoping he could feel my passion. "I love you, Josh. If you walk away now, I'm not sure I could ever forgive you."

He slid his arms up and down my back and pulled me tighter. He stopped kissing me and pressed his forehead against mine. The explosions stopped—the ones in the sky and the ones inside my body.

"I'm not walking away. I'm asking for time. I need to be alone and sort through my feelings. I love you, and I'll be back for you." He peeled me off of him and set me down on the ground. "I love you, Lizzie. I have to do this." He climbed into his truck and drove away.

I fell to my knees and clutched the grass in my hands, pulling and clawing at it as the man I loved drove out of my life. I trembled as the tears gushed down my face and I ugly cried.

NINTEEN
Gray

Business was booming, and life was headed in the right direction. My divorce was official, crazy Kitty Cat was in jail, and it would only be a matter of time before the custody of Janie was official. I was sure the judge would grant custody to Lizzie. Sitting at my desk, I looked at my calendar to see what meetings I had today. Tonight was the office dinner celebration. I wanted to take Andra and Lizzie to dinner to thank them for their hard work and success.

I was about to make a call when Lizzie came into my office. Her eyes were puffy and swollen. She looked sick. "Are you not feeling well?"

"I've had a rough couple of days." She managed to get a few words out before she flopped into the chair by my desk. "Josh left."

I blinked. *Did I hear her correctly?* "What do you mean, Josh left?"

"I mean, he left. He decided a few days ago on the Fourth of July. I haven't seen or heard from him since." I handed her a tissue so she could blow her nose.

"Take it from someone who's been with you. He'll come to his senses. Trust me."

"It's fine. I'm fine. We have work to do, so let's get to it." She threw the tissue in the trash and stood up in a huff.

"Lizzie, if you need to take the day off, I understand. I can reschedule dinner tonight."

"Dinner. I forgot about dinner. It's fine. I need to keep moving." She grabbed another tissue and walked out the door.

Damn, that woman drives me insane. Even when she's distraught and crying, she's sexy. She doesn't even know how incredible she is.

I leaned back in my chair and crossed my hands behind my head. For the first time, I was truly happy. I didn't have Lizzie, but I was coming to terms with that. Our DNA was wrapped together in our beautiful daughter. I would always be connected to Lizzie, and being Janie's father made me look at the world through a different lens. I couldn't believe it, but I adored this quiet little town. I didn't miss New York even a little.

A knock at the door caught me off guard, and I almost fell out of my chair flat on my ass. I leaned forward and grabbed my desk for balance. Once I composed myself, I said, "Come in."

Andra entered the room wearing a fluffy white dress and emerald green high heels. *Her taste is a mystery.* Green eye shadow covered her eyes from lid to brow and red lipstick was smeared on her lips. "How can I help you, Andra?"

"I'm not going to make dinner tonight. Is that a problem?"

"No problem. We can reschedule. Is that all?"

She stood awkwardly, staring at me like she had something else to say.

"Andra?"

"Never mind. That's all. Thank you." She turned and left.

She was an interesting character. She does a decent enough job and has some good ideas, but she's socially awkward. It's like she doesn't understand how to read the room. I can't put my finger on it—she's just weird.

The day flew by. I walked to Lizzie's office, and she was already packing up to go home. "Knock, knock."

She looked up. "I was getting ready to come say goodbye. I'm headed to daycare to get Janie. I'll meet you at the restaurant. What time again?"

Should I tell her Andra isn't coming?

"Sevenish is good. We have reservations."

"Okay, great. I'll see you there."

"Don't forget we changed to Fisherman's Café on the water."

"Yep, got it." She threw her bag over her shoulder, walked past me down the hall, and out the front door. The scent of lavender captivated my nose as she passed.

I locked up the office an hour later, put the top down on my new Maserati, and let the wind blow through my hair. Blasting *Free*

Falling on the stereo, I sang at the top of my lungs. Life was good. I couldn't remember a time in my life when I felt this content.

When I arrived home, my front door was cracked. *What the hell?* I pulled my phone out of my pocket and dialed 9-1-1 but didn't press the call button. I carefully opened the door and looked around. The condo appeared to be empty. I walked through all the rooms and checked all the closets with my phone at the ready. Nothing.

I went into the kitchen to get a drink of water and spotted an envelope sitting on the table with my name in cursive written across the front. I contemplated whether I should open it or call the police. I opened it. Inside was a picture of Janie screaming at the Fourth of July parade when she freaked out about the clowns. With the picture was a note that said, *I'm coming for you.* Startled, the picture slipped out of my hand. *This is insane. Who'd be doing this?* Catalina's in jail. I really thought her threats were empty, but maybe I need to take her more seriously. *Did she get out?*

I called Mr. Stallard. He answered on the second ring. "Hello, it's Gray Stone."

"Hello, Mr. Stone. What can I do for you?"

"Have you heard anything about Catalina getting out of jail?"

"No. Her parole hearing isn't until the end of August. Why?"

"I was just wondering. Thank you. Have a good night."

I hung up.

I stared at the note. This doesn't make any sense. Is Catalina an escape artist now, too? Should we add that to the list of things she's capable of? I put the picture and the note back inside the envelope and tucked it in my top desk drawer. I finished getting ready and walked the few blocks to Fisherman's Café.

I greeted the bubbly hostess with a smile and confirmed we had a table on the water. She said, "Yes, sir. Follow me." Dressed in all black with matching high heels, she guided me to the table. Typically, I would have bought out a section of the restaurant, but I wanted to show Lizzie that I do listen to her. I decided not to do that tonight. However, when I sat down at the table, and the man next to me was wearing a plastic bib with a giant red crab on the front, cracking crab legs and sending shells flying every which way, I regretted my decision.

The waiter came to the table, and I ordered two waters and two glasses of wine. I could see Lizzie as she walked through the front door. She looked incredible. Her brown hair flowed past her shoulders, and her skin seemed to be glowing. She wore a long-flowered sundress that accentuated her breasts. *Stop it. You're friends—no more thinking about her breasts.*

I stood and waved so she could see me.

"Hi. Sorry, I'm a few minutes late. Janie didn't want to eat her dinner."

"That's okay. I haven't been here long."

"Andra must be running late, too," Lizzie said as she hung her purse across her chair and sat down.

I hesitated. "She's not coming."

Lizzie's face immediately hardened. "Is there no end to your manipulation?" She stood up to leave. "Damn you, Gray."

"Wait. Don't go." She turned to face me. "She was supposed to come. I swear. She canceled this afternoon. I didn't tell you because I didn't want you to cancel, too. Please, sit."

She paused. *Come on, Lizzie. Stay.*

"Yes. This was a work celebration dinner. That was the plan. But, when Andra canceled, I took the opportunity to talk to you alone. I'm sorry I didn't tell you she couldn't make it. Selfishly, I knew you wouldn't come."

She eased back into her seat but set her purse on the table so she could flee at a moment's notice. "If this is ever going to work, you need to be honest with me. I want to trust you, but there's so much history. It's not easy for me."

"I understand. I'm sorry." I was sorry. If I could rewind time and do things over again, I'd make different choices, but I can't.

"We need to be able to talk through things even if you don't get the answers you want." She looked adorable when she was trying to be stern. Her beautiful eyes peered over her menu as she spoke. *Why didn't I see how special she was when I had her?*

"I understand," I said. She raised an eyebrow, and a faint smile appeared on her face. I could feel my eyes light up as I smiled back at her. "What are you going to order?"

"I'm thinking about the salmon or maybe some crab legs. I haven't had crab legs in a while." Just as she said crab legs, a shell from the table beside us flew through the air and landed in her hair.

I burst out laughing. "Salmon it is." I reached across the table to pull the shell from her hair and said, "And this is why I buy out the surrounding tables. I can't have my dinner guest attacked by crab legs."

Her face softened, and she laughed. Her smile caused my insides to melt like a chocolate bar sitting out in the sun.

Lizzie ordered salmon and a shot of vodka. The girl knew what she wanted when she wanted it. There was no denying that. I admired a girl who liked to drink her liquor straight. I ordered the surf and turf and a martini with two olives.

"Are you nervous about the judge's custody ruling?" I wanted to set her mind at ease.

"Yes. Incredibly nervous."

"Don't be. I think the judge wants to do her due diligence or at least give the appearance of doing her due diligence. You deserve custody of your daughter, and Judge Marshall will see that."

"Easy for you to say. You have custody." *This was my chance.*

"About that," I said calmly. A look I didn't recognize flashed across her face. She looked out at the water. A clear sign she wasn't sure she wanted to hear what came next. "I want to talk about you, Josh, and Janie."

She snapped her head to look at me. "Josh? What does he have to do with any of this?"

"He has everything to do with this. He's going to be your husband, isn't he?"

"I don't know. Right now, he's on a mission to find himself." She rolled her eyes, opened her mouth, and swallowed her shot of vodka in one huge gulp. She beckoned to the waiter with her empty glass in hand, signaling she wanted another.

"Okay, well, let's pretend for a second that you are still going to marry him. He's going to be a part of Janie's life. I want to give you a few things to consider." I reflected on what I wanted to say next. I took a sip of my martini, then another. "I love you, Lizzie. I won't deny my feelings for you." She pursed her lips and looked out toward the water again. "I love you and Janie both. But-"

"Oh great. There's a but," she muttered under her breath.

"I see the way Josh looks at you. At first, I wanted to punch him. But he's a good man, and I see how genuinely happy he makes you."

The waiter approached and gave Lizzie her second vodka shot. Lizzie said, "I'll take another." She raised her glass and said, "To Josh." I'd never seen a woman throw back a shot of vodka quite like Lizzie Levine. *Perhaps I should cut her off.* She slammed the glass down on the table and breathed out a tasty breath of satisfaction.

I took both of her hands in mine and said, "Lizzie. I see now the mistakes I made. I want you to know that I love you enough to let you go. Your happiness means everything to me. I won't be a problem for you and Josh. If you ever decide you want me back, I'll come running. But as long as Josh is your choice, I'll respect that."

She blinked. Then looked down at our hands and pulled away like she didn't notice they'd been holding mine. "Are you for real right now?"

"What do you mean? I'm trying to be honest. That's what you asked me to do."

"Is this a trick? Are you trying to get me to fall for you again?"

"What? No. I'm telling you how I feel. I see how much you and Josh love each other. He's been far better to you than I have. I'm trying to respect that." The third shot of vodka arrived. Before the waiter could even set it down, Lizzie snatched it from his hand.

"Keep 'em coming," she slurred. "Yep. Josh has been sooooo good to me. He's such a good man." She opened the hatch and threw back her third shot.

"Here, eat a piece of bread," I said, and handed her a large roll with butter. I can't have this conversation while she's intoxicated. I need her sober.

"I'm fine. Am I not allowed to have some drinks?" she snapped.

"Sure, you can, but this isn't normally like you."

She groaned and shoved half the roll into her mouth.

"I would like to be Janie's father. I want to share custody with you. I'll agree for her to live with you and Josh, but I'd like her to be able to stay with me some, too."

She wiped crumbs from the table into her hand and dropped them onto her plate. "I know you want to be her father." She blinked at me again, like I was speaking in a foreign tongue. The waiter brought over two shot glasses of vodka this time.

Lizzie dropped her napkin and reached down to pick it up, and I mouthed to the waiter not to bring any more.

When she sat upright again, her hair was messed around her face. I snickered. She gave me a playful, dirty look and smoothed the stray hairs.

"I don't have any right to take your daughter away from you. I wish Josh were her father, but he isn't." Her words cut me deep, and from the look on her face, she knew it. "I'm sorry. I didn't mean that." She threw back her fourth shot of vodka.

"Yes, you did, but I understand. Doesn't mean it didn't hurt, though."

She dropped her head into her hands and sighed. "I'm tired. I feel like all I do every day is fight. I don't want to fight anymore."

I put my hand on her chin and lifted her face to look at me. "Janie and Josh are worth fighting for." I can't believe I'm encouraging her to fight for Josh. What am I doing? This would be the perfect time to take advantage of the situation. My old self would have.

"I like Southport Gray." Lizzie's words slurred out of her mouth. "Southport Gray is much better than New York Gray."

Our food arrived, and we talked about Janie while we ate. Lizzie's eyes lit up like a Christmas tree as she told me how Janie liked to babble to herself in the morning. She laughed when she told me about the food Janie didn't like and how she'd throw it on the floor. She went on and on about how she'd point and say "wassat," at anything new.

I could listen to this beautiful woman talk about our daughter for hours. I cleaned my plate and wiped my mouth. "Janie's the perfect mixture of both of us. I have no doubt she'll grow up to be a kick-ass woman. She won't take shit from anyone, like her mother."

Lizzie smiled, then burped. Her eyes widened so large they might have popped right out of their sockets. Embarrassed, she covered her mouth and said, "Excuse me."

I practically had tears coming out of my eyes. "The great Lizzie Levine burps. Who knew?"

She stuck her tongue out at me. "I should go. Helen's at the house with Janie." She picked up the last shot of vodka. "Can't let this go to waste." Before I even had time to react, down the hatch it went. Lizzie stood to leave and fell back into her chair. She looked at me and said, "Whoopsie, daisy." Her head flew back, and she erupted in uncontrollable laughter.

I put my arm around her. "Come on. I've got you."

"You're so hot, Graaayyyssooon Stooooonnnneeeee." She criss-crossed her feet in a zigzag pattern as we walked. "I wish you weren't such an ass. Things might have been different," she slurred.

I propped her in a seat at the bar. I slipped the bartender a hundred and said, "Make sure she stays right here. I need to pull up our golf cart."

Lizzie pressed her forehead to mine. I could smell the vodka radiating from her breath. "I want to kiss you now." She puckered her lips, and it took every ounce of strength I had not to give in. I wanted her. I wanted her badly, but deep down, I know she wanted Josh. She lost her balance and fell out of the chair.

"Stay here," I said firmly, putting her back in the seat. I dug through Lizzie's purse and found her keys. "Lizzie. Do you know where you parked?" She shrugged and laid her head on the bar.

Great. Just great.

Ten minutes later, I found the golf cart a block away. I squealed in on two wheels, uncomfortable that Lizzie was unattended at the bar for so long. When I walked up, she was throwing another shot back. I glared at the bartender. "How many did you serve her?"

"Two. Then I realized she was pretty inebriated. She had three more, but they were water. I didn't tell her and she didn't seem to notice."

I pulled Lizzie to her feet, and like a rag doll, she leaned forward and backward, unable to focus. She was like a slinky, bobbling all over the place. *Screw it.* I hoisted her over my shoulder and carried her to the golf cart. She was mumbling words I couldn't understand. Then she said, "something, something, Josh."

"I know Lizzie. You love Josh. He'll come home soon. Don't worry." She passed out, sprawled across the backseat.

As the words came out of my mouth, someone tugged hard on my shirt, spinning me around. Before I even realized what was happening, a fist connected with my jaw. Pain shot through my cheek and I tasted blood. Blinking to gain focus, I saw Josh Miller standing in front of me. "What the hell, man?"

He reared back again, preparing to deliver another blow. I threw my hands up in surrender. "It's not what you think." The second punch landed squarely on my nose. Warm sticky liquid dribbled down my face.

Bent over in pain, my hands on my knees, I took a deep breath and backed up to put distance between us. "I don't want to fight you. I deserved the first punch and I'll let the second punch slide, but hit me again and you'll regret it."

"You're a piece of shit, Gray. What did ya get her drunk so you could seduce her?"

Lizzie came to and sat up. "Hi, Joshua." She accentuated the U-A.

"What the fuck, Lizzie? Are you with him now?"

"Maybe I am? What does it matter? You don't want me, re-member?" Her words were hard to understand, but from the look on Josh's face, he definitely heard her. "Gray wants me. He *really* wants me." I could feel the rage building in Josh's veins as she spoke. Lizzie tried to get out of the golf cart and fell into me. I hoisted her to her feet, and she leaned in for a kiss. I turned my head away, and she passed out again. Josh helped me put her back in the golf cart.

Squaring off, face to face with Josh, I said, "Look, man, she was drinking because she's devastated that you left."

"Don't pretend you don't want her," Josh yelled.

"I do want her. But she loves you. I told her to fight for you." I pushed my index finger into his chest.

"Fuck you, Gray."

"Yeah, fuck me. I'm doing my best here, man. Don't fuck this up like I did. Trust me, you'll regret it."

Josh launched a wad of spit out of his mouth and said, "I'm not you. I'd never treat her that way."

"No. You're better than me. That's why she deserves you. Get your head out of your ass and fix it." I used my hand to wipe the blood off my face.

He smirked. "I hit you pretty good, didn't I?"

"Yep."

"Sorry."

"That's your one freebie." I offered my hand in truce. Josh's eyes wandered to my blood-soaked hand and back up to my face.

"We can shake later."

I nodded. "Helen's at the house. Your girl needs to get home. I was going to take her."

"I got it." He hopped in the driver's seat and popped the brake. He drove a few feet and stopped. "Hey Gray."

"Yeah?"

"You're still an asshole."

"I know." I waved and crossed the street toward my condo.

TWENTY

Lizzie

Slowly, the room came into focus, and I saw that a trash can had been positioned by the bed. I sat up and ran my hands over my clothes. I was in a tank top and my underwear. *Shit. Did Gray see me naked? Did I change myself?* Panic shot through my veins, and I hopped out of bed, only to feel vomit rising to my throat, and I immediately sat back down. *Oh, dear God. Did Gray and I...?* The possibility set alarm bells ablaze in my head. *No. I couldn't have. I wouldn't have.*

Think, Lizzie. Think!

I remembered going to dinner with Gray. I remember being pissed that Andra didn't come. I remembered him telling me he loved me. Like a mathematician who cracked an impossible code, I remembered where it all went wrong. Shots. Oh my God, I drank vodka shots and a lot of them. Ugg! I moaned.

I reached for my phone and checked the time. It was eleven o'clock. *What the hell? Janie!*

Ignoring the need to vomit, I sprinted into Janie's room. It was empty. I pulled the blanket out of her crib as if she was hiding underneath it. I ran down the stairs, taking them two at a time. As I turned the corner, I could see Janie sitting in her booster seat, eating chicken nuggets.

Shit. Shit. Shit. Was Gray here?

"Hi, Mommy." She smiled big.

Josh was standing behind the kitchen island, drinking coffee. He lifted the pot and said, "Coffee?"

I froze, rubbed my eyes, and opened them again. *Am I dreaming?*

Unable to get any words out, I nodded. *Does he know about dinner with Gray? Did he show up this morning? Was he here last night?*

The questions swirling around my head did not help the incessant pounding. *Ugg, so much vodka. What was I thinking?*

I walked carefully to the kitchen table and slid into the chair. Josh brought me a mug of coffee the way I like it and then sat across from me. "You had some fun last night, huh?"

I opened my mouth to speak and bolted to the bathroom. Clinging to the toilet bowl, last night's dinner flew out of my mouth. I lingered a few extra minutes. I wasn't ready to face Josh again.

"You okay in there?" Josh called from the kitchen.

I went back to the table and took a sip of my coffee. I could still taste the vomit in my mouth.

Fidgeting, I said, "I don't remember much of last night."

"Do you remember seeing me?" He raised his eyebrow.

"You?" I said, confused. "No. I didn't see you."

"I brought you home." He got up from the table and put two pieces of toast in the toaster.

Great. I didn't accidentally sleep with Gray.

"I saw you and Gray on a date, and I punched him."

I gasped. "You punched him?"

"It's a long story. But yeah. I punched him twice." He smiled.

My brain cannot process any of this. *Maybe I'm dreaming.* You know, one of those dreams where you wake up so you think you're awake, but it's still a dream. *Yeah, that must be what's happening.*

"It wasn't a date," I said. "Is he okay? Am I allowed to ask that?" Sarcasm dripped from the words as I spoke them.

"He's fine." Josh shrugged and threw the dish towel he was playing with over his shoulder.

I furrowed my brow as my eyes darted from left to right. *I'm confused right now. I'm being punked. That's what this is.*

"You weren't in any shape to be a mom last night. Gray agreed, so I brought you home and put you into bed." He cleaned up Janie's hands and turned to face me.

"Don't worry, I slept on the couch in the loft. Someone needed to be here for Janie this morning." I was a terrible mom last night. I didn't plan to be irresponsible. It just kind of happened.

My shoulders slumped, and I stared into my cup of coffee, contemplating if I could jump in. I exhaled and watched the ripples in my mug. "I think the weight of everything caught up to me, and I wanted to forget for a little while."

Josh scoffed. "Oh, you forgot. That's for sure."

I was out of patience for his shit. I didn't need anyone rubbing my nose in my mistakes. It's been the best I can do to get out of bed and face each day while he's off finding himself.

"If you're here because you want to talk things out, fine, let's talk. If you're here to make me feel bad, leave. I don't have time for that."

"I'm here for Janie."

Ding.

The toast popped out of the toaster. "Butter?"

"Yes, please." I had the urge to punch him, but it would have to wait until after he made me toast.

"Dad's moving into his assisted living place today. I need to help him."

"I can help." I looked at Janie, who flung some grapes to the floor.

"I'll manage." He brought me the toast and picked the grapes off the floor.

"Will you be back after?"

"No."

Just no. That's it, no explanation. No discussion. Just no.

Maybe it was the hangover or the lack of patience for my life right now, but I had enough.

"Fine," I spat. I ripped my ring off my finger and threw it at him. "I'm done."

I lifted Janie out of her seat and went upstairs. I didn't mean it, but I was pissed. I didn't know how to fix our situation. *He didn't even chase after me.*

I popped on Bubble Guppies and snuggled in the bed with Janie. I texted Gray.

Me: I won't be in today.

Gray: I figured. Laugh face emoji.

After three rounds of the same show, I switched to Paw Patrol and told Janie to stay in bed while I took a shower. As the hot water sprayed over my skin, I cried. We'd heard nothing from the judge, and I was tired of waiting. The stress and worry were taking a toll. Keeping Janie was on my mind every day.

Living in this big house alone sucked. The view wasn't as beautiful when I looked out at the ocean alone. I thought of Len. His stories, his wisdom. I loved listening to him talk about the past and Josh as a boy at dinner. *Maybe I should move back to my apartment.* I was furious with Josh. I understood things were difficult right now, and the stress was piling up like last week's laundry, but we were supposed to help each other. Instead, he kept pushing me away.

I could hear Janie giggling from the bedroom. I turned the water off and called out to her. "Hi, Janie bug."

"Hi, Mommy."

I got dressed, carried Janie to her room, and changed her diaper. It amazed me how much poop could come out of a toddler. "Pee you, Janie bug. This one's a stinker." I wiped her clean and put on a new diaper. I pressed my mouth to her belly and blew, making a rumbling sound. She giggled furiously. I did it again. From deep down in her gut, she belly laughed. I carried her to the rocking chair and opened my latest book, Lessons in Chemistry. Sometimes, I would rock Janie and read the book I was reading to her. In this case, she was learning about a female chemist trying to make her way in a man's world.

After two chapters, Janie was fast asleep, and I laid her in the crib. I took the book and walked downstairs. On the kitchen table was a note. When I picked it up, my ring fell out.

Lizzie,

> *Please keep the ring. I'm sorry I can't stay right now. I'll find my way back to you.*

I love you, Josh

I rolled my eyes and set the ring on the table. I wasn't ready to put it back on, but I wasn't ready to give it back, either. I was glad he left it. Pulling my phone out of my pocket, I clicked my favorites and hit Josh. I decided to text him. I wasn't finished with what I had to say.

Me: I know you didn't ask for the crazy in my life.

Me: But

Me: You did sign up for it. When you asked me to be your wife, you knew what you were getting into. And you asked anyway.

…

…

…

I waited. No response.

Me: You're pushing me away and I don't deserve it.

…

…

…

No response.

Me: The ring's at the house. You want me to wear it? You'll have to put it on my finger. AGAIN.

Josh: Thumbs up, emoji.

Thumbs-up, emoji. Fucking thumbs-up emoji. Seriously? I screamed.

Startled by a knock at the door, I went to look through the peephole. I didn't see anyone.

I opened the door and looked around. Nothing.

As I pulled the door closed, I noticed a manilla envelope resting on the doormat. It said Lizzie in the top right corner. I picked up the envelope and looked down the street. No one was there.

Walking back into the kitchen, my pulse elevated, and I nervously undid the metal clasp. Inside was a piece of paper. Typed in bold, large font, it said, MOTHER OF THE YEAR. I stuck my hand inside the envelope and pulled out several photographs. I threw my hand up to cover my mouth as I gasped. Still images of my indiscretions last night stared back at me. A freeze frame of me slamming down a shot at the dinner table with Gray. Another one of me at the bar, practically falling out of my seat. Another one of Gray carrying me over his shoulder to the golf cart. One of me passed out in the golf cart, and the final picture was of Josh punching Gray in the face.

My stomach sank, and my nerves tingled. As if the photos weren't damning enough, someone was watching me. My hair stood on the back of my neck.

With my hand shaking, I picked up my cell phone and called Mr. Stallard.

He answered right away. "Hello, Lizzie."

"I need to speak with you as soon as possible, but I just laid Janie down. Could you come to my house? I received an envelope full of photographs. I'm freaking out."

"I'll be right there." He disconnected.

TWENTY ONE
Josh

NorthStar Assisted Living was the nicest, most expensive care facility in the area. The monthly fees cost an arm and a leg, and I might have to sell my boat to afford it, but I didn't care. My dad deserved the best. Since his stubborn ass refused to come home, I needed to find a place where I could feel comfortable leaving my father.

I spent the first few hours meeting the staff and interviewing Stella, who would be my dad's primary care nurse. She was in her mid-thirties and had worked at NorthStar for ten years. She was strict as hell, but seemed to take pride in her care for her patients.

"Your dad's in good hands here. I promise," Stella said. Her olive-green scrubs complimented her gentle chestnut eyes. "I'll treat him like my own father."

"Thank you, Stella. I really appreciate that."

She walked me to his room. "You can unpack his belongings while I take him to get some lunch."

After several trips to the truck, I carried the boxes, his lounge chair, and a bookcase into the room. The space was roomy but needed a personal touch to feel like home. I hung his favorite pictures on the walls and unpacked a stack of books. His clothes fit nicely in the drawers and closet. I didn't want him here, but I did feel better after meeting the staff and seeing his room. They even had a beautiful walking garden. I neatly folded his favorite blanket and nestled it on the end of his bed. Organizing the last of his books on the bookcase, I was almost finished when Stella wheeled him back into the room.

"See, son. This place is great. I'll be fine here." He looked so frail. His cheeks were sunk into his face. "They'll take care of me."

"I know, Dad. I wish you'd consider coming home with me instead. I can take care of you."

His tired eyes looked over at the bed. "Josh, I need full-time assistance. You have a life to live, and I want you to live it. I'll be happy here."

"I don't have much of a life right now." I helped him to bed and pulled the covers up to his chest, taking special care to fold the top back so he could keep his arms out.

"Ah. Lizzie. You're still an idiot, then. Haven't you gone home yet?"

Annoyed, I slumped into the chair and breathed out a sigh. "I'm not an idiot. I was planning to go home last night and apologize."

"Plans are great, Josh. But you have to follow through." He folded his arms on top of the covers and turned to face me. "She isn't going to chase you down. You're the one that left. You need to go to her."

"I went to the house last night."

"Yeah. And?"

I groaned. "She wasn't there. Helen said she was at a work dinner." I said the word *work* in air quotations and rolled my eyes.

"I see. Gray equals work." Len's eyes closed slowly and popped open again.

"You're tired, Dad. I'll leave you to rest." I adjusted his pillow.

"Oh, no, you don't. Did you go find her at dinner?" His eyes widened, waiting for my response.

"I did. She was drunk and hanging all over Gray. He was carrying her over his shoulder. She tried to kiss him. I lost it, Dad. I completely lost it."

"Did you talk to her?"

"She passed out. I was so mad. I punched Gray in the face. I don't know what came over me. The two of them were together and I lost my shit."

Len laughed, then coughed, and laughed again. "That's my boy. Get your girl the good old-fashioned way."

I smiled. "Oh, Dad. I screwed up. I should've never left. I know it's only a matter of time before she leaves me for him. He's Janie's father. She loves him. I can see it in her eyes when she looks at their daughter. I want to fix things, but last night just pissed me off all over again."

He grabbed my arm and squeezed. "She loved him—past tense. But you're right. If you don't get your head out of your ass, you might lose her. You need to decide if you want to fix it. If you do, fight for her. If you don't, tell her so she can move on with her life."

"Why are you taking her side?" I said.

"Because I see the way she looks at you. She's smitten." He laughed.

"Love you, Dad. Thanks for the talk."

"Son, when you find a good woman, you do everything you can to hold onto her. Don't let her go. Trust me."

"Thanks, Dad." I fixed his covers and placed a book on his nightstand. "I'll be back tomorrow."

TWENTY TWO

Lizzie

“Do the police have any idea who's sending me these pictures?” I asked Stallard.

Sitting at the kitchen table, he thumbed through the latest delivery of threats. “They don't have much to go on. So, no.”

“This doesn't make any sense. Who else besides Catalina would want to threaten us?”

“You'd know better than me. But I'll make sure these get to the police with the rest of them and make the usual copies of everything, too.”

I paced the kitchen, biting my bottom lip. “I don't know. Catalina's the only person I can think of.”

“Well, I have to say, Lizzie. You're handling this very well.” He scooted his chair and turned to face me. “Gray told me he'd hire security for you if you want it.”

“Gray? When did you talk to Gray?”

"He got some pictures, too. Didn't he tell you? They were of you and Janie at the Fourth of July Parade." I didn't want Stallard to think I didn't know, so I played it off like I was confused. "Anyway, he said he'd pay for protection. Do you want protection?"

I stopped pacing and put my hand on the counter for support. "No. I won't have Janie growing up that way. I won't be afraid. We're fine. Everything's fine. Thank you for following up with the police and coming over here today."

"No problem. If you get any more, call me immediately. I think you should consider Gray's offer. Even someone watching the house might not be a bad idea."

"Thanks. I'll think about it."

Catalina

Impatiently, I waited for my shit ass attorney to arrive. This place was a complete hell hole, but I've been careful to be a model prisoner. I did my job and then some. Against my typical personality, I had been a perfect angel, except for that one bitch I punched in the bathroom, but she deserved it.

Mr. Jacobs arrived wearing his usual white dress shirt. He removed his plaid jacket and smoothed his brown tie as he sat down.

"It's about damn time. I haven't heard from you in weeks. What happened in court?"

"Good day to you too, Catalina."

"Don't be a smart ass. I'm paying you an obscene amount of money to win."

He put his briefcase on the table and pulled out a folder. Flipping through the pages, he grabbed a document and handed it to me. "Here's a copy of your divorce papers. You're a free woman." I glared at him. "Sorry, poor choice of words."

"I don't give a shit about the divorce. Am I going to get my daughter or not?"

"The judge wants to review the information before she decides."

"Did Gray tell the court that I should be Sophie's mother?"

"Not exactly." His eyes darted around the room. "He spoke highly of Miss Levine and encouraged the judge to consider her parental rights as Sophie's biological mother."

I slammed my hand on the table, causing the guard to approach. Mr. Jacobs assured him everything was okay and waved him away. "He'll pay." With my teeth gritted, I said, "I'll make him pay handsomely for that."

Sweat beaded on Mr. Jacobs's forehead and he picked at the bottom of his tie. This was not a good sign. "You're fucking useless." I rolled my eyes.

"I have some good news."

"Oh goody, you mean you did something, right?" *God, he's such a pissant, an incompetent shit.* I've practically made his case for him, and he can't even follow the breadcrumbs and get the job done.

"Your parole hearing is scheduled for the end of the month. Assuming you don't do anything stupid between now and then, I believe you'll be released with community service."

"Well, it's about damn time." I sarcastically clasped my hands together.

"You won't be permitted near Elizabeth Levine. If you violate that order, they'll put you right back in your cell for a very long time."

I flicked my hand at his nonsense. "What do you think my chances of getting Sophie are?"

"Not good."

"Do I need to take matters into my own hands, Stew?" He wiped the sweat from his brow. His beady little eyes looked down at his briefcase.

"I'll see what I can dig up."

"Look, Stew. Gray is a narcissistic bastard with no business raising a child, and Lizzie is an awful mother. Dig deeper, you'll find something," I snapped.

He closed his briefcase and stood. He threw his jacket over his shoulder and said, "I'll keep you posted."

Useless.

TWENTY THREE
Lizzie

I made it a ritual to get up early and visit Len a few mornings each week. NorthStar Assisted Living made it easy for me. Len had me added to the family list, and I was given a pass that granted me access to the front door. I could swipe my badge at the counter in the lobby. When the screen lit up green, I could go straight back to his room. If the screen lit red, that meant he was receiving medicine or treatment, and I had to wait for someone to tell me when it was okay to visit.

The place had one doctor and several nurses on staff. Len was required to do physical therapy every day, which he loathed. The hallways smelled of Vics Vapor Rub and vanilla. I pushed Janie in the stroller down the hallway and stopped at Len's door.

"Good morning, Papa." Len was sitting in his chair by the window. I couldn't see what he was reading, but he slowly placed his bookmark on the page, closed the book, and looked up toward the door.

"My two favorite girls." His eyes were tired but wide with excitement at the sight of us. His breathing was shallow and quick.

"I brought you some Burney's," I said, holding up the box of croissants.

He laughed. "Stella, might kick you out if she sees those."

His room was decorated with photos of him and his wife. There was a photo of Josh on a swing as a little boy. A more recent photo of Josh and Janie and several photos of just Janie. He had stacks of books on his bookshelf, and across the foot of the bed was his favorite blanket from home.

I pulled out a bag from under the stroller and held it up. "I brought you something. I thought you'd like a new pair of cozy slippers."

He smiled. "Thank you. Let's walk in the garden."

He enjoyed our walks when I pushed him around the grounds. The facility had a beautiful walking path for the residents.

"Okay, Len. I'll let Stella know."

After my first visit here, I figured out how to MacGyver the stroller and wheelchair handles together so I could push both Janie and Len at the same time. Len liked for Janie to sit in his lap while we walked, but I didn't think that was a good idea.

The air was hot, but the humidity was bearable. The sky was a radiant clear blue, and it was a beautiful day. The trail weaved around the garden and was lined with azalea bushes. As we walked,

I wondered if Len would still be here in April when they were in full bloom. Gigantic oak trees provided much-needed shade throughout the walk. Under each tree was a wooden bench dedicated to a local or deceased resident.

"How are you, Lizzie?"

"I'm doing okay." I did my best to sound genuine.

"Has Josh come home yet?"

"No. I'm not sure he's going to. It's been a month." I paused to watch two cardinals flitting about a bird bath nestled in the garden.

"He'll be home. Have faith."

"What am I supposed to do? He's shutting me out. I know we've both been through a lot, but I need him to come home." The cardinals flew away.

Len looked up at me over his shoulder and reached for my hand. "He loves you. He's in pain right now. He'll come around. Give him a little more time." His breathing had become more labored.

I looked into his tired eyes. I wanted to believe him. "He hurt me. I'm not sure I can forgive him. I'm going through a lot, too, and he left me."

"He's a fool." He shook his head and laughed. "He's still pissed that I made him put me here. He's pissed that I'm going to die. And if I'm being honest, he's trying to figure out how to be okay with Gray being part of your life. Janie's life, too."

I inhaled and exhaled slowly. "I know." I dropped my head and kicked a pebble off the pathway. "I haven't made things any easier for him. But he still broke my heart when he left. I'm in this limbo, waiting and wondering if he's ever going to come home. And Janie. She loves him. She knows he isn't around as much. I have my daughter to think about now. He needs to come back."

Sweat started to bead on his forehead. "He'll come around. He's stubborn." Len started to cough violently; blood droplets fell into his hand. Fear consumed his eyes as he pushed the button around his neck. I held his hand and wiped his mouth with a clean tissue. "Oh, Len. You need to rest."

A nurse appeared outside a few minutes later, and she wheeled him away. Janie and I waited in the lobby to make sure Len was okay. She entertained everyone who walked by. Smiling and flashing her dimples, she sang and danced with a big smile on her face. They laughed and then she'd giggle, causing the sprout on top of her head to bobble.

"He's in his room lying down, but you can visit with him briefly if you'd like," Stella said. I pushed Janie back into Len's room. The oxygen mask swallowed half his face, but his eyes smiled when we entered the room. He pulled the mask down around his chin.

He reached for my hand and said, "There's nothing that you don't have the strength to rise above. I admire your courage and tenacity. Josh's acting like a fool, but you love him, and he loves you. Don't give up on him just yet." He squeezed my hand. A tear trickled down my cheek from the corner of my eye. He was right. "He'll return to you. Your love will be stronger on the flip side of adversity."

I retrieved the book he had resting on the nightstand, sat in the chair next to the bed, and read him a chapter. When I finished, he was snoring peacefully. I kissed him on the top of the head and left.

I worked with Helen less and less, but I loved the time I could spend at Bayview Books. When I left my New York City life behind and took the job with Helen, I had no idea the haven the store would become. Helen was the friend I didn't know I needed.

The bookstore was hopping today. People were stocking up since summer was starting to wind down. Early August brought excitement for fall, and everyone was ready for cooler weather, pumpkin spice, and reading books. Mrs. Demur bought ten books and hung out on the couch most of the day, reading. A group of older gentlemen played chess for a few hours. It was the most raucous game of chess I'd ever seen. Generally, chess was a quiet game, perfect for a bookstore, but not for these clowns. They whooped and hollered, and we cracked up at their antics. Even the pirate manuscripts were viewed several times today.

Drew worked at the counter and skipped lunch because the checkout line never ended. I was happy to see the bookstore full of life. Word had spread about the magic in this store, and everyone in town desired to experience the action. Our next event was towards the end of the month, an adult-only trivia night with a BYOB.

I came in today to help with the crowds, but Helen said the store had been so busy the past few weeks that she also needed help with inventory and freshening up. Good old Helen, constantly cleaning and moving things around. She closed the store at 5:00 PM, and I stayed to assist. Renee offered to help out, too, and was picking up pizza on her way.

"Whew, what a day," Drew said as he flopped onto the couch, opened a water bottle, and chugged. "I'm not sure the store's been this busy since I started."

Helen scooted up next to him on the couch and laid her head on his shoulder. "It was a great day."

"Yoohooo. Did someone order a pizza?" Renee's voice bellowed through the metal slot on the giant wooden door.

"I'll get it." I hurried to the door and pulled it open.

"Oh, my goodness. Look at your baby bump. It's finally popped out a bit," I exclaimed. I took the pizza boxes in one hand and rubbed her belly with the other. "There's a little baby in there."

Randy walked through the door behind Renee. "I didn't know you were coming?"

"I can't stay, but Ren and I have some news to share." He closed the door and took the pizza from me. As we rounded the corner, we caught Helen giving Drew a little smooch.

"Get a room," I shouted.

Helen squished her nose up and puckered her lips. "Yeah. Yeah."

Randy set the pizza on the table by the couch. "Lizzie, open the top box first."

As I opened the lid, the inside of the box was painted pink and in capital white letters it read: IT'S A GIRL!

I squealed like a schoolgirl. Randy and I embraced and jumped up and down. Helen hugged Renee and then me. I hugged Renee while Randy hugged Helen. Drew hugged Renee, then me, then Helen. There were lots of hugs, cheers, and excitement, but most of all, love.

"And look at her little baby belly. It's so cute." I leaned down and spoke directly into Renee's stomach. "Hello, little girl. I'm your Auntie Lizzie. I'm going to be your favorite Auntie."

"You're her only Aunt." Randy patted me on the back.

"Oh, our girls can grow up together. It's going to be so much fun," I said, as I gave Randy another hug.

"I hate to celebrate and run, but I'm the babysitter tonight."

"Oh, that's right. Gray picked Janie up from daycare, and Randy's picking her up from Gray's," Helen said. "How's that going? Having Gray be an active father."

"It's going well. He's a good dad. I haven't let her stay the night with him yet. We're working up to that."

"How's Josh handling it?" Helen said.

"And that's my cue to leave," Randy said as he waved and walked toward the front door. I followed him, gave him another hug, and locked the door behind him.

"Did I step in shit?" Helen said when I returned.

"Josh's been living on his boat. Between Gray, the custody battle, and Len, he needed time to get his head on straight. His words, not mine. He claims he's doing this for us. I haven't seen you to tell you."

"So what? He left? I don't understand. This is Josh we're talking about, right?"

Renee and Drew sat quietly, eating their pizza, watching Helen and I go back and forth as I filled her in on the events of the last few weeks.

"You're not wearing your ring," Helen said.

I raised my eyebrows and exhaled. "Yeah, it's been a crazy time."

"This is so unlike Josh," Helen said, with her hands on her hips.

"He comes by to see Janie, but I go upstairs. It hurts too much to be around him while he's…" I put my hands up, bent my fingers, and made air quotes, "getting his head on straight."

"I don't have any words," Helen said.

Renee piped up. "I had plenty, but I think it was mostly hormones talking."

"Len thinks that Josh's angry because he refused to let Josh take care of him. He knows he's dying and needs round-the-clock care. He said that Josh's pushing me away on purpose. He's afraid he'll lose me, too. The funny part is, if he keeps this up, he will."

Helen patted Drew's knee. "You're a man. What do you think?"

Shaking his hands in the air, he said, "Oh, nooo. I know better. I'm not getting in the middle of this."

I looked over at Drew and said, "You're the perfect person to get in the middle. You're a guy. What do you think?" We egged him on a little longer, and finally, he relented.

"Josh doesn't seem like he's the type of man to play games. He's genuine. If that's true, then it's simple. He really does need time to get his head on straight."

In unison, we all called bullshit and heckled Drew for his answer. "I'm just saying. Sometimes a guy needs a minute."

Changing the subject, I said, "We have work to do. Sargent Helen expects this place in tip-top shape by 10:00 PM."

TWENTY FOUR

Lizzie

"What do you mean, she isn't here?" I bit the inside of my lip to remain calm. The pale yellow walls of Apple A Day's tiny lobby were closing in on me. My heart raced.

"Janie wasn't here today," the teacher repeated. Cortisol shot through my veins as the fight-or-flight response set in.

Raising my voice, I said, "She most certainly was here. I dropped her off this morning." I pointed to the electronic check-in kiosk. "The other girl said this was broken, and she'd sign Janie in when it got working again. She wrote her name on a note or paper or something."

Concern flashed across the young girl's face. With a quiver in her tone, she said, "Let me get Mrs. Rappapure."

"Please do." I began to pace in a circle. Inside, I was freaking out like a swan flapping its little feet ferociously under the water. *This can't be happening. This cannot be happening.*

Mrs. Rappapure was the owner. According to her resume, she received her degree in early childhood education back in the early nineties. She worked for years in the classroom until she opened Apple A Day ten years ago. It was supposed to be one of the most renowned daycares in town.

The young girl returned a few minutes later, with Mrs. Rappapure following a few steps behind. Both women were wearing matching red t-shirts that said Apple A Day in white letters. The "A" in Day was an apple with a bite taken out.

"Hello, Miss Levine, I'm Delvi Rappapure, the owner. Ms. Kate tells me we have a situation with Janie."

"A situation? I'd say we have a situation. I dropped Janie off this morning, and she isn't here."

"We don't have any record of Janie being here today. Are you sure she came this morning? Janie isn't usually here on Mondays."

Politeness went out the window. "For God's sake. I brought her here this morning. Like I told Kate, when I dropped her off, your thingy wasn't working. The other girl wrote down Janie's name and said she'd check her in. I kissed Janie goodbye, and she walked her to the classroom."

"I understand Miss Levine. We don't lose children. There has to be a perfectly good explanation." She clicked a button on the intercom and asked Janie's teacher to come to the lobby.

Miss Jessica appeared a few moments later and said she didn't see Janie today. My throat was closing, and I couldn't catch my breath.

Sucking in huge gulps of air, I clawed at my chest and fell against the wall.

Delvi said, "Kate, get her some water."

I pulled my phone from my pants pocket, and I dialed the Southport police station. I asked for Detective Wilson. A few seconds later, I was connected to his voicemail. In between breaths, I left him a message. "Detective Wilson, it's Lizzie Levine. It's an emergency. Call. Help."

"You need to calm down. Take some slow deep breaths," Delvi said in a calming voice.

"Calm down. You want me to calm down," I raged at the top of my lungs. "My child is fucking missing."

"Miss Levine, this is a difficult situation, but there are children here. Please monitor your language." *Monitor my language. Is she for real?* I should have throat punched her.

"My child is missing," I screamed again at the top of my lungs. "Search every classroom. I want you to search the entire building right now. I'm going to scream obscenities from the top of my lungs until you search every single cranny of this building."

"Yes, Miss Levine. Please sit here. Try to calm down. We'll search the building straight away." She instructed Kate to put the daycare in a soft lockdown. I started screaming Janie's name. "Janie! Janie bug! Are you playing hide-and-seek? Janie! You're scaring mommy. Come on out, Janie."

Kate insisted to Delvi that Janie was not at school today. I should have throat punched her, too. I dialed 911. Delvi replied, "I know, but we need to do a thorough search anyway."

These people cannot be for real. Do they think I'm lying? I freaking brought her here this morning. I left her with the other chick. *The other chick?*

"Delvi, who's the other girl that works the check-in station?" I said, trying to keep my tone calm.

"What other girl?"

"I don't know. There was another girl here this morning. She's the one that said she'd sign Janie in." I pointed frantically at the front desk as if I could make the girl materialize in front of us.

"She was filling in for Kate this morning. She only works occasionally when we are short-staffed or need a substitute," Delvi said.

"Call her. Call her right now. She saw Janie. She knows that Janie was here."

I opened a new text. I sent the first one to Gray.

Me: Janie's missing.

Me: She was taken from school.

Me: I'm freaking out.

I sent the next to Randy and Renee together.

Me: Janie was taken from daycare.

I hit copy and paste and sent the same message to Helen.

Gray: This is a joke, right?

Me: Not a joke.

My chest tightened again. *This is a bad dream. This has to be a bad dream.*

Gray: Where are you?

Me: Daycare.

My phone started to ring. It was Randy. I didn't answer.

Gray: I'm on my way. Does your family know?

Me: Yes.

Randy called again. I answered this time, sobbing into the phone.

"She's gone." More tears. "They think I'm crazy." More tears. "They say she wasn't here. She's gone." Uncontrollable tears spilled from my eyes.

"Lizzie. Slow down. I can't understand you."

"Wilson. Go get Wilson."

"I'm on it." He hung up.

The New Hanover police arrived ten minutes later and took my statement. Gray arrived shortly after. I never expected to appreciate a hug from Gray Stone again, but I clung to him like a dryer sheet stuck to a pair of stockings, and sobbed into his chest. Terrified that I'd only found my daughter to lose her once again. His arms felt safe and strong.

"Everyone's calling and texting, wanting to know what's going on. Can you please deal with that? I can't talk to anyone right now."

He wiped the hair off my face and kissed the top of my head. "Yes. Have you spoken to Josh?"

"No. He doesn't know."

"Okay. I'll take care of it."

Holding his phone to his ear, he walked outside.

I felt numb. The room was a blur. Fuzzy images of the daycare staff and police talking and walking around the facility came in and out of focus. Flashing lights flooded into the room from outside. A police officer sat beside me and offered me water. I stared blankly at him.

"Miss Levine, we've issued an Amber Alert for your daughter. We have a description from Janie's teacher, but I'd like to review it with you. Do you think you can manage to do that?"

I nodded.

Fear had paralyzed me. My heart thumped inside my chest like a mallet as it slammed into my rib cage over and over. The thumping grew louder and louder, muting the officer's voice. The daycare walls closed in again. I could feel my eyes rolling in the back of my head and my body fell backwards. Gray came out of nowhere and caught me in his arms.

"Lizzie! It's okay. You're going to be okay. Breathe."

My eyes re-focused on his lips as they moved. I blinked and leaned into him.

"Are you Mr. Levine?" The officer said.

"No. But, I'm Janie's father."

"As I was explaining to Miss Levine. We issued an Amber Alert. We got a description of Janie from her teacher. Miss Levine was about to review it. The more accurate, the better."

"Okay. We can do that."

"She's approximately two years old, light skin, light brown hair. Is that correct?"

"That's correct."

"Can you describe what she was wearing today?"

Gray looked at me. "Lizzie, do you remember what she was wearing today?"

I closed my eyes and played back the memory of the morning in my head. It was a beautiful morning. Since Josh left, I started the habit of rocking Janie on the bedroom balcony and reading to her. The memory slowed my heart rate and filled me with temporary joy. She giggled and laughed at the birds as they flew by, and I sipped my coffee. I took her to her room to get dressed. I slathered baby lotion on her arms and legs and we celebrated her wearing big girl bottoms now. I pulled a clean pair of pink shorts with a small ruffle out of her drawer and chose a white shirt with small pink flowers scattered on the front and back. I tied her hair in a ponytail on top of her head and clipped on a small white bow. I loved my little girl more than life itself. I'd already lost so much time with her. Feelings of despair flooded my heart. I started to lose control again.

Gray took hold of my hand. "It's okay, Lizzie. It's going to be okay. We'll find her. Can you tell the officer what she was wearing today?"

Allowing Gray's voice to ground me, I opened my eyes and described her outfit to the officer.

"Typically, when a child goes missing, especially in a split house-hold, we start with the non-custodial parent as our first suspect or a close relative. I think we can rule both of you out. Is there another parent or family member that would want to kidnap Janie?"

Kidnap. My child's been kidnapped. Hearing that word was too much. I laid my head on Gray's shoulder and stared at the pale yel-low wall behind the front desk. My eyes studied the bulletin board that hung on the wall boasting this month's birthday wishes.

"No one in our family would take Janie," I said in a flat tone.

"Do either of you have a significant other that would want to take Janie?"

"I don't," Gray said. "Lizzie's fiancé's name is Josh Miller. He's already been contacted, but he wouldn't have taken her."

"We would like to question all the family members, including Josh. Can you provide me a list of names and contact informa-tion?"

Gray nodded.

"Is there anyone else that would want to kidnap your daughter?"

I sat up, shoulders hunched, and plain faced. "Crazy Catalina."

The officer looked at me, confused.

"Catalina Stone. She's my ex-wife," Gray said. "But she's in jail."

"This has all been very helpful. One last thing. Do you have a few recent pictures of Janie we could use?"

"Yes. I can send you some," I said.

He handed me his business card and said, "You can email them to the address on the card. The sooner the better."

I began scrolling through my phone, looking for the best pictures of Janie. *The best pictures. Seriously?* What's the right picture to use for your child's Amber Alert?

"We'll call you if we need anything else." The officer tucked his notepad in his chest pocket and walked to Delvi's office.

"Everyone's coming to the GSM South offices. Renee and Helen are working on posters we can put around town. Do you want to go to the office and help, or would you prefer to go home?" Gray wrapped his arms around me and held me for a few minutes. What I wanted was my daughter.

Puffy eyed, red nosed, and broken, I walked into the office. Randy, Renee, Helen, and Drew were making piles of fliers as they came off the printer. A somber quiet of fear was thick in the air.

A beautiful picture of Janie was front and center on the bright yellow-colored paper. MISSING was printed at the top of the flier in bold, black letters. Underneath her picture it read: *If you've seen this child or know her whereabouts, please contact the New Hanover Police Department.* The number was listed below the sentence.

I was still clinging to Gray's arm, unsure if my legs would hold me up, when Josh came out of the bathroom. The sight of him sent my emotions into overdrive. I craved his love and strength right now. But I didn't know where we stood. I wasn't sure how to react. I froze, squeezed Gray's arm tighter, and held my breath.

Josh's eyes filled with tears the instant ours connected. Gray gently pulled his arm away from me and gave me a subtle nudge toward Josh. Josh stepped forward and pulled me into his arms.

His comforting strength enveloped me, and I melted into a puddle of goo. He kissed my head and face over and over in between his words.

"I'm sorry." Kiss. "I'm sorry for everything. This is awful." Kiss...kiss. "I'm sorry, Lizzie. I can't believe this is happening." He leaned away from me. "Let me look at you. Are you okay?" He pulled me back into his chest and held me until my legs were strong enough to hold me upright. He kissed me again and again, then whispered into my ear, "I'm here. I'll never leave your side again. We'll get her back."

Josh had shattered my heart when he left. The time without him had been agony, but despite the hurt, he was the anchor I needed to get through this. His embrace didn't erase the betrayal, but in Janie's absence, it was his familiar arms that steadied me. As I looked up into his eyes, a torrent of fear was met with the silent vow reflected in his gaze. "I can't lose her again," I breathed, barely a whisper.

He tightened his hold, and in that moment, he was more than the man who had run—he was my lifeline. "We're all here for you. For Janie. None of us are going to lose her," he assured me with a firmness that I desperately needed to believe in.

Randy said, "The axe team is on their way to help."

"My teacher friends are coming, too," Renee said.

Helen said, "My entire block will be here any minute, and Mr. Stallard and his employees."

Josh smiled and said, "The construction crew is rounding up friends and they'll be here too."

Josh looked at Gray and nodded. "It was Gray's idea. He suggested we use the office to make the fliers and call as many people as we could from our small town to help. He called me to fill me in and everyone snapped into action."

Helen put her arms around Drew's waist. "The whole town loves that little girl, Lizzie. We'll find her."

Pride swelled from the tip of my toes to the top of my head. I can't believe everyone was pitching in to help find Janie. For the first time all day, my fear was replaced with hope that she'd be in my arms soon.

"Deputy Wilson and some other Southport officers and fire-fighters are coming out to help, too," Gray said.

About thirty minutes later, at least one hundred people gathered at GSM South. Gray took charge and called everyone to order. "Helen's passing out stacks of fliers. Organize yourselves in groups of ten. An officer or firefighter will participate in each group and guide you through the route."

Deputy Wilson stood next to Gray and said, "We'll start at Apple A Day Daycare and fan out from there. I want a flier on every telephone pole, in every storefront window, and checkout counter. If you see the kidnapper with Janie, do not approach. I repeat, do not approach. Call 911."

Gray shook Deputy Wilson's hand and turned back to the room. "On behalf of myself, Lizzie, Josh, and the rest of Janie's family, we thank you for your support."

The crowd dispersed.

TWENTY FIVE
Lizzie

The minutes ticked past into hours. By midnight, bright yellow fliers papered every building, telephone pole, and window from Wilmington to Southport. I could not believe the amount of support we received, but sadly, my hope had dwindled.

Josh, Gray, and the rest of the family sat around my kitchen table as we waited for any news at all. The New Hanover police had called Gray a few times to let them know they had a few leads, but so far, nothing had panned out. They opened a tip line, and the calls poured in, but most amounted to nothing.

At one o'clock in the morning, Helen and Drew said their goodbyes and insisted I call them the second we heard anything. At two o'clock in the morning, Randy and Renee decided to stay the night.

Josh fixed up the spare bedroom upstairs with clean sheets. "The room's all set."

Renee rubbed her belly. "Thanks, Josh. I need to lie down. It's been a long, stressful day, and I'm not feeling great."

I hugged Renee. "You need to take care of that baby. Go lie down." I handed Randy some peanut butter crackers and two bottles of water. "We'll wake you up if we hear anything."

Josh paced the kitchen while Gray checked his phone every three seconds. I sat at the table, slumped over, with my head resting on my arms. There wasn't anything we could do at this hour, but sleep seemed a luxury for parents who were desperate for their child to come home.

I must have eventually fallen asleep because I jumped out of the chair and onto my feet in a flash at the sound of Gray's phone ringing. Slobber dripped down my cheek, and crust had formed in my swollen eyes. Josh was by my side in two giant steps as Gray frantically hit the green button on his phone to connect the call. It was now five-thirty in the morning.

He put the phone on speaker and laid it on the table. "Gray Stone," he announced.

"Hello, Mr. Stone. We have excellent news."

My hands flew to my mouth as I sucked in and held my breath. *This should be good, right? He said excellent.*

"We believe Janie was returned to the police station this morning. We need you and Miss Levine to come down to the station and confirm."

Josh and Gray were holding their breath, too. Gray exhaled, took the phone off speaker, and walked into the living room. He tried to speak quietly, but I heard him. "You said excellent news. Is it safe to assume she's unharmed?"

Gray made a shrieking sound that I'd never heard before. Josh and I hurried to the room and found him doubled over, sobbing like a baby. "What? What's happened? What happened to our baby girl?" I wasn't sure I wanted the answer, but I needed the answer.

Gray stood. A grin the size of Texas appeared on his face. "She's fine. They said she's happy as a clam entertaining the entire police department. They even commented on her dimples."

Josh immediately wrapped me in his arms and pressed his lips to mine. He pecked my face several more times, and we cried tears of joy. Josh and Gray did a handshake and pulled each other into a bro-hug, and finally, Gray and I embraced. "Thank you. I couldn't have survived yesterday without you. Thank you for calling Josh. I needed you both."

"Let's go get our girl." Gray pumped his fist in the air. We raced toward the door.

"Wait, I need to tell Randy and Renee."

Josh turned me back around and pushed me out the front door. "Go. I'll tell them. You call me the minute you confirm it's Janie, and then I'll tell everyone."

"It's Janie. I can feel it." I threw my arms around his neck and kissed him.

Later that night, half the town showed up to congratulate us. Janie was the center of attention, and she loved every minute. The police said that she was buckled into a stroller, sitting outside the front door of the precinct. They reviewed the security cameras but couldn't make out the person who dropped her off. She didn't have a scratch on her. The only thing that appeared out of place was her missing white hair bow. The doctor checked her out this morning and gave us a clean bill of health with no signs of trauma or maltreatment. Of course, I wanted answers, but for now, I didn't care. My Janie bug was home, and that was all that mattered.

I told her to wave goodbye to her guests as I headed upstairs to put her to bed. As I went through our normal bedtime rituals, I asked Janie questions like she could answer me.

"Who would want to take you?"

"Why would they take you only to drop you off at the police station?"

"Oh, Janie bug, I wish you could tell us what happened. At least you won't remember this day."

I rocked her a little longer than normal, then stared at her for what seemed like an eternity when I laid her in her crib. I didn't want her out of my sight. I considered putting her to sleep in the pack-and-play downstairs while I helped Josh clean up the kitchen. *Ugg, Josh.* I was glad he was home, but we had so much to discuss. I had to "will" myself to leave Janie's room. *Relax Lizzie. She's home safe and sound.*

I made it to the door and turned back around. Peeking into the crib, I smiled. Janie was sound asleep. She looked peaceful and content, completely unfazed by the last twenty-four hours. *See, she's fine. Go talk to your fiancé.*

Part of me needed to deal with one thing at a time. We just got Janie back. Can we take the win for today and deal with our messy relationship tomorrow? The other part of me needed to rip the band-aid off. Whatever is going to be, will be. I had my daughter back. Not much could ruin this day.

As I walked down the steps and turned the corner, Josh was washing dishes at the sink, and Gray was drying them. I wanted to be angry and resentful towards Josh for the last several weeks, but I couldn't bring myself to find the anger. "Well, isn't this a sight?" I said. "A few weeks ago, you two were duking it out in the parking lot of Fisherman's Café, and now you're bro-hugging and doing dishes together."

Josh flicked his soapy hand at me and said, "Don't get it twisted. He's still an ass, but Janie has a way of bringing people together."

"She sure does," Gray said. "Well, gang. I guess this is my cue to leave." Gray flashed finger guns at both of us, winked at me with a secret thumbs up, and showed himself out.

I picked up the dish towel and started to dry the dishes.

The air between us was heavy with so many things we needed to say.

Josh turned off the water and reached for a towel to dry his hands. His movements were jerky, betraying his inner turmoil.

"I'm sorry, Lizzie." His voice emerged raw and strained, as if each word scraped against his throat. The usual spark in his eyes was now dampened, revealing layers of guilt and remorse that shimmered in the dim light. "I was a complete fool, full of jealousy and grief. I couldn't see things clearly. I convinced myself it was only a matter of time before you went back to Gray." The words seemed to cost him, each one a brick in the wall he'd built around himself, now crumbling down.

"Josh, I..." My voice trailed off as he silenced me with a gesture, a finger pressed gently to my lips—a touch that once would have sparked a different kind of silence between us.

"When my dad got sick, the grief hit me like a freight train, and I spiraled out of control." His voice cracked. "It's been me and him for so long. I felt like my life was off the rails. As long as Gray was Janie's father, he would be part of your life." He reached for my hand, and I pulled away. The space between us was a chasm of hurt and misunderstanding.

"I figured pushing you away now would protect me from the inevitable later. When you spent the night at his house, and I got the news my dad was going to die, I fell apart." His gaze dropped to the counter, where his fingers began an anxious dance with the ladle.

"When Gray told me that Janie was missing, my stomach twisted into knots. The pain of losing our little girl was paralyzing, and I realized how you've been feeling this entire time." The raw edge in his voice scraped at the walls I had built around my heart. "I've been horrible to you. You needed me, and I ran away. I know I hurt you, and I'll spend the rest of my life trying to make it up to you if you'll still be my wife."

He pulled my ring out of his pocket and dropped to one knee. "Lizzie, if you can find it in your heart to forgive me, I promise I will stand by your side no matter what. Will you marry me?"

A whirlwind of emotions tugged at me. I yearned to leap into his arms, to seal his plea with a fervent yes, yet a part of me demanded he understand the depth of his betrayal. "Maybe."

His head jolted back in shock. "Maybe?" A flicker of panic flashed through his eyes.

"Yeah, maybe." He stood up and put his hands on the counter, trapping me between his arms. His presence radiated around me like a force field. He was almost impossible to resist. *Almost.*

"Do you believe that I didn't sleep with Gray?"

"Yes. I know you didn't sleep with Gray." His certainty rang clear.

"Do you believe me when I tell you I love you? He's Janie's father and part of our life, but I don't want to be with him. Do you finally believe that? Like, for real? Fully believe it and aren't just saying so?"

"I believe you. Yes. I see clearly now." He scooted a little closer. I could feel his breath on my skin. My defenses started to slip. *God, it's been so long.* My skin tingled with desire.

"Do you understand that we're supposed to share and work out our burdens together? That's the point of being husband and wife." I put my hand on his chest to ensure a little distance. My resolve was weakening, but I continued to resist a little longer.

"Yes. I understand. It's easy for me to be strong and help you with your problems. It's my problems I struggle with, but I recognize that now and I promise that I'll do better. It's you and me, babe." He tilted his head, and his sorrowful eyes connected perfectly with mine.

His stomach pressed against me, and his chest grazed my nipple. Chills shot down my spine, and my skin was set ablaze with longing for him. *Stay strong, Lizzie. Just a few more minutes. Stay strong.*

"And you promise never to leave me again, no matter how bad the fight? No matter how angry you are, no matter what the situation? We stick together?"

"I promise." He brushed his lips along the nape of my neck, sending electrical pulses through my body.

"You hurt me." My voice shook. "You can't ever do that again. I won't stand for it." I slapped his chest as I said each word.

"I'll spend forever making that up to you." He reached his hands under my shirt and ran them up my back. "I was afraid I was going to lose you. I screwed up."

I wasn't sure I could resist much longer. I pushed him off me, raised an eyebrow and said, "Ask me again."

"Ask you again?"

"Ask me to marry you again."

He got down on one knee for the second time tonight, held the ring in his fingertips, and said, "Lizzie Levine, you are the most incredible woman I've ever known. You make me want to be a better man every day. I want to love you until the day I die. Would you give me the pleasure of being my wife? My partner in crime in this thing we call life."

I held out my left hand. "Yes!"

He slipped the ring on my finger, and I lunged toward him like a hungry animal. He smashed his lips to mine, and fire ignited inside my stomach. It had been six long weeks without his touch, and every inch of my body desired him. He picked me up and set me on the counter, stepped back, and pulled his shirt off. I ran my fingertips along his firm, glorious chest as I gazed directly into his warm, soulful eyes. Undoing his belt buckle, I brought my lips to his and used my feet to push down his pants. Kissing him like a ferocious lion devours a fresh meal.

He swiped the countertop, knocking the clean dishes and pots to the floor. A plate shattered as it hit the ground. He laid me onto my back, tugged, and pulled my pants off in one swipe. Placing gentle kisses up my legs, he bit the top of my underwear and used his mouth to slide them down my legs. I exhaled a moan. He took a moment to soak in the image of my naked body on the kitchen counter. "You're beautiful, Lizzie, in every way." He climbed on top of me like a cat. His body hovered above mine. He lowered his face down and placed a short, sweet kiss on my lips.

I gasped. "I want you right here, right now."

He nodded as my hands dug into his ass cheeks. He pulled away and hopped off the counter. "I have a lot to make up for. It starts today." He kissed my neck, then my collarbone, and then moved down to my breast. He teased my nipple, and I cried out. I ran my fingers through his hair and tried to pull him back on top of me. He slid me to the edge of the counter and kissed my thighs. I squeezed my fingers into his skin and left indents on his shoulder. He flicked his tongue back and forth between my legs. My back arched as I moaned. *I love this man.* He continued to pleasure me as I exhaled breath after breath. He lifted me, and I wrapped my legs around him as he eased inside me. He carried me a few steps toward the open pantry door. I wrapped my fingers around the top of the door and pressed down as he slid me up and down.

I cried out, "Don't stop."

His thrusts grew frantic as he whispered, "I love you," in my ear.

He carried me wrapped around him to our bedroom on the second floor and laid me on our bed, the bed we hadn't slept in together for six entire weeks. He walked to the porch and opened the door. Sounds of the water crashing into the sand and rocks flooded the room. He climbed into bed and pulled me on top of him. Caressing my back with his hands, he looked into my eyes. We made love again to the sound of the ocean waves and then fell asleep in each other's arms.

When the sun peeked over the horizon a few hours later, he rolled over onto me. His lips touched mine, and once again, desire shot through every cell in my body. My heart exploded. I could handle anything with Josh in my life. We made up for our lost time over and over until Janie woke up.

TWENTY SIX

Lizzie

Flipping through a magazine, I sat in the office of Stallard Law. Janie was in her stroller beside me. I had pulled her out of daycare, obviously. Mr. Stallard texted me this morning and asked if I could stop by. Josh insisted on coming with me. "Together," he said. "We do things together."

I told him I didn't think it was a big deal and that I'd fill him in when I got home. At this point, I'd been through a great deal of shit, and I didn't think much more could shake me. That was until today. I was so relieved that Janie was returned safely that I didn't consider how it could impact my custody.

Mr. Stallard escorted me to the small conference room. He cooed at Janie and patted her head. He sat at the table, crossed his legs, and wrapped his fingers around his knee. "Well, Lizzie. I'm afraid I don't have great news today."

I sat up a little straighter. My first thought was that the judge had made her ruling, but I waited for Stallard to continue.

"The hearing will be next Thursday, but in light of recent events, I'm afraid you may not like her decision. I was made aware that she received the photographs of your drunken escapades. If you're granted custody, you may be court-ordered to attend rehabilitation."

I ran my hand through my hair and looked at my sweet baby girl. "I'm not an alcoholic. But if that's what I have to do, I'll do it."

Stallard clicked his pen and said, "I know that, but the pictures don't look good. Add to that, Janie was kidnapped under your care."

His words stung like a bike of murder hornets. How much guilt can one mother hold? Every day was a battle to love myself. "Do the police have any leads on where these pictures are coming from? I don't like the feeling of being watched."

Stallard shook his head. "No, they don't have any leads." He uncrossed his legs and continued. "I know that's not what you want to hear, and I'm in no way suggesting you've done anything wrong. Please hear me when I say that, but Catalina's attorney has quite a bit of ammunition to paint you as an unfit mother between the photos and the kidnapping."

My throat went dry, and my tongue felt like sandpaper. *Haven't I been through enough?* I took a sip of water and said, "What do I do now?"

He leaned forward and paused. "Gather as many friends and family as you can who would be willing to speak on your behalf. We might need them. In the meantime, be the best mother you can be, and don't put yourself in any more compromising positions."

Frustrated and defeated, I left his office and walked home. As I pushed the stroller, I sang to Janie. Her legs bounced up and down as she mumbled along the words to the song. I loved this small town, but I couldn't stand the feeling of being watched every time I walked down the street alone. *I'll be damned if Catalina's going to affect my everyday life. What if it isn't her?* I pushed the thoughts out of my head. I refused to allow myself to be afraid. I stopped at the corner and pulled out my phone. I sent a text to Gray and Josh.

Me: Stallard's didn't go well. Are you both available to meet for lunch to discuss our daughter?

I was still getting used to the fact that we were one happy, dysfunctional family communicating together when it applied to Janie. I was glad that Josh and Gray didn't want to beat the shit out of each other anymore, but I had to admit I was still getting used to our new Partridge family normal.

Josh pulled in at the same time I did. "Is everything okay?"

"Sort of."

He helped me fold up the stroller and carried Janie into the house.

"She needs to eat, then lie down for her nap."

Josh put some dinosaur chicken nuggets in the microwave while I cut a block of cheese into small pieces.

Gray walked into the kitchen a few minutes later. "What happened?"

I placed the nuggets, cheese, and some grapes onto the red plastic plate. Josh poured some milk into a sippy cup and handed it to Janie.

I blew out a long breath of air. "Stallard implied that the collection of inappropriate photos, in addition to the kidnapping, may significantly impact my chances of getting custody. He said that Catalina's attorney will paint me as an unfit mother."

Josh immediately wrapped his arms around me and pulled me into him. "We won't let that happen. You're a great mother."

Gray went off. "That's ridiculous. She freaking stole our child. She's in jail. How in the actual fuck could she ever keep custody of Janie?"

Janie said, "Uck." She smiled, her dimples in full view. "Daddy."

"Ah, shit. I guess we're at the stage where we can't say those words around her." He slapped his hand on his forehead. "I did it again."

"Yes. She's starting to repeat everything she hears. Mostly, she doesn't make sense yet, but she's trying." I laughed.

"What did Stallard recommend?" Josh said.

I filled them in on the rest of the conversation with Stallard.

"We can ask our friends and family to stand up for us. I'll ask everyone we know. We'll have more people than a river has fish."

Gray tilted his head and raised an eyebrow. "I have a suggestion."

"By the look on your face, I'm not sure I want to hear it."

Gray blew me off and continued. "I bought a farm several years ago. I paid cash. There's no record of the transaction. I planned to retire there, but also thought it would be good in a pinch, in case I ever needed a place to lie low."

Josh and I looked at each other and then back at Gray. "Lay low?" I inquired. *What the hell kind of shit was Gray into that I didn't know about?*

Gray waved his hand and said, "Nothing bad. I mean, look. I'm an asshole, right? I've pissed a lot of people off over the years. A guy like me with as much money as I have might need a place to lay low." He shrugged. "But that's not the point. The point is, we could go there and take Janie. They'll never find us. No one even knows I own it. Except you two and my staff that lives on the ranch."

"Are you seriously suggesting that I run away with you and our daughter in front of my fiancé?"

"Yeah, bro. You can't be serious?" Josh said.

"You could go. I didn't mean I had to go, or we could all go."

I shook my head. "This is insane. We aren't discussing this anymore. I'll get custody legally."

"If there's one thing I know for sure, Catalina won't stop. Janie will never be safe," Gray said. I didn't want to hear it. We have a justice system for a reason. We have laws for a reason. I had to believe in that.

"I'll get to work on gathering friends and family to speak on your behalf," Josh said.

"I appreciate you trying to help. But those of us who aren't billionaires don't think quite like you. We don't have the same resources. I want to believe in the justice system."

"I'm saying the law doesn't work the way you think, Lizzie. We'll see how it plays out. I have the resources. You just have to ask."

Gray was freaking me out a little bit. I stared at the lines on his face and the white strands of hair mixed with his sandy blond locks and realized that maybe I didn't know everything there was to know about Gray Stone.

"I can see I'm making you nervous. You don't like when I flaunt my money." He wiggled his fingers in the air. "But I do have a lot of it. Janie's my daughter. There's nothing I wouldn't do to protect her and keep her safe. Away from Catalina is the safest place for her."

Josh and I stood speechless.

"All right, well...gotta go," Gray said nonchalantly. "Business calls. My second in command is busy today, so someone has to work." He winked at me.

I rolled my eyes and walked him to the door.

"What was that all about?" Josh said when I returned to the kitchen.

"I don't know. Let's just do what Stallard said." I bit my bottom lip.

"You're worried, aren't you?" Josh said.

"I think Gray had a point. Catalina will never stop. I don't want Janie's entire life being a battle with her father's batshit crazy ex-wife."

He hugged me. "Let's see what happens. I think you're doing the right thing."

TWENTY SEVEN

Gray

GSM South was booming. I needed to hire more help, but it wasn't easy to find the right people. I had the bright idea of contacting the local university to see if their marketing department needed any internships. I could start with a few college students and then scoop up the best ones to train into full-time positions once they graduated, but first, I had to create a system to train up good help. Experienced marketing personnel weren't coming out of the woodworks here in Wilmington.

I offered to do a few pro-bono marketing campaigns for the university to build a relationship and hopefully a pipeline of students I could train up.

"Andra," I called from my office.

"Yes. Mr. Stone," she said as she appeared in my doorway. Today she chose a sort of goth look with thick black boots, fishnet stockings, black skirt, and a silk navy blue blouse. A dark black line was smeared under her eyes.

"Meet me in the conference room in fifteen. Dig up every picture you can of campus life for UNCW and be ready to display them in the meeting. We need to develop a quick landing page that will entice students from around the country to move from their happy little towns to Wilmington, North Carolina, for school."

"Yes, sir. On it." She disappeared.

"And call Lizzie. Tell her to come straight to the conference room."

From a distance, she shouted, "Calling now, Mr. Stone!"

I walked into the conference room and hooked my computer to the television. I had some bullet points laid out, but I wanted Andra's inside college eye and Lizzie's brilliance for the layout.

Andra carried her open laptop as she searched for pictures and sat at the table. Lizzie flew in a few minutes later, pushing Janie's stroller with her briefcase and baby bag slung over her shoulder. She was adorable, even when she looked disheveled.

Janie's eyes lit up when she entered the room. She pointed to Andra and said, "Adda." Proud as peacocks, Lizzie and I looked at each other and smiled.

"Wow, she must remember you from before. She's getting good at repeating words and names."

Andra tensed a little. *Maybe she doesn't like kids.*

I pulled Janie out of the stroller and propped her on my hip while Lizzie got settled.

"All right, girls. Give me some quick bullet points on why any high schooler should want to come to the University of North Carolina, Wilmington."

Lizzie responded immediately. "The beach. We need to focus on the beach."

Andra agreed and added that we should include the university's top majors and capitalize on key areas where the school excelled. She also described some of the unique features and student activities we could highlight.

We had a great brainstorm session, and I put together a beautiful landing page with place holders for pictures. Lizzie and Andra made a shot list from the photos Andra found online. I insisted we take our own photos to drop into the landing page, and then the marketing piece would be set.

Pleased with our progress, I hugged Janie goodbye, told the girls I was off to pick up lunch, and stepped out into the parking lot, only to find Andra's silver Nissan Maxima had blocked me in. I went back inside the office and asked Andra for her keys so I could move her car. She barely looked up from her work and dangled the keys over the counter. With keys in hand, I started the ignition, put the car in reverse, and backed into another spot that was clear of my car.

As I pushed the shifter into park, my foot crunched something on the floorboard. I leaned over to get a better look, hoping I hadn't crushed something important.

Resting on the floor of Andra's car was a child's white hair bow.

No fucking way.

TWENTY EIGHT
Gray

Andra was in the conference room cleaning up when I went back inside. "Did you forget something, Mr. Stone?"

Stay calm. "Yes. We need to discuss a few more things." I stopped in the conference room doorway.

"I think we wrapped up nicely," Andra said with some pep in her step.

"I have something else on my mind. Where's Lizzie?" I remained in the doorway, intentionally blocking the exit.

"She went to lay Janie down in her office."

I leaned back and turned my head toward Lizzie's office. "Lizzie. Can you come back to the conference room, please?"

I could hear her groan. "Yeah. Be right there." She liked to go through her customary naptime ritual with Janie. I was disrupting that. *I wish I could tell her somehow.* I couldn't take the risk of Andra bolting out the door. Lizzie turned the corner, and I did my best to alert her with my eyes. I was widening my eyes and darting them from her to the conference room. She furrowed her brow and raised her hands in confusion.

As we walked in, I quietly closed the door behind us and turned the lock. I sat at the table and waited for the girls to take their seats. I placed my phone on the table, but before I walked into the room, I set it to record. None of this made any sense. There had to be a perfectly good explanation for this hair bow, and I was going to find out right now. Why would Andra kidnap Janie?

I pulled the bow from my pocket and threw it on the table. Lizzie instantly gasped. "That's Janie's bow. Where'd you get that?"

Knowing that we were still working on our trust issues, I could see her wheels starting to spin that I somehow had the bow. I didn't waste any time. "Andra blocked me in this morning."

"I'm sorry Mr. Stone. I was in a hurry and planned to move it after the meeting, but I forgot."

I waved my hand to let her know it was okay. "Turns out, everything happens for a reason. When I moved your car, I found this white bow on the floorboard." I could tell by the look on Lizzie's face that she wasn't quite following yet. Andra squirmed in her seat.

I continued. "I believe this is Janie's hair bow. Andra, do you know the last time she wore this bow?"

Andra laughed nervously. "How would I know that?"

Lizzie's eyes widened with understanding.

"Can you tell me why you have a toddler's white hair bow in your car? You wear some crazy things, but I've never seen you wear such a bow."

She shifted in her seat. "Are you accusing me of something?"

"I'm just asking questions. Where'd the bow come from?"

Lizzie's neck turned red, and I could feel the anger radiating from her skin like steam rolling off a hot tub.

"Where'd you get the bow, Andra?" I said more firmly.

Andra bit her bottom lip as she glanced up to the right as she searched for an answer. "I remember now. My baby cousin spent the weekend with me. It must be hers."

Lizzie snapped. "You're a liar. That's Janie's bow. I know it's Janie's bow because it has a yellow stain on the top corner."

I decided to play good cop in this scenario. "Lizzie. I know you're upset. Janie's kidnapping was terrifying, but we have no reason to believe Andra had anything to do with it. She said the bow belonged to her little cousin." Andra let out a breath and relaxed.

I didn't think Andra was a criminal, but I believed the bow was Janie's. The question was why and how?

"What's your baby cousin's name and her parent's name? I'd like to confirm with them. I'm sorry if this is uncomfortable, but surely you can understand. Once we confirm, you're in the clear. No harm. No foul."

Lizzie picked up what I was putting down. "Really? It's Janie's bow. This is ridiculous. I'm calling the police." She pulled her phone out of her pocket.

I reached over and touched Lizzie's arm. "Let's not be hasty."

Reaching for the bow, I turned back to Andra. "You don't mind giving me that information, do you?"

Andra stiffened. "I do mind. I don't have to prove anything to you."

Lizzie snapped. "Do you like working for GSM South?"

"Of course, I do."

"Then start talking. I know this is my daughter's bow. I'll beat it out of you if I have to."

Andra's lip quivered, and she burst into tears. Hysterical blubbering type of tears. "She made me do it."

Lizzie looked at me, and we froze. I grabbed a tissue from the box sitting on the center of the conference room table.

Between sobs, Andra said, "I'll tell you everything. I didn't want to do it."

Lizzie and I both sucked in air, anticipating what information she would share. I gave her a few moments to collect herself.

"Start from the beginning."

"Last year, I needed a roommate during my last semester. I was up to my eyeballs in debt and running out of money to finish college. My roommate at the time moved home and I couldn't afford to stay. I joined a few Facebook groups and found a post from a woman who recently moved to the area."

The red in Lizzie's neck now covered her entire face. I was afraid she might completely blow a gasket.

"She said her name was Kit, and she had an infant little girl. She offered to let me live rent free and agreed to pay me to be her live-in nanny. I thought it was a dream come true. Her only stipulation was that I couldn't ever have friends over. She also insisted I use a P.O. Box to get my mail." Andra blew her nose and pulled another tissue from the box. "I loved little Sophie. Kit was supposed to be my friend."

Oh, Kitty Cat, you crazy bitch. Catalina Stone had struck again. If it wasn't enough that she changed her name to Kit Moltisini and stole our baby from Lizzie's womb, she had now ruined Andra's life.

Lizzie opened her mouth to speak, but cleared her throat instead.

Andra continued. "When she got arrested, she threatened to kill me. I believed her. I still do. She told me I needed to continue to live in the apartment and visit her every two weeks in jail. She's the reason I applied for this job. I wanted the job for real, but she told me I had to work here to get close to you both. She made me follow you, take pictures, and deliver them to you. She's determined to get custody of Sophie." Andra began sobbing, and her shoulders bobbed up and down uncontrollably. "I'm terrified of her. She'll ruin me."

Lizzie was unable to control herself. "Her name is Janie. If you call her Sophie one more time, I'll jump across this table and punch you in your damn mouth."

Terrified, Andra leaned back in her chair as far as she could. Her eyes were as wide as silver dollars. The waterworks started again, and I waited for her to collect herself.

"On my last visit, Kit went on and on about how her attorney was useless and she wasn't going to win custody of Soph—I mean Janie. She said if I took Janie from the daycare and spent the day with her, she'd pay me one hundred thousand dollars and cut me loose. I could be free from her threats and move on with my life. I had a hacker friend from college fiddle with the daycare's electronic check-in system, and I sneaked her out. Janie remembered me, so it was relatively easy."

My heart began to race, and I could barely stay under control. But I needed the entire story. I took a deep breath.

Lizzie gasped. "You took my little girl. What's wrong with you? Like what in your actual mind makes you think that's okay? I don't understand. Janie's entire family was scared sick about her."

"I know. I'm so, so sorry. I wish I could take it all back. Kit's crazy. She threatened my family. I was supposed to take the money and leave town."

Lizzie was losing her temper, so I tried to regain control of the situation. "You picked her up from daycare, and then what? What did you do then?"

Andra sucked up the snot in her nose. "As I said, I loved Sophie. Sorry, Janie. I took care of her. We walked around the park. I fed her lunch. Laid her down for a nap. Then we went to the playground, got some ice cream, and hung out for a while. I waited until the middle of the night when security was low and dropped her off at the police station."

Sarcasm oozing from Lizzie's every word, she said, "Oh okay, that's perfectly fine, then. You loved and cared for her. I completely understand now."

Andra relaxed and let out a breath. "Oh wow. You're so gracious, Miss Levine. I'm so glad you understand. I'm truly terrified of Kit. You can understand that, right? I only did it because she threatened me. I'd be so grateful if I could keep my job."

I recorded the entire conversation and had everything I needed. I looked at Lizzie, who was white knuckled from clenching the handles of her chair. I nodded to let her know that she could have the floor. I sat back and marveled at her fierceness.

"Pardon my French, but are you fucking serious? No, no. You must be an idiot. Keep your job? Ha. You're fired. I'm calling the police and perhaps you can share a cell with your friend Kit—Catalina, whatever the hell she goes by these days. You kidnapped my daughter! Why do you people think you can do this and get away with it? Janie's my daughter! She's mine. She grew inside my belly." Lizzie pointed to her stomach for visual effect. "Right here. She grew right inside here. Your crazy ass roommate ripped her from my body and stole her. She fucking stole her. I'm sorry that you got tangled up in this mess, but you chose to do what she asked—stalking us and threatening us with those photos. You kidnapped my daughter. She's *my* daughter. Mine!"

She stood up and slammed her hands onto the table. "I'm so sick and tired of having to prove this point. I'm sick and tired of that crazy bitch thinking she can take her from me. I don't care what Catalina said or did. You had no right to take her. None." Lizzie turned and slammed her hand into the wall. "Ugg. I'm sorry for cursing so much, but damn."

I had already texted the detective working on this case and attached the audio recording I had made of Andra's confession.

By the time Lizzie finished her rant, the police were on site and putting Andra in handcuffs.

"Keep her job?" Lizzie mumbled under her breath. "She's as crazy as Catalina. Keep her job?" She huffed. "Tell crazy Catalina I said hello. She'll never have my daughter. Never!"

TWENTY NINE

Lizzie

I entered the courtroom with confidence. Josh managed to get fifty friends and family that would vouch for my ability as a mother. The courtroom was packed. Some even wrote me letters. I read through them last night, and they gave me all the reassurance I needed to push through the hearing today. My meeting with Mr. Stallard yesterday didn't hurt either.

Stallard came to my house, and Gray and I shared the audio recording of Andra's confession. Josh and the rest of the gang were there, too. I was grateful for the support of my family and friends. For more than a year, it had been one battle after another. I would not have survived without everyone's support. I believe moving to Southport was the best decision I'd ever made.

Mr. Stallard was confident the new information would ensure that I would win custody. He wanted to make me aware of the possibility that the judge would claim that neither Gray nor I were fit parents, but he assured us this scenario was highly improbable. Considering I didn't want to see Catalina ever again, I asked if he thought she'd get out on parole, given the new information.

He said, "It depends if they can prove her involvement. Andra will do some jail time, but Catalina will deny she had anything to do with the pictures and kidnapping and suggest that Andra acted on her own. Andra's attorney will have to prove that Catalina was involved for more time to be added to her sentence."

I hated his answer, but for now, I was focused on the custody hearing. Today could be the day I finally became Janie's legal mother. I didn't want to get too excited, but I couldn't help but feel jubilant.

As I took my seat next to Mr. Stallard at the little desk in the front of the courtroom, I inhaled a breath. I turned to the rows of benches behind me, where my family and friends sat eagerly awaiting the verdict. Sitting next to Drew, Helen gave me a thumbs-up with a massive smile on her face. Renee was tucked under Randy's arm with her hand on her belly, which was more noticeable. They both smiled and waved. Josh held Janie on his lap and mouthed, "I love you." He leaned down and kissed Janie's cheek and whispered something into her ear. Janie put her hand over her mouth and blew me a kiss. I caught it and pulled it to my heart and pretended to hug her from my seat.

Mr. Jacobs and Gray sat at the table across the aisle from me. I hated he had to sit over there with "her" attorney, but technically, Gray and Catalina were the legal guardians. Gray smiled and raised his eyebrows as if to say, *here we go*. He gave me a subtle thumbs-up and turned to stand and face the judge. The bailiff had announced her entry.

"This has been an interesting case, to say the least. I've reviewed all the facts, and I'm ready to make my decision. We consider many factors in child custody cases. It appears to me that Janie is a healthy, well-balanced little girl surrounded by a lot of love and family. I have scrutinized the mental and physical well-being of both parents. I'm aware of a few indiscretions, but I believe both Gray Stone, currently Sophie Stone's legal guardian, and Elizabeth Levine, whom I am decreeing to be the biological mother, are both mentally stable individuals. I believe that Elizabeth Levine has the capacity to raise her daughter in a loving home and see no reason why she should not be granted legal custody."

My knees buckled, and I gasped as I collapsed into my chair. Renee squealed, and Randy let out a whooping sound. Cheers erupted in the courtroom. The judge banged her gavel.

"Order in the court. Order." The judge banged her gavel again. "Miss Levine, I want to say on behalf of this court that you've been through enough. Please take your daughter home." She banged her gavel, and the custody battle ended.

I pinched myself because I couldn't believe Janie was officially my daughter. *Is this really happening?* Tears of joy trickled down my cheeks as Josh handed me my beautiful baby girl, who was officially mine. I held her tightly and kissed her face a million times. I could finally stop holding my breath.

"It doesn't seem real," I said to Randy and Renee as we hugged. "So many days I didn't think this moment would ever come."

Gray shook everyone's hand and gave me a hug.

Helen walked up with her arms open wide and said, "It's a great day, Mama."

It was a great day indeed. We exited the courtroom and gathered in the hall.

"Hey, while we're all here, I have an idea." Everyone stood and stared, waiting for me to continue.

"Who's got time for a wedding?" I shouted. "I don't want to wait another second."

Josh raised his hand and said, "Let's do it."

Drew stepped forward. "I'm actually an ordained minister if you're serious. I took one of those online courses so I could marry a friend a few months back."

"I'm absolutely serious." I laughed. "How long does everyone need to get ready?"

Randy said, "Sis, you tell us when and where, and we'll be there."

"Josh and I will go to the Register of Deeds and get our marriage license. Then meet you at the Waterfront Park in two hours. You're all invited." I looked at Helen. "Will you be my maid of honor?"

"I'd be honored. Yes." She squeezed my hands and pulled me into a hug.

Gray stepped forward to Josh and said, "I'd like to throw together some decorations if you'll allow me to help."

"That would be great. Thanks." Josh shook his hand. "But you're still kind of an ass."

"I know. I know." Gray shook his head and smiled.

Josh put his arm around Randy and said, "You ready for this, bro?"

Randy, being the sap that he was, was already crying. "My baby sister's getting married. I need a minute to process."

THIRTY

Lizzie

Josh came home to get his suit and then disappeared. He said he'd meet me at the Waterfront Park. He didn't want to see the bride before the wedding. Helen came over to help me get ready. I curled my hair and tied it up in a strategically messy bun. Helen whipped up a crown of white daisies with some items she had on hand at the bookstore and bobby pinned the crown to my head.

I dug through my closet and pulled out every dress I owned that had a shred of white. Helen and I agreed on my white chiffon sundress with large blue iris flowers that covered the bottom and trailed off as they swept upward toward the waist of the dress. The top was sweetheart cut with white spaghetti straps. I paired the outfit with a strappy pair of blue heels.

Helen dressed Janie in a powder blue sundress and white sandals. She braided her hair and weaved a few white flowers into the braid while I took my time carefully applying my makeup. I wanted to look perfect—a dab of concealer, some foundation, a little bronzer, blush, and highlighter.

Beaming, Helen said, "You look beautiful." I finished my eyes and added some lip gloss. I was more than ready to get married. My heart was leaping out of my chest with excitement. I was finally going to get my happily ever after. I had my daughter, and I was about to marry the man of my dreams.

"I want to cut up some strawberries and put a bottle of champagne on ice for you two crazy love birds to have later. You go ahead. I'll be right behind you." Helen was the best.

I drove Janie and me to Waterfront Park. Gray was finishing the last of the decorations with Renee's help. Every lamppost was covered with a garland of baby's breath, and twinkling lights lined the pier. A large archway stood on the beach, covered in white lilies and giant white lights. A few picnic tables were moved onto the sand and decorated with white tablecloths and gorgeous crystal vases holding a dozen red and white roses.

"My goodness, this is beautiful! How'd you pull this together so quickly?"

Renee tied the last of the baby's breath to the lamppost and said, "I just got here. It was all him." She pointed with her thumb at Gray.

"I rounded up some help," he said. I raised an eyebrow, knowing there was more to the story. "I paid the florist a ginormous amount of cash. It was an offer she couldn't refuse."

"That's the Gray I know. Seriously, though, thanks."

"You look beautiful, Lizzie. I'm happy for you. Truly. You deserve all the happiness in the world."

I hugged him, then kissed his cheek. "Thank you. Are you going to stay?"

"I'm going home as soon as I finish up here. This is your special moment. I'm not meant to be a part of it. Plus, someone has to talk to the caterer and get the food and drinks. I'll have them bring everything over. You don't worry about a thing. A Burney's croissant tower, too."

He put his hand in mine and said, "Unless you want to change your mind. There's still time to marry me instead."

I slapped his arm. "Grayson Ethan Stone."

"You can't blame a guy for trying. It's hard to love a woman who loves someone else."

I snorted. "You'll manage."

"I'll take care of everything. You enjoy your special day." He kissed my forehead as if he were saying goodbye.

He'd always be Janie's father, but he was letting go and handing me over to Josh. I looked into his eyes and said, "Thank you." He understood what I was thanking him for, and I understood he had let me go. We didn't need to say the words out loud. Oddly, I was happy and sad about it at the same time.

Distracting me from my thoughts, Randy pulled up in my golf cart, fully decorated with white streamers. A sign affixed to the back that said JUST MARRIED in black letters and empty cans tied to string dangled from the back bumper. I shook my head and laughed.

"I did the best I could with such short notice."

I wrapped him in a bear hug and said, "It's perfect."

His eyes were glistening. "I'm so proud of you, little sis. You're so strong and brave. Josh's a good man, and I'm thrilled for you two."

"Are you ready to walk me down the aisle?"

"No." He chuckled. "But do I have a choice?"

"Have you seen Josh?"

Randy looked around. "Now that you mention it, no. I haven't."

Drew was sitting on a bench by the waterfront, not a hair out of place. He was wearing tan dress pants and a short-sleeved Tommy Bahama shirt with light brown palm tree leaves all over. "Have you seen Josh?"

"I don't think he's here yet."

I've spent so much of my life on the edge of disaster, waiting for the proverbial shit to hit the fan, that I couldn't help it when my stomach dropped. *He wouldn't stand me up. Would he?*

About ten seconds before I went into full-blown panic mode, Josh's truck pulled into a parking spot a few feet away. He stepped out onto the sidewalk, his dark hair glistened in the sunlight—my man. Josh Miller looked more handsome than ever. My heart skipped a few beats as I swooned. His black dress pants weren't quite as sexy as his jeans, but they fell perfectly over his bottom, and that was good enough for me.

From where he stood, he hollered, "I'll be right there." He walked to the bed of his truck and pulled out a wheelchair, opened it, and pushed it next to the passenger door. As the door opened, Len sat bright-eyed in the front seat.

"We can't have a wedding without the best man," Len said.

Stella climbed out of the backseat in pale green scrubs. "This's my dad's nurse, Stella. They wouldn't let him come without her." It wasn't the time to tell Josh that I had already met Stella, so I waved and said hello.

Josh and Stella helped Len into the wheelchair and pushed him to his spot opposite Helen. Holding Janie's hand, Renee stood beside the archway.

Randy looped his arm through mine. We walked down the aisle to the sound of ocean waves and sea birds singing like a choir in church. When I looked into Josh's eyes, they were filled with love and admiration. There was a hint of mischief in his gaze, subtly suggestive, as if he were peeling away layers without ever touching me. I returned his gaze with a playful flutter of my eyelashes and a coy smile. Randy hugged me like a big brother who was letting go of his baby sister, content she would be taken care of. He shook Josh's hand as he passed me over to him and stood beside Len, who had a tear dangling in the corner of his eye. Helen stepped forward, squeezed my shoulders, hugged me tight, and then took my bouquet.

Drew began. "We're here today to join this happy couple in the sacrament of marriage and to bear witness to the miraculous power of love. A love that has brought this bride and groom together. Today, they stand before God and their closest friends to pledge their love and join together as one." Drew motioned for us to face each other and then nodded to Josh to begin his vows.

Josh took my hands. "Lizzie, from the moment I bumped into you at the general store, I knew you were special. I'm in love with you more today than I was yesterday, and I look forward to loving you more each day forward. Your beauty radiates from the inside out. To know you is to love you. We are the sum of our experiences, both good and bad, but you handle every situation with grace and tenacity. You make me want to be a better man, husband, and father every day. Lizzie, you are an incredible person, friend, businesswoman, and mother. How you manage to be all of those things is a mystery to me." He looked out at our friends and family and said, "I think she has Hermione's magic clock." Everyone chuckled. "You're my best friend and the love of my life. I vow to love you through good times and bad. I vow to protect you and Janie and always do my best to keep you safe. I'm honored to spend the rest of this life with you and every life we may live throughout eternity."

I took a moment to collect myself, and with a shaky voice, I said, "Josh, you're my soulmate, my one true love. I'm stronger and more confident every day because of you. You make me feel like I can do anything. Your embrace gives me peace, and I know I can do anything with you by my side. You are a loving, wonderful man and father. You make me laugh, you make my heart sing, and you make a mean cup of coffee." He laughed and nodded. "I vow to love you in good times and bad. I vow to put you and Janie first. Janie and I are the luckiest girls in the world, and I can't wait to spend the rest of my life with you. I love you with all my heart for today and every day forward."

Drew clasped his hands together and said, "Love that is rooted in faith, trust, and acceptance will be the foundation of an abiding and deepening relationship. Josh Miller, do you take Elizabeth Levine to be your lawfully wedded wife in sickness and in health until death do you part?"

Josh pushed the ring onto my finger. "Yes."

"Elizabeth Levine, do you take Josh Miller to be your lawfully wedded husband in sickness and in health until death do you part?"

I slid his ring onto his finger and said, "Yes."

"I now pronounce you husband and wife. You may kiss the bride."

Josh wrapped his arms around me, spun me around, and dipped me almost to the ground as his tender lips kissed mine. Our family cheered in excitement.

The kiss lingered, and Randy said, "Yo, bro. That's my little sister."

Josh pulled me back upright, said, "Yes. But now she's my wife," and kissed me again.

After the celebration, Randy and Renee took Janie to spend the night with Gray. Helen took Stella and Len back to the nursing home. Josh and I rode in the wedding golf cart and clanked all the way back to the house as the cans clattered along the pavement.

We both undressed the second we walked into the house, dropping clothes along the path to the bedroom. We lay naked in our bed, sipping champagne straight out of the bottle and feeding each other the strawberries that Helen had prepared earlier.

"I can't believe it's over." I sighed in relief. "Janie's legally my daughter, and you're legally my husband." I laid my head on his chest. "I don't think I've been this happy in my entire life."

Josh rolled me on my back and poured champagne down my chest. The cool, bubbly liquid ran down my stomach and puddled in my belly button. "I plan to make you happier each day we're together." His tongue met my skin and licked the trail of champagne. I spread my legs and wrapped my thighs around his body. My fingers slid through his hair, I balled my hands into fists, and tugged slightly, signaling for him to come up to me.

He slid his body slowly up until our lips met. He delicately poured champagne into my mouth and followed it up with a strawberry, then another slow, supple kiss. "I want to make love to my wife." He spilled more champagne on my chest, spilling it onto the sheet. He cupped his hand around my breast and kissed my nipple. His tongue teased me, sending chills down my spine and my toes curled.

"I want to make love to my husband," I whispered into his ear, then kissed his neck, and slid my hand down his stomach. My hands wrapped around his body and pulled him close.

"I'm ready, wife." His sultry tone ignited my passion and lit me on fire.

"I'd say you are," I teased.

As husband and wife, we became one, consummating our marriage until the sun peeked over the horizon.

THIRTY ONE

Lizzie

Bayview Books was packed. It had been one week since the wedding, and I was still on cloud nine. Josh and I planned a honeymoon for December in Hawaii, and I couldn't wait. We were going to spend a week in paradise at a five-star hotel in Maui. I was daydreaming about Luau's when Helen said, "Yoo-hoo. Lizzie. It's almost time to start. Are you ready?"

"Sorry, Helen. I feel like a teenager in love for the first time. I can't stop thinking about my man." I winked at Josh, who was sitting a few feet away. "I have the QR code cards ready. Do you want me to pass them out?"

"Sure. Go ahead," she said and took off.

Helen rented ten televisions and placed them all over the store. She even had one in the loft upstairs. I walked around and handed every few guests a card with a QR code on it. I explained as I walked they needed to use their phone to scan the barcode and download the app. Once the app was downloaded, they should select Bayview Books Trivia Night.

Helen grabbed the microphone. "Welcome to Bayview Books Trivia Night. This is our first trivia night, and we're looking forward to a good time." The crowd cheered and hollered in excitement. "Thank you, Randy Levine, for helping to set up all the televisions you see around the room and a special thanks to the newly married Lizzie Miller for organizing tonight's event." She continued to announce the game instructions and get the crowd hyped up about the bragging rights they would have if they won.

My job was to walk around and help the guests. Randy and Renee were paired with Josh and Drew. I checked on them often. The first question appeared on the screen.

What's the oldest house in Southport?

Millie, Helen's neighbor, exclaimed, "Ooh, ooh. I know." Her friend put her hand over her mouth and said, "Great. Don't tell everyone. You select the answer on your phone."

A minute later, the answer appeared on the television—the Walker-Pyke House.

A few groups erupted into cheers and high-fives. One guy said, "See. I told you that was the answer."

Randy shouted, "Shit, Ren! I knew that. Why didn't you tell me I knew that?"

Renee burst out laughing. "I guess I didn't know you possessed that fact in your brain."

The next question popped on the screen.

What are people from Southport known as?

The entire place shouted in unison, ignoring the rules of the game. "Sandgrounders."

I looked at Josh and shrugged. "I didn't know that."

A third question emerged on the screen.

Which famous pirate visited Southport in the 1700s?

"Ren, Ren. I think I know this one," Randy said as he patted her leg.

Drew said, "I know it. Do you want me to answer it?"

"Are you sure you know it?" Randy said sternly. "The Levine's play to win. If you're sure you know it, then yes. Answer it."

"Well, now, you're making me nervous." Drew laughed.

Renee slapped him on the shoulder and said, "Answer before we run out of time. I'll keep Randy man over here, in line."

The answer flashed on the screen, and Drew hissed. "Yes."

The game went on for over an hour, and everyone seemed to have a ball. Helen gave away twenty books to random winners throughout the night. As Randy and Renee were leaving, I said, "Don't forget, 'I'm the mama' party this Saturday to celebrate that I'm the mama." I pointed both thumbs toward my chest and did a little happy dance.

Josh said, "Yep. I'm cooking shrimp and steaks. It's going to be great."

"We wouldn't miss it," Renee said as she waved. "Hey Lizzie, there's an envelope out here." Renee started to bend down, and

Randy stopped her. "You're twenty-eight weeks pregnant." He bent over, picked it up, and handed it to me.

"Aww. Such a chivalrous man," Helen said.

I handed her the envelope. "You're coming Saturday, right? You and Drew."

"Heck yeah, girl. Because you're the mama." She threw her hip into mine, and then we chest bumped and burst into laughter.

"It was a good night, Helen. The store's really hopping these days. I'm so proud of you."

"I couldn't have done it without your help. I miss you around here. But Drew takes good care of the store and me." She winked as she opened the envelope to see what was inside.

"Gross." My teasing turned serious when terror spread across Helen's face.

THIRTY TWO

Lizzie

Josh and I prepped for the party all day. I scrubbed the house from top to bottom while he tended to the yard. He even helped me at the grocery store, which was a good thing because we needed two carts for all the food, drinks, and paper products. This was a much-needed distraction from the photo bomb we received on trivia night. The image sent chills up my spine every time it popped into my head. A beautiful photograph of our wedding day, but someone scratched mine and Janie's faces out of the picture. Written on the note in black Sharpie marker were the words *Not happily ever after.* The police have the photographs and have offered to keep an extra watch on the house and on our street.

Today we were officially going to celebrate the end of a horrible chapter in our lives and the beginning of our new family. Josh personally went to Gray's condo and invited him. They even talked about going fishing together. I would not let anything ruin this celebration.

Every morning since the hearing when I lifted Janie out of her crib, I spun her around and sang, "I'm your mommy." She'd smile and giggle, then wrap her arms around my neck, and say, "Mommy." Hearing those words from her mouth and knowing that I didn't have to fear losing her anymore filled my heart with tremendous joy. I was free. Free from Catalina Stone. Free from Gray Stone. Free to live my life with Josh and Janie. Gray was still a part of our lives, of course, but on my terms. Not because I had to keep the peace to see my child.

Helen came early to help me set up for the party. I ordered heart-covered paper plates and napkins online and filled in extras with solid red ones from the grocery store. She whipped up a buffalo chicken dip while I worked on the pigs in a blanket. I used a small heart cookie cutter to create heart-shaped pieces of cheese. I borrowed Valentine's Day dishes with red hearts from Renee, who had a dish for every occasion. I decorated with hearts everywhere to celebrate our love.

Randy and Renee arrived first. Randy immediately went out back to the grill to help Josh. Renee, whose belly entered the room before she did, wandered to the counter and sat down on a stool. "Any news on the photos?"

I immediately responded, "We aren't talking about that tonight. We're celebrating."

"All right." Renee nodded. "How can I help?"

I held up my knife and said, "You can help by sitting there and relaxing."

Helen held up a cup and said, "Can I get you some water or lemonade?"

Usually, Renee would argue and insist on helping, but it was too hot, and she was pregnant.

"Have you guys decided on a name yet? She'll be here before you know it," I asked.

Renee's eyes lit up as she spoke. "We haven't decided on a middle name yet, but we know her first name will be Ava."

I repeated the name. "Ava Levine. It has a nice ring to it."

Helen poured some water for Renee, finished mixing the dip, and scraped it into the mini-Crockpot. "I assume the nursery's ready?"

I cupped my hands over my mouth and gasped. "Oh, my God. I'm the worst sister-in-law ever. We need to have a shower. Next weekend. Shower weekend. We'll plan it tomorrow."

Renee laughed. "It's okay. Next weekend will be great. And yes, Helen, the nursery's almost finished. I had no idea how many gadgets and gismos an infant needed these days."

I picked Renee's phone up off the counter and shoved it in her hand. "That's what you can do. Go online right now and create a registry. My niece will not be born without everything she needs."

Helen clapped her hands. "Oh, this'll be fun."

"Hello," called a voice from the foyer.

"We're in the kitchen," I shouted.

Gray walked in wearing a white t-shirt with a red heart painted on the chest. Drew followed behind a few steps.

I said, "Nice shirt, goober."

Gray looked around the room and noticed that no one else was wearing hearts. "I thought it was a heart-themed party."

I laughed. "Yes, for the decorations, but not the attire."

He shook his head. "Oh, well." He picked Janie up out of her pack-and-play and sat her onto his lap at the kitchen table. "I'll hang out with this cutie."

We munched on the snacks until Randy, and Josh finished cooking the food. I set out homemade potato salad, macaroni and cheese, pasta salad, corn on the cob, and a garden salad. The scent of fresh food filled the kitchen. "Hope everyone's hungry."

Randy brought the steak and shrimp inside a few minutes later, and everyone made a plate. Seated around the table with my family and closest friends, I finally felt complete. Randy and Renee were talking about the baby. Helen and Drew were passing cute looks to each other; they didn't think anyone witnessed their affection, but I did. Janie was now on my lap, and Josh was by my side. Even Gray was part of the group, chatting it up with everyone.

"The food's delicious," Drew said.

"This potato salad's to die for," Renee said. "The baby totally agrees and wants seconds." She laughed.

I raised my glass of water and said, "I'd like to make a toast." Everyone raised their glasses and waited for me to speak. Janie reached up and touched the bottom of my glass. "To family and great friends. I couldn't have survived without you, to my husband, whom I adore, and to Janie, who's already a strong survivor. This little girl is going to kick ass at life."

"Cheers." Each person went around the table and clanked their glasses.

"To Lizzie," Josh said as he raised his glass again.

"To Lizzie," everyone said, clanking their glasses.

After dinner, Helen washed the serving dishes, and Randy dried them and placed them onto the island for me to put away. We worked together seamlessly through the pile of dirty pots, pans, and bowls. Out of the corner of my eye, Randy held the corners of his wet dishtowel and swirled the towel into a roll. "Don't even think about it."

"Oh, come on, sis, for old times." He tilted his head as his mischievous eyes alerted me he wasn't going to give up. "Okay. Okay. I won't do it."

I let my guard down. Standing on my tippy toes, I reached up to slide the casserole dish into the cabinet and *"Thwack."*

A searing pain shot through the back of my thigh as Randy erupted into laughter. He had flicked me with the towel. "Holy Christ. That hurt like hell." I took off chasing after him with a dish towel Gray handed me. I sucked at the infamous towel flick, but I chased him around the house anyway, trying to get him back. Helen said, "Oh, the joy of siblings."

"I'll get you one of these days," I promised Randy with a shake of my finger.

"What's all the commotion about?" Josh said as he came down the stairs into the kitchen with a fresh, clean Janie. He had just given her a bath and put on her jammies.

"Your friend Randy here whipped me with the towel." I twisted my body into a pretzel to stay facing Josh but to show him my hamstring at the same time. Craning my neck around, I said, "Look, it left a welt." Josh shook his head and high-fived Randy.

"Wow. No sympathy. That's disappointing."

The evening was fun and right. Josh held Janie as we walked to the front porch and said goodbye to everyone. Hugs and kisses all around. "We should do this again," I said. Janie waved and blew kisses.

Josh and I lingered on the front porch. He pointed to the sky and turned to Janie. "See that bright orange star in the sky? That's Jupiter."

She clasped her hands together and said, "Doopy."

Josh chuckled. "Yes. Doopy."

Janie leaned towards me and practically leaped into my arms. "She wants her mommy," Josh said.

I took her into my arms, and she rested her head on my shoulder. "There's a few more things to put away, but I'll do it in the morning. Janie's ready for bed."

Josh stepped into the house first, and I squeezed his ass cheek as I stepped in behind him.

Turning to look over his shoulder, he said, "Did you leave the back door in the kitchen open?"

"What? No. I didn't leave the door open."

As we entered the kitchen, the electricity went out. "What the hell?" Josh said as he closed the back door. He pulled his phone out of his pocket. "I'll check online to see what's going on with the power."

I carried Janie to the pantry in search of a candle. *Ohh, even better.* "I've got a flashlight." I turned around and froze. Every hair on my body stood on end. Josh was still looking down at his phone, oblivious.

He said, "The electric company doesn't have any info," then looked up at me. He must have glimpsed the terror in my eyes because he turned to see what I was looking at.

Catalina Stone stood inside the living room off the kitchen. Her arms extended in front of her. I could see the flecks of a silver gun in her hand. "Did you miss me?" she snickered.

Josh's phone clattered as it crashed to the ground.

THIRTY THREE
Lizzie

My throat went dry. Clinging to Janie, I muttered, "How?"

"My parole hearing went swimmingly. Got out yesterday."

I blinked. *Maybe, I'm imagining this.* Nope, not imagining it. Catalina was still there.

"No time for chitchat," she quipped. "Give me my daughter, and no one gets hurt."

Over my dead body.

"Get the fuck out of my house, and *you* won't get hurt," I snapped.

"I'll shoot her," Catalina said as she pointed the gun directly at Janie. "I'm leaving with her, or no one does. She's my daughter."

What kind of sick individual would point a gun at a child? Adrenaline coursed through my veins. I pressed my feet firmly into the ground and stood tall. "You're psychotic."

Josh took a step toward her. "Move again, and I'll blow your brains out." She fired a warning shot past his head that crashed into the microwave. Josh stopped in his tracks.

I coached myself to keep my breathing calm. "It's okay Janie. It's going to be okay."

Out of the darkness, a voice called from the hallway. "I'm back. I forgot my phone."

"What the fuck?" Gray said as his eyes fell on the scene for the first time.

Protect Janie.

Bang.

Bang. Bang. Bang.

Four deafening shots rang out through the house like an explosion. The sound reverberated in my eardrums, and my heart stopped beating.

Everything in the room moved in slow motion, and my lungs struggled to draw breath. Through the ringing in my head, I could hear Janie screaming. Her shrieks penetrated my eardrums as my brain processed what was happening.

From my gut, I screamed, "Janieeee."

Josh called out to Gray as he grappled with Catalina. "She was aiming at Janie. Get Janie."

Gray rushed toward me.

Janie cried and screamed. The sound of her anguish elevated louder and louder.

Gray gently scooped her up into his arms and laid her on the kitchen island. Her cries echoed through the house.

Josh managed to get the gun away from Catalina and hit her on the head. He rushed over to help Gray.

Gray cried out, "She's covered in blood."

Josh shrieked, "Lizzie. Call 911. Oh my God, Lizzie, call 911."

I heard his words, but I couldn't comprehend them. My mind was focused on one thing and one thing only. Breathing. My lungs constricted, causing each breath to be more and more difficult.

Gray snatched his phone from the counter and used the light to scour our daughter's body. "It's okay, Janie. It's going to be okay," I whispered, my voice shaky.

"I can't find where the blood is coming from," Gray said. The two men were frantic. "She's covered in it. It's got to be coming from somewhere."

Gray lifted Janie and put her in the sink while Josh held the light. I could hear the water coming out of the faucet.

I looked down. My hands were shaking violently and covered in blood. I tried to speak, but no sound would come out. I felt a writhing pain of terror as I waited for Gray or Josh to report that Janie was okay. My legs were weak, but I commanded them to remain standing. In the faintest light, I could see Catalina escape out the back door. I tried to point, but my arms were heavy like they had been cast in cement blocks. I tried to scream. Nothing came out. Janie cried louder, and the sound crushed my heart. The oxygen must have left the room. I gasped for air as my knees shook.

"Lizzie? Lizzie? Call 911," Josh shouted again as he assisted Gray.

Everything happened so fast, but moved in slow motion at the same time. The room blurred out of focus.

Gray said, "I think Janie's okay. I can't find any wounds. The blood must have come from somewhere else."

A bright light burned my cornea as Josh turned the light in my direction. I could feel more adrenaline rush through me like a tidal wave. My skin burned where the bullets had torn through my flesh.

A still image of my daughter's face was frozen in my mind. Her beautiful smile and her gigantic dimples stared back at me. *I love you, Janie bug. Mommy loves you.*

Josh's green eyes sparkled in the darkness like freshly cut emeralds. Our time together flashed through my head like the movie of our life on a big screen. Moments spent on our balcony, moments we spent reading and playing with Janie—a collection of our time together. His eyes met mine, and I mouthed to him, "I love you. Keep her safe. No matter what. Keep her safe."

Suddenly, I felt no pain. No terror. The room blurred from the outside inward. I fell to my knees. *I love you, Janie bug. I love you so much.*

Filled with complete calm. Everything went black.

THIRTY FOUR

Josh

"Lizzie! Oh my God, Lizzie," I screamed.

Gray was holding Janie now. "Shh, shh. It's okay, baby girl. Daddy's got you. You're okay."

"Call 911," I yelled.

My heart stopped. Under the faint light, I watched Lizzie collapse. A pool of blood flowed from her body. The thick red liquid inched its way across the floor like tentacles. I slid down next to Lizzie and lifted her onto my lap.

"Lizzie," I shouted. "Lizzie. Stay with me."

I could hear Gray on the phone with the 911 operator. "The first responders will be here soon."

In a strained and faint whisper, she said, "Keep her safe."

Tears gushed down my cheeks. "Come on, baby. Stay with me. Lizzie, stay with me." Her stomach was covered in blood. I pressed my hand to the wounds, but it wasn't enough.

Her face was pale. A smear of blood spread across her cheek. I could barely make out her words. "You're the best thing that happened to me. I'll find you in our next life," she sputtered. Her eyes closed, then slowly opened again. "Promise me you'll keep Janie safe. Even if that means letting her go." I pressed harder into the holes that riddled her body.

"Stop it. You're going to be okay. We'll keep her safe together." I rocked her back and forth.

Coughing, she said, "Promise me."

"I don't need to do that. You're going to be okay."

Life escaped through her eyes, and her body was limp in my arms. "Noooo. Wake up. Come on, Lizzie, wake up."

Desperate to save her, I laid her body flat on the floor and tilted her head back. My knees slipped in a puddle of her blood as I positioned myself toward her head. I leaned down, covered her mouth with mine, and blew two long breaths. I pressed my palms down into her chest and pushed. Down. Down. Down. Down. Several more times.

Gray flipped the breaker, and the lights flicked on. My eyes burned as my corneas took in the blood—it was everywhere!

"Come on, Lizzie. Breathe! *Breathe*, Lizzie." Two more breaths.

Down. Down. Down. Down. Down. Down. Down. Down. Down. Down. Down. Down. Down. Down. Down.

I checked for a pulse. Nothing. Two more breaths. I repeated the cycle over and over.

Gray touched my shoulder and, in a gentle tone, said, "Josh, it's been 10 minutes."

I pushed him away. "Get off me." Blood spirted out of Lizzie's midsection as I pressed down hard on her sternum, trying to bring her back to life.

Exhausted, I sobbed. I pulled my beautiful Lizzie into my arms, her lifeless body draped over me. I rocked back and forth as I cried out, overcome with grief, a ferocious grief I'd never experienced before.

"Why?" I screamed through tears. "Why did this happen?" I kissed her face and clung to her lifeless body.

I leaned against the island cabinet and held her in my arms. I stared at the wall in front of me.

I looked at Gray as he consoled Janie. "Go."

Gray's eyes were moist with tears as his mind processed the scene around us. "I can't leave you."

I snapped. "Go. Get Janie out of here. Go to Randy and Renee. Call Helen. We need to keep Janie safe. Catalina's gone."

Gray's eyes widened. We were both so focused on Janie and Lizzie that we hadn't realized Catalina had fled the scene. He leaned down and stroked Lizzie's blood-soaked hair and face. He hung his head in silence for a moment. I could tell that he was doing his best to control his grief.

I put my hand on his arm and said, "It's okay. I know you loved her, too."

Upon hearing my words, Gray erupted into a full-blown wail, the kind that a grown man usually keeps to himself.

Janie leaned toward Lizzie with her arms outstretched and said, "Mommy. Mommy, night night." She didn't understand that her mother was dead, that her soul had moved on.

Her sweet little voice took my breath away. Lizzie had fought so hard to be her mother, and now she would never have the chance. Her love for Janie was fierce. She saved her life. Whatever happened in those few seconds, Lizzie sacrificed herself so that her daughter could have a chance at life.

I was confident in what Janie needed, and I'd do exactly as Lizzie asked.

Or fall apart trying.

THIRTY FIVE

Josh

After the police took my statement, I asked if I could leave. I couldn't spend another minute in the house. Connor Clifton was the detective in charge, and he informed me that my house was now a crime scene. They'd contact me when I could re-enter. He gave me his business card and told me to call him if I could think of anything else.

"No detail's too small," he said. "If we need anything else, I'll be in touch. Don't go far."

As I walked outside, policemen were placing crime scene tape on the front of the house. My house...the scene of a crime and not just any crime. The crime where Catalina Stone murdered my wife, my beautiful Lizzie Miller. Where my wife selflessly had taken four bullets to save her daughter's life.

Now, I needed to say goodbye to Janie.

My shoulders were hunched as I walked the ten blocks to Randy's. My feet scuffed the road with every step. My body was sluggish, like it weighed a thousand pounds. A few hours ago, everything was perfect. Lizzie was happier than she'd ever been. She said so herself. I was giddy. Through crazy odds, we found each other and stuck through the chaos. Janie was finally Lizzie's, and we were going to raise her together and be a family.

How did I get here? How can I survive without my wife, the love of my life? The pain was too much. My body trembled.

Distracted by my grief, I wandered past Randy's house. I was three houses down the road before I noticed. I backtracked, stepped onto the front porch, and knocked on the door. Drew greeted me with a somber look.

Randy and Renee were crying at the kitchen table. Gray and Helen were whispering about Janie at the counter. Through her tears, Renee cried out, "Josh, you're here!"

"I can't be at home right now. I don't want to be, but the police kicked me out."

As she composed herself and took in my appearance, she gasped. "You're covered in blood." More tears came faster now.

Randy stood up and said, "Follow me. I have a change of clothes you can borrow."

I washed my hands in the sink and changed into gym shorts and a T-shirt. I was a zombie. The numbness already creeping in.

"I laid Janie down. She's finally asleep," Gray said.

Helen cried. "That sweet child witnessed her mother die. She's traumatized. She may not understand it, but she must feel it."

Randy shook his head. "None of this seems real." He put his head in his hands and cried. "How did this happen? Catalina should've never been released from jail. We tried to tell them something like this would happen."

Drew said, "Where's Catalina now? Is she in custody?"

Gray sighed. "She got away."

"You mean she's still out there? Oh, dear God," Helen shrieked.

I took a deep breath and scratched my head. "The police are going to put cars out front and at Gray's condo. They have an APB out for her arrest, but everyone needs to be on high alert."

Randy kept shaking his head. "None of this feels real. I keep thinking that Lizzie's going to walk through the door any minute."

The image of Lizzie's lifeless body flashed through my mind, an image I wish I could delete from my memory banks. *She isn't walking through that door ever again.*

Gray ran his fingers along the edge of the placemat in front of him at the table. "She was aiming for Janie. We need to talk about how we keep her safe. I can hire private security for her and all of you. I should have done that already." He rubbed his forehead. "What do you guys think we should do? Until Catalina's behind bars, we can't take any chances. Lizzie sacrificed herself to protect Janie. That can't be for nothing."

"What if Catalina isn't caught? Then what?" Randy said in a huff.

Renee looked up. "Even if she's caught, I don't feel safe. She's certifiable. She won't stop until she gets what she wants."

Helen said, "I've called Mr. Stallard to fill him in. He may have a few suggestions."

I sat quietly, listening to everyone talk through different options, and what they felt was best for Janie.

Keep her safe, even if you have to let her go. Lizzie's last words played on repeat in my head.

I stood up slowly and moved to the head of the table. "In her final breath, Lizzie made me promise that I'd keep Janie safe, even if I had to let her go. I didn't want to listen. I didn't want to believe that Lizzie was going to die." I wiped my eyes. "She repeated herself and demanded I promise this to her. I didn't know what she meant, but I do now. She realized Catalina would never give up, and Janie would always be at risk."

Randy frowned. "What're you talking about?"

Gray's eyes grew wide with understanding. "No."

Frustrated, Randy shouted, "What're you talking about?"

I wrapped my hands around the back of the chair for support. "Gray owns a secret farm." I nodded to Gray as I spoke. "You need to take Janie and disappear. This is what Lizzie wanted. She said, 'Promise me you'll keep her safe even if you have to let her go.' This is what she meant."

Renee blew her nose. "How are we even having this conversation? This is crazy talk."

Randy put his hand on her arm and said, "Maybe it's a good idea, at least for a little while. Catalina will go to prison for murder this time. Once they catch her, Gray and Janie can come home."

Gray shot me a sideways glance. "Janie's family's here. I don't feel comfortable with this plan. She needs all of you in her life."

"But it's possible, right?" Looking him directly in the eye, I said, "You have the resources to disappear."

"Theoretically, yes. It's possible. I have enough money for Janie and me to live off the grid for the rest of her life if we need it. I have people that'll help, and no one would know who we are and where we're from, but you couldn't know either. You could never contact us."

Randy let out a sigh. Renee started to cry again. Alarmed, Helen and Drew looked at each other.

"This is what Lizzie wanted. I'm certain. She'd want us all to do whatever it takes to keep Janie safe," I said more firmly.

"I'm not ready to make this decision," Randy said. "Let's give it some time. Maybe the police will find Catalina tonight. I don't want to be hasty."

Gray nodded eagerly. "I agree. We can wait. I'll start getting things in motion, but we can wait a little longer to decide."

Grief filled the air like a fog hovering above our heads. The room was thick with despair, sadness, and anger. We sat in silence, except for the occasional wailing outburst and sniffle. We found comfort in each other as we shared our silent but devastating pain.

Suddenly, a loud clatter rocked the living room, and everyone ducked in reflex.

"What the hell?" Randy shouted.

A brick was hurled through the living room window, and I bent down to pick it up. A note was affixed to the brick with a rubber band. The note said, "You're all going to pay for taking my daughter."

"Oh, my God." I turned to show Gray the note. He snatched it out of my hand. Before he could respond, Renee screamed.

Flames blazed through the kitchen window at the back of the house. I rushed outside to see fire licking the side of Lizzie's old apartment. The smell of burnt wood and smoke filled the air around me. "Call 911," I hollered.

"There's a police officer out front. How'd she get past him?" Helen said, looking around frantically.

Randy looked at Gray and said, "Josh's right. You need to take Janie and go."

THIRTY SIX
Gray

Janie and I were packed and ready to flee. I put the essentials in a duffle bag I could easily carry on my back and laid it by the door.

Randy and Renee arrived at my condo first. Renee sat on the couch and pulled Janie next to her. "I love you so much, baby girl. Be a good girl for your daddy. We'll always be with you." She put a small necklace around her neck with a Saint Christopher medal. "St. Christopher is the patron saint of travelers. He'll always keep you safe."

Randy stood inside the doorway with wet eyes as he watched his wife say goodbye to their niece. My heart was breaking. I had grown to adore this family. I valued the strength and love of Lizzie's people, the ones she chose to surround herself with. Janie should grow up surrounded by this very family. She needed them. Hell,

I needed them. These people and this town had shaped me into a better man.

Randy walked over to the couch and kneeled in front of his niece. "Janie bug, you are so loved. We don't want you to go, but we need to make sure you're safe." Janie leaned forward and wrapped her arms around Randy's neck. He sniffed back his tears.

Josh knocked on the door. Standing with him was Helen, and I let them both in.

Randy tickled Janie and said, "Say hi to Josh and Helen."

She waved. She didn't smile or flash her signature dimples. She didn't speak. She just waved.

Josh said, "Hello, beautiful girl."

She slid off the couch and bobbled over to Josh. Her arms were outstretched, and she opened and closed her hands. He picked her up and spun her around, dancing with her. I choked back my tears.

"She hasn't spoken since the incident. Not one word," I announced to the group. "She's been impacted by this trauma in ways she can't express."

Janie was clearly struggling, which made leaving even harder. These wonderful people are exactly who she needed to get through this. "I'm not sure I can do this alone."

I begged Josh to come with me, but in the end, we agreed Janie would be safer with me. The more people that needed to get off the grid, the greater the chance of Janie being found, and Josh needed to stay here to be close to Len.

Josh put his hand on my shoulder. "We talked about this. You can and you will. You don't have a choice." He pointed at Janie. "That little girl needs you. She's counting on you. We all are. But..."

Gray smirked. "I know. I know. I'm still an asshole."

Josh shook my hand and said, "Actually, I was going to say you've turned out to be a decent guy and a great father."

I wrapped my arm around him in the tightest hug we'd ever exchanged. Everyone said their final goodbyes. The room was somber, filled with light sniffles.

"I'll make sure that Janie knows all of you. When she's old enough to understand, I'll tell her everything. When it's safe, hopefully sooner rather than later, I'll bring her home. This is her home. You're her family."

Josh picked up the duffle bag and handed it to me. Randy and Renee gave Janie one more hug. Helen tucked a book into Janie's bag.

"As soon as we are settled, and I know it's safe, I'll send a letter to the bookstore and let you know that we're okay."

I walked out the door with my duffle bag on my back and my daughter in my arms. Southport was a beautiful place full of community and family. I was terrified that without this place and the people who lived here, I'd fail at the most important job I ever had, being a father.

THIRTY SEVEN

Josh

How does one prepare for a funeral? How can one event encompass everything in a person's life? For those who survive, we are left alone, haunted by our grief and figuring out how to live a new life. A life without the person we've lost. I decided to have a celebration of life for Lizzie. Is this what she would have wanted? I don't know, but I think so.

I selected an antique urn for her ashes. Etched into the center was a gold lily like the bouquet I gave her shortly after we first met. Selecting the canister that would hold your wife's ashes was an odd experience. On the one hand, I wanted the best for her. On the other hand, who gave a shit. What I really needed was her. The urn I chose couldn't give me that. I would have to wait for my next life to see her again.

I could still smell the lavender scent of her lotion in the morning when I woke up. I rolled over each morning and reached for Lizzie out of habit. My heart shattered when my hand fell against her empty pillow. She was gone. Each day, it was like realizing this truth again for the first time, or at least, that's how the pain in my chest felt when she wasn't there.

When the scent of coffee wafted through the house, I thought of her. I loved the look she gave me and the gratitude that filled her eyes when I handed her a cup of freshly brewed java to start her day. I loved bringing her coffee. It was the best part of my morning. It's the little things you remember after someone is gone. It was the little things that haunted my sleep and brought me to tears in the solitude of my morning showers.

I remembered the smile that lit up her eyes when she watched the sunrise. The way she spread butter on her toast. The way she had to wash the dishes before putting them in the dishwasher. The way she looked at me on our wedding day. So many little details that went unnoticed when she was alive, but knock the wind from my chest now that she was gone.

I left Janie's room completely untouched. Sometimes, I liked to sit in the rocking chair and pretend she was in my arms while I read her favorite stories aloud to no one.

My house was empty. I considered putting it up for sale. Helen told me to wait at least a year. This house had been with my family for generations, but I no longer enjoyed living here. Gray left me the keys to his condo. He told me to rent it or use it. He didn't care which. He planned to keep it for when he and Janie returned someday. I might stay there for a while.

My dad didn't take the news of Lizzie's murder too well. Stella, his nurse, said he was declining rapidly, and they didn't know how much time he had left. I hadn't gone to see him much lately, and I hated myself for that. My world was closing in on me, and I couldn't breathe.

I wasn't sure how I would continue. Randy said we had to keep putting one foot in front of the other, but I was broken, shattered like a fragile piece of glass. Most days, I wanted to lie in bed and cry, but I reminded myself Lizzie would not want that. She'd want me to keep going. It was the only reason I got out of bed each morning.

I lay in bed and did my best to prepare for the day ahead. The day we said goodbye to Lizzie. My phone needed a charge, but I had left my charger in the kitchen. I checked in my nightstand for an extra but had no luck. Reluctantly, I opened the top drawer of Lizzie's nightstand to see if I could find one in there. Tucked neatly in the drawer were two items: a yellow spiral notebook with a sun in the center and the words You Are My Sunshine written across the top. Stuffed in the flap was a black ballpoint pen. I had never seen Lizzie with these items before. Curious, I pulled out the notebook and opened it.

At the top of the page was the date *August 15* and the words *Dear Janie.* I thumbed through the pages as tears trickled down my face. Lizzie wrote Janie a journal of sorts. She wrote something practically every day since Janie returned to her life.

How did I not see her doing this?

I was too emotional to read the journal. I tucked it back into the nightstand drawer and decided I would read it later. Lizzie always intended to write a book. Maybe I could publish her journal someday, and when Janie returned, *if she ever did*, I could give it to her.

Several of our local Southport friends, each holding a candle, gathered on the road by the Yacht Basin. They offered words of condolence as I passed. My legs faltered as I walked down the dock toward my boat. Celebrating her life today made her death seem even more real. Randy and Renee were already waiting for me when I arrived.

"You look like shit," Randy said as I approached.

"Thanks, brother. I appreciate the honesty." I hadn't left the house in a few weeks.

"Are you eating?" Renee said. "You look like you haven't eaten in days. You need to take care of yourself."

I didn't respond. She was right, but I didn't care. I was doing the best I could right now. I clung to the urn as we climbed onto the boat. Helen and Drew arrived moments later. I went into the cabin and told the captain we were ready to shove off.

I had the boat covered in pink, purple, yellow, and white lilies. I must have ordered a thousand of them. Helen gazed around the boat deck and said, "Josh, the flowers are beautiful."

"Thanks, Helen. I think Lizzie would've liked them."

Everyone took a seat as we pulled out to sea. I asked the captain to take us to Lizzie's favorite fishing spot. "There's snacks and drinks inside the cabin. The staff will help you with whatever you need. Today should be as easy as possible for everyone. When we get to Lizzie's spot, we'll spread her ashes."

With our plates of snacks, we sat outside on the upper deck in awkward silence. No one wanted to say goodbye. The sound of water beating on the bottom of the boat as it chugged through the ocean was our sermon for the day.

Helen stood up. "Lizzie was my best friend. I still see her prancing around the bookstore every day. She loved coming up with new ideas and fun events for the store. Bayview Books wouldn't be what it is today without her. I plan to honor Lizzie by having a section of the store dedicated to her and her favorite books. I'll donate a portion of all my event proceeds to the local community to help foster children find families. I think Lizzie would really like that."

Renee said, "That's wonderful, Helen."

"She was my little sister. There's no denying she was a spitfire. Even hell on wheels sometimes, but her personality was big. She was the life of the party. Somehow, through everything, she always found the good in people. She was kind and selfless," Randy said.

"She was a wonderful mother. Regardless of everything she'd been through, she opened her heart to love. She was the best sister-in-law. She would have been the best aunt," Renee said as she rubbed her baby bump. A tear trickled down her cheek.

"She was my everything." I started to cry, unable to finish my words.

Randy put his hand on my back. "As a little girl, Lizzie would dig up worms. She loved to play with earthworms. She wasn't afraid to get dirty, and she preferred to play with boys. She didn't like frilly dresses or anything pink." Everyone laughed. "She was a fierce student who worked hard to get good grades. She liked to beat to her own drum, you know." Everyone nodded their heads.

Helen said, "That sounds like our girl."

"When our parents died, we were both technically still kids. I was the older brother, so it was my job to take care of her. It turns out she was the one that taught me. She taught me how to take chances. She taught me to chase my dreams. I never told her that." He paused to collect himself. "You all know her past. She went down a dark path for a bit, but she pulled herself up by her bootstraps and forged a life for herself. She landed a job at the best marketing firm in New York City. She knew what she wanted, and she went after it. I admired that about her."

Renee smiled at Randy. Being on the boat with everyone and listening to old stories was surreal.

"She came here to reinvent herself and to heal. She never gave up on that. When she learned her daughter had survived, she fought tirelessly to get her back." Randy lifted his eyes to the sky and said, "I am so proud of you, Lizzie."

"I'll be right back," I said to everyone and disappeared into the cabin. I returned a few minutes later with a tray of Fatorade and one Gatorade for Renee. "A toast to Lizzie." Randy chuckled. The kind of small chuckle that brought a smile to your face, but it was full of sadness. Fatorade was Lizzie's made-up drink. It was vodka and Gatorade mixed, and she loved it.

Everyone took a glass. "To the best woman I've ever known. My wife, Lizzie." I raised my glass, the gang responded in kind, and we drank to Lizzie. We remained silent after the toast until we reached our destination. Taking in my new reality, as did everyone else, I stared off into the water. We shared our grief with unspoken words. The boat slowed, and I handed everyone a silver glass of Lizzie's ashes. Randy, Renee, and Helen, each took a turn stepping to the edge of the boat and saying a quiet goodbye as they poured Lizzie's ashes into the water. I went last.

"I'll never love another. You were my greatest gift and my greatest blessing. I'll live the rest of my days for you. Fly, my sweet Lizzie. Fly." I slowly turned the cup upside down and cried as the remainder of my wife's ashes blew into the water.

THIRTY EIGHT
Helen

About six months had passed, and it was an ordinary Saturday. Drew and I were at the bookstore serving our customers when the postman arrived. "Drew, I'm going to grab the mail and pick up lunch."

He was watching Mr. Paul and his friend play chess. "Okay. I'll be here."

Every day, my heart missed Lizzie. I rarely spent any time with Josh since his dad passed away a few months back. I kept in touch with Randy and Renee, but with the new baby, it was hard to spend a lot of time together. I'd given up hope that we would hear from Gray. We all had to assume that no news was good news and that he and Janie made it safely where they were going.

I pulled the mail out of the mailbox and began flipping through it. In the stack was the water bill, the power bill, a supply invoice, and a plain white envelope with no return address. My heart did a flip-flop in my chest. Immediately, I ran back into the store for my phone.

I texted the crew in a group message.

Me: I think I might have a letter.

Randy: Where are you?

Me: I'm at the bookstore.

Randy: Renee's napping, but she won't want to miss this.

Me: I'll come to you.

Josh: I'm working. Go ahead without me.

Me: Joshua Miller, angry face emoji. You get your ass to Randy's now.

Josh: I'll try.

I sprinted back downstairs and hopped into my golf cart, popped the brake, and took off like a bat out of hell. *Shit. I forgot to tell Drew what I was doing.* I called him to fill him in and asked him to man the store. A few moments later, I lurched to a stop in Randy and Renee's driveway.

Randy was on the front porch waiting for me. "Do you think Josh's coming?" he asked.

"I don't know. Let's give him a minute. He hasn't been the same. Losing both Lizzie and his dad has taken a toll on him."

Randy ushered me inside, and we sat on the couch. "Ren's getting the baby changed. She'll be right out."

I was excited to see the beautiful Ava Elizabeth, or Ava Lizzie for short. I met her a few days after she was born but haven't seen her since.

Renee was holding little Ava when she came into the living room. I sprang to my feet, gave her a side hug, and took a peek at the baby. "Oh, my God. She's beautiful and growing so big. She's so alert." Her curious eyes looked at me, taking in all my facial features.

"She's growing, that's for sure. Now, if I can get her to sleep through the night. I'm exhausted."

Renee was still in her pajamas, and her hair had not been brushed. "I'm happy to babysit anytime. Just say the word."

My phone buzzed. It was Josh.

Josh: I'll be there in five.

Me: Great.

I dawdled over the baby while we waited.

Upon his arrival, we sat together in the living room. I opened the envelope. "I'm going to feel like a dummy if this isn't what I think it is."

Impatiently, Randy said, "Open the damn thing."

I took a deep breath and ripped open the seal. Inside was a handwritten note. I carefully removed the note like it was a bomb that might explode in my face. My heart raced inside my chest. I opened the folds and read the note aloud.

Hello,

We made it to our destination, and the little one's safe. She's enjoying the farm and the chickens. She collects eggs from the coop every day. I'm teaching her about horses, and eventually, I'll teach her to ride. Don't

worry. We'll start with ponies.

Her mother would be pleased to know that I read to her every morning.

At night, I tell her stories about all of you and her home. She still hasn't

spoken a word since we left, but I'm hoping soon we can settle into our new

identities, and I can take her to the doctor.

She misses her mother and her family. So do I. I'll write again as soon as

I can. In the meantime, I'll cling to Hope. Maybe someday soon, Hope

can return to you in Southport.

Lovingly,

The Asshole

PS - Burn this letter.

PPS - I'm not kidding.

I dried my tears and handed the note to Randy. "I think he named her Hope. Look at the letter. The H is capitalized."

"I wonder where they are," Renee said as she rocked little Ava Lizzie.

Pain flooded Josh's face, and it broke my heart. I moved next to him and wrapped my arm around his shoulder. He leaned into me and cried. "I miss her so much."

I squeezed his arm. "I do, too."

Randy handed the letter to Renee so she could read it again. "I don't think they'll ever find Catalina. I'm starting to think Janie will never come home." He laid his head on the back of the couch. "I still can't wrap my brain around how this crazy person invaded my sister's life."

"If it's the last thing I do, that bitch will pay," Josh said through gritted teeth and then slammed his hand on the coffee table. "Janie will come home someday."

Acknowledgments

Writing any book can be challenging. It's difficult to put yourself out there and hope you can find the right audience who'll appreciate your story. There were times I wanted to give up, times I didn't think I would finish, and times I wanted to cry from exhaustion.

I couldn't have done it without the help of my team, who encouraged me every step of the way. I am so grateful for the amazing editors I've found and how wonderful and diligent they are. Thank you, Kim, Jenn, and Adele, for your hard work and for helping to make this story come to life.

Thank you, Mo, for putting up with my numerous cover design revisions. Your patience and willingness to get it right are astounding.

My husband, Chris, whom was willing to sit for hours and talk about the plot, characters, and story development. I appreciate your participation in the process and your reminder that it is okay when I don't have all the answers. You've always been my biggest cheerleader and fan. I thank God for you every day.

My children think it's cool that their mom writes books, and my daughter is my best salesman. Thank you for putting up with Mom's late-night and weekend writing sessions. I love you both to the moon and back.

I must acknowledge my college roommate Steph, who is by my side, cheering me on every step of the way. Reading draft after draft, discussing plot holes and character development, and reminding me to believe in myself when I start to doubt my ability.

I would also like to thank Robin Strickland, who again took time out of her busy schedule to help me ensure that Keeping Janie's legal aspect was as accurate as possible. I am forever grateful.

My launch team—there are hundreds of you, and you know who you are. Marketing Keeping Janie would be a daunting task without you. Thank you for your time and effort in spreading the word. I will always be grateful to each of you for your support. I am lucky to be surrounded by amazing people who will jump into the book with me and buckle in for the crazy ride.

Last but definitely not least, I thank my family and friends who support and root for me. I am grateful to you. I could not do this without your love and encouragement. I love you all.

From The Author

Several years ago, I decided I wanted to be a writer. I started with my debut novel, The Secrets We Conceal, a coming-of-age fiction based on a true story. After releasing the book and deciding I wanted to write another, I needed time to figure out my next story.

I was going through some personal difficulties, struggling to find gratitude each day. My siblings are a huge part of my life, but I rarely see them because we live in different states. I decided I needed to take a trip to visit, and I did. Spending time surrounded by the comfort and love of my brother and sister was exactly what I needed to get back on track. Enjoying the beautiful weather and the small town of Southport, NC, catapulted me into a story. I couldn't move my fingers fast enough to write. Sitting at a picnic table on the water, I whipped out an outline and feverishly developed characters and plot lines. It was exhilarating, and Call Her Janie was born.

It wasn't long after starting Call Her Janie I knew the book needed to be a series, and Keeping Janie came to life.

Everyone should have someone they can lean on to lift their spirits and show them they have the strength to get through anything. In the Southport Series, Lizzie leans on her brother and Helen to lift her up and find her way again. I hope you enjoy the Southport Series as much as I enjoyed writing it. Stay tuned for book three and many more books to come.

Do you have a story to tell? Would you like me to join your book club and discuss my books? I'm happy to help. Reach out any time to srfabricoauthor@gmail.com. If you feel so compelled, please leave an honest review on Goodreads, Amazon, or anywhere books are sold.

Book Club Questions

1. Which scene stuck with you the most?

2. What was your least favorite scene?

3. What part of the book, if any, made you cry?

4. Did you expect the ending?

5. What ideas do you have for an alternate ending?

6. Do you feel that Gray really turned over a new leaf and grew as a person?

7. Do you think they should have stayed in Southport?

8. Do you think Lizzie will return in book three?

9. What do you think Josh might do now?

10. What do you think might happen in book three?

About The Author

S.R. Fabrico is an award-winning author whose literary talents have captivated readers worldwide. With her debut novel, The Secrets We Conceal, and her second novel, Call Her Janie, she has emerged as a rising star in the literary realm.

With a remarkable 25-plus-year career in business, marketing, and sports, S.R. Fabrico brings a unique perspective to her writing. As a World Champion Dance Coach and esteemed speaker, she infuses her stories with passion and insight.

Residing in Tennessee with her husband and children, S.R. Fabrico continues to create captivating narratives that will transport you to new and extraordinary worlds. Prepare to be enchanted by her exceptional storytelling prowess.

In addition to her passion for writing novels, she has published a series of sports journals and a journal for women. She believes that journaling is good for the soul.

CALL
HER
JANIE
S.R.
FABRICO

KEEPING
JANIE
FABRICO

JANIE'S
HOPE
S.R.
FABRICO

Summer 2024

THE SECRETS
WE CONCEAL
S.R. FABRICO

GYMNASTICS

MY
FIREFLY
JOURNAL

DANCE

SWIM

CHEER

SOCCER

BASKETBALL
JOURNAL

MY
VOLLEYBALL
JOURNAL

Connect With SR. Fabrico

Subscribe and follow S.R. Fabrico to stay up to date on new releases and important updates.

Email srfabricoauthor@gmail.com to set up a virtual book club meet and greet with the author.

www.ingramcontent.com/pod-product-compliance
Lightning Source LLC
Chambersburg PA
CBHW032341310726
48973CB00007B/1798